DRAGON'S COVE

RIVIAND LOST
BOOK 3

KRISTY DIXON

Book Cover by Miblart

Edited by Lawrence Editing

1st edition 2025

ISBN 978-1-960841-37-7 Paperback

ISBN 978-1-960841-38-4 ebook

For Malia April

Riviand
Colter's Lake
Goblin Mountain
Tyran
Troll's Retreat
Troll City
Serpent's Hill
Desert
Pyramid
Kinton
Dragon's Cove

1

CHAPTER 1

Smoke billowed from the dragon's nose, and Odie took a step back. "Easy, girl," he said, squatting down. He held out a piece of jerky and the small orange dragon stepped closer. "That's it." The dragon looked at him and then at the jerky. She sniffed it and snatched it from his hand, then ran to the corner of the dungeon.

"Well, I think we made some progress." He wiped his hand on his britches. With luck, he'd gain the dragon's trust and she wouldn't have to stay down here. Dovin said bantam dragons didn't breathe fire, but they were keeping her down here until they were sure. The smoke coming from her nostrils wasn't reassuring.

Odie grabbed his black feathered cape from the floor and climbed the stone steps. He and his friends needed to get ready to go to the upper continents, but every time it seemed like they were ready to go, something happened and it was pushed back. This last time it was a stomach bug that had affected most of the castle. They couldn't go anywhere when some of their group were throwing up.

"How's the dragon?" Mateo asked, coming down the hall toward him. "Did you name her yet?"

"She took something from my hand. I don't know what to call her yet. I'm sure it will come to me. Are you better?"

"Yes. That was brutal. I'm not sure if it was the worst sickness I've ever had, or it just seems that way because I don't have my mom to wait on me. I haven't felt sick since last night, so I think I'm over it."

"Well, don't come near me. I haven't gotten it and I don't plan to." Odie would have to trust him on the mom thing. He didn't remember his actual mother, and his goblin mother had never waited on anyone.

"Are the girls still sick?" Mateo asked.

"Yes. I've been keeping away from everyone. I think Dovin and I are the only ones who haven't had it."

"This has interrupted everything. We could have gone up to Akkron, researched dragon shifters, and been back already if all this stuff didn't keep happening."

"How long do you think we'll be up there?"

"Not too long. How long can reading a few books take?"

Odie shrugged. "What if there aren't any books about it?"

"I bet there are. Who wouldn't want to learn about people who can change into dragons? I just hope Durdessa gets better soon. Once she's well, we can go. We don't have to wait for the others since they aren't coming."

"We won't be going until tomorrow at the earliest."

Mateo nodded. "I'll see you at supper."

"I'm eating in my room until people aren't sick." Odie went to his room and fed Gregor. The puffin was finally getting to a healthy weight now that Odie's brother Tipp wasn't sneaking him treats all the time.

Odie had only been to the upper continents once, and he wasn't completely sure what to expect. He could only hold so many things in his cape pockets, so he'd have to choose what to take carefully. They weren't going into trouble, so he probably didn't need anything for protection, but it was always good to be prepared.

After placing his feathered cape over his shoulders, he began loading the pockets. He had put at least five pockets in every cape he made. The trick was to load the pockets and not break any of the vials while he was running around doing things. He stuffed a vial of sleeping potion in one. He wished he had magic. The sleeping potion only worked if it was set on fire, so if he couldn't start a fire, it was useless.

He should probably leave a few of his inventions with Claret and Kaylee. He frowned when he thought about Queen Claret. She hadn't spoken more than a few words to him since they escaped the goblins. He hoped she didn't blame him for the time she spent in the dungeon, and he really hoped she hadn't changed the way she felt about him.

He shook his head to rid himself of those thoughts. Falling for the queen was probably a mistake, but he hadn't done it on purpose. He stuck a stink bomb in one pocket. They were always good if you needed a quick distraction. He filled the rest of his pockets, then carefully took off the cape and hung it in his wardrobe. He'd be ready at a moment's notice.

Kaylee groaned and held her head. "Being sick in Riviand is worse than being sick on Earth." She turned sideways in bed and looked over at where Claret lay, staring up at the ceiling in her own bed. When they had gotten sick, they had decided to stay in one of the spare rooms so they wouldn't get their own rooms germy and gross.

"Why is it different?" Claret asked.

"Because Riviand doesn't have toilets or TV."

"And what are those?"

"A toilet is like an outhouse that's inside."

Claret frowned. "That sounds disgusting."

"It's better than an outhouse. It has water at the bottom. You push a lever and the water goes down some pipes and cleans away the mess."

Claret turned to her side and scrunched her forehead. "I still don't quite understand."

Kaylee blew out a breath. "I'm just glad we aren't throwing up anymore."

"Do you think the others will leave soon? It's still so strange to know that people can leave Riviand after thinking it was impossible for thousands of years."

"I'm glad. I was worried I'd be trapped here forever."

There was a knock on the door and then Odie peeked in. His mouth was covered with a bandana. "Are you two doing any better?"

Claret turned to the other side, with her back to him.

"Lots better," Kaylee said. "Now it's just a colossal headache."

Odie nodded. "It looks like we might leave tomorrow morning. I wanted to leave you two with some things." He entered, carrying a small box. "I labeled everything. There are some smoke bombs, stink bombs, and one sleeping potion. If you use that one, you need to throw it at the ground, then start it on fire." He placed the box on a small table near Kaylee's bed.

"Thanks," Kaylee said. "We aren't planning on leaving the castle, so we should be fine."

He nodded and glanced at Claret. "You never know when a vorcraw might come around. I just want you to be prepared."

Claret didn't turn, and Odie frowned.

"We appreciate it," Kaylee said. "Good luck tomorrow."

"Thanks." Odie looked at Claret once more, then left, closing the door behind him.

Kaylee waited a few seconds, then sat up. "What's your deal?"

Claret rolled back to face her. "What do you mean?"

"You've been ignoring Odie since we got back from the goblins."

Claret's mouth turned down. "I don't know what you're talking about."

"You didn't even look at him when he came in."

"That's because I look dreadful."

"And that's all?"

"What else would it be?"

Claret didn't want to explain anything to Kaylee. She didn't even know what she was thinking, so telling someone else would be impossible.

"Don't you like him anymore?" Kaylee asked.

Claret rubbed her lips together. "It's complicated."

"You know it wasn't his fault the goblins captured you, right?"

"I know. It's just... Odie was my enemy for so long. As the queen, I should have control and make good decisions. As soon as Odie showed me kindness, I completely fell for him. What if Durdessa is right? What if I only have these feelings because he is the first boy I've ever spent time with? The first person who ever saw me as a person and not a queen?"

Kaylee ran her fingers through her curly black hair and tilted her head. "I guess that could be. You've spent time with Mateo, though, and you still chose Odie."

Claret pushed herself up and leaned against the headboard. "When the dragon took Odie and me to the goblins, I admit I had my doubts. I wondered if Odie had betrayed me. It's gotten me thinking. I don't know him that well. He spent most of his life with the goblins. Could he really change that fast?"

Kaylee shrugged. "I guess you'll have to figure that out."

Claret twisted the top of her blanket. She was trying to protect her heart, but she knew it was too late. If Odie didn't turn out to be what he seemed, she was going to be crushed.

"I trust him," Kaylee said, "but I didn't know him when he was working for the goblins."

"He was never mean, just the goblins' messenger."

"And you didn't like him then?"

"No, I hated him. When he appeared, it meant he was asking for gold for the goblins. He says he regrets it now."

"Do you believe him?"

"Yes, but I don't always trust my judgment. Don't you think it seems odd to go from hate to... something else in such a short amount of time?"

"I don't know."

"I need to make sure I know what I really think and that I'm not just letting his new hairstyle influence me."

Kaylee laughed. "What do you mean?"

Claret felt her face heat. "Odie used to wear his hair slicked back. Now that he's stopped, he looks so much more appealing."

Kaylee laughed again. "Ouch. Laughing hurts my head. I'm not a great one to give advice. I've never been in love or anything. Not even close."

"I'm not in love," Claret protested, although she wasn't sure. Odie filled a hole in her heart, but that could be because she was inexperienced.

"Just be careful," Kaylee said. "Don't let your mind lead your heart or the other way around. If you push Odie away now and then realize you love him, he might not put himself out there again. I think you need to talk to him."

Claret sighed. "That sounds awkward."

"It might be, but is it worth it?"

Claret frowned. "I suppose it is. I believe love is the most important thing in the world."

Mateo ran around the streets of Tyran. He was still weak from being sick, but if he missed his run again, he was going to get out of shape. He'd been pushing himself a little harder ever since Odie had beaten him at a race. Losing wasn't his thing. He usually focused on endurance over speed, but that was before. The next time they raced, he was going to win.

A scream behind him caused him to spin around. He scowled as a vorcraw came around the corner of a house and picked up a water barrel. His tiger eyes locked on Mateo and he roared. The people walking the streets all ran. Mateo looked around for something to use as a weapon. If he could break the water barrel, that would be the end of the vorcraw. They couldn't survive water.

The vorcraw lifted the barrel above his head and threw it with amazing force. Mateo jumped out of the way and the barrel burst into pieces, only steps away from him. Water splashed his legs and a piece of wood hit him, but it was harmless.

Mateo ran as the vorcraw charged him. Outrunning one wasn't hard. Their gazelle legs should be faster, but since they only had two and their bodies were bulky, it made them slow and clumsy. He scanned the road, trying to see another barrel. One splash of water would kill a vorcraw and that would be easier than engaging one in a fight.

Water guns would be epic right now. It was too bad they weren't found in Riviand. If he ever went back to Earth, he'd grab some and bring them back. That would solve the problem with little effort. The vorcraw roared again, and he turned to find it gaining on him.

Mateo frowned. He wasn't going as fast as usual since he was still feeling weak. Mateo turned to face the monster. He wouldn't be able to make it to the castle before it overtook him at the pace he was going. He scooped up a rock and threw it with everything in him. The rock hit the vorcraw in the chest, barely slowing him down.

Mateo concentrated on a larger rock nearby. He raised his hand and tried to levitate it. The rock trembled but didn't rise. The vorcraw was going to be on him any second.

"Duck!" someone yelled from behind him. He wasn't sure if they were talking to him or not, but he dropped to the ground. Something whizzed past his head and hit the vorcraw in the chest. Mateo stood up and watched the creature try to pull a sword from himself. He growled and fell to the ground. Smoke rose from the monster and it disappeared. The sword clattered to the dirt road.

Mateo turned to see Trio, one of the city's blacksmiths, standing tall. His long beard blew in the breeze. He walked over to the place the vorcraw had been and picked up the sword, then wiped it on his dirty white apron.

"Thanks," Mateo said.

Trio grinned, showing several missing teeth. "Glad to help. Now I know this sword is good. You are a curiosity to me. Not many people have vorcraws sent after them."

"I'm just lucky, I guess."

Trio held out the sword. "Take it. It's a good one."

Mateo took the sword and turned it in his hand. It was simple but obviously sharp. It hadn't had any trouble stabbing the vorcraw. "How much?"

"You can have it. I don't know what you and your friends are up to, but I know you are on the right side of things. You put the replica Blade of the Phoenix I made in place of the real one. I figure that's because you are keeping the real one safe and away from prying eyes. I'm honored that my sword is good enough to pass for the real one."

Mateo thought about denying it, but Trio wasn't stupid. The Blade of the Phoenix had been stolen once before, and that meant it could be stolen again. Placing a duplicate and having it protected seemed like the best plan.

"I only hear rumors," Trio said, "but the people in Tyran and probably all of Riviand are talking about you and the others. Most people find hope when they hear about the way you saved Riviand from rising. Others see you as a threat. Don't go running around without a weapon. It's dangerous."

Mateo nodded. "Thanks." He ran a hand through his black hair. "Vorcraws die if they get wet. We need to figure out a good way to carry water with us, besides for drinking."

Trio rubbed a hand over his beard. "Hmm. I think I could come up with something. If I do, I'll let you know." He turned and left Mateo standing in the road with the sword.

2

— · —

CHAPTER 2

Odie, Mateo, Dovin, and Durdessa stood in the main hall of the castle. They all had a pack over their shoulders and they were ready to teleport to the cave on the goblin mountain. From there, they would go to Akkron and try to find information on dragon shifters.

Kaylee had come and told them all goodbye but not Claret. Odie told himself he didn't care, but he knew it was a lie. He needed to move carefully or some of his vials might break. He needed to come up with something less breakable to store his things in. The problem with that was, most of them only worked after the glass broke.

"Are we ready?" Dovin asked. They all nodded.

"Wait!" Claret said, hurrying toward them, her green dress flowing after her. "Can I talk to Odie for a few minutes?"

Durdessa frowned but didn't say anything.

"I'll be right back," Odie said, following Claret into a room off the side of the hall. There was no furniture in the room, but the walls were covered in paintings of former kings and queens. He turned to Claret. He ignored the sweat running down his back.

"I didn't want you to leave until I spoke with you."

Odie nodded. She looked serious. He supposed this was the time she was going to tell him she wasn't interested in spending any time with him anymore. He knew it was coming, but it still put a lump in his throat.

She twisted her hands together and looked at the floor. "I don't know you well, Odie. When the dragon took us to the goblins, and I spent time in the dungeon, I couldn't help wondering whether you had betrayed me."

"I would never. I know it's hard for you to trust me after everything I put you through in the name of the goblins."

She nodded and looked up at him. "I think Durdessa might be right. We need time to get to know each other better before—"

"You can fully trust me?"

She nodded. "I feel in my heart that I can, but you were part of the goblins for most of your life."

He looked at his boots and nodded. "I understand." He did, but that didn't make it feel any better.

"I just wanted to let you know what I was thinking before you left. I know I've been distant, and I want you to know why."

"Being *distant* won't help us get to know each other."

"I know. I've been working through my thoughts."

"I hope you'll trust me someday." He pulled his black ring from his pinky finger and handed it to her. "This is the only thing I have from my life before the goblins took me in. It was on my thumb when King Ummi found me. It's the most important thing I own. I want you to take it."

"I can't do that," she protested, trying to hand it back.

"You can. I want you to see the trust I have in you." He turned and put his hand over the doorknob.

Claret grabbed his arm and pulled so he would turn. She looked up at him and frowned. "I want to be honest, Odie. That's why I'm telling you these things. My head says to be careful, but my heart says that I already love you." She threw her arms around him and gave him a hug. The glass containers in his cape clinked together. Odie couldn't make his eyes wider if he tried. She opened the door and disappeared around the corner.

Odie waited for a moment and took a deep breath. He stood tall and walked out. Mateo, Durdessa, and Dovin all stared at him. He shrugged. "What?"

"Are we ready to go?" Dovin asked. "Mateo, try not to run us into any cave walls." They had decided Mateo would take them to the cave, then Dovin would take them to Akkron. Dovin hadn't ever been in the cave, so he couldn't teleport them. Dovin turned to grab his bag.

"What did Claret say?" Mateo whispered next to him.

Odie shook his head. "Girls are really confusing."

"This is going to be so boring," Kaylee said at lunch. "What are we going to do until everyone else comes back?"

Claret swallowed a bite of carrots. "I hate to say this, but you are going to have to be bored by yourself most of the time. I have a rigorous schedule that I've been neglecting. After lunch, I need to meet with people and address their concerns. It takes hours and doesn't leave me a lot of time."

Kaylee stabbed her meat. "I guess I'll have to keep myself busy. I wish we hadn't promised to stay in the castle. Willow and I could try to fly together better." Kaylee thought riding an alicorn would be as easy as a horse, but the alicorn was larger and didn't always notice Kaylee's attempts at steering.

"I wonder how many vorcraws Isadora has sent after us," Claret said. "I thought they were only after the two of us, but since one attacked Mateo the other day, who knows? What if they attack everyone?"

Kaylee didn't see that happening. Isadora wouldn't waste efforts on people she wasn't after. "I've been keeping a glass of water in any room I'm in."

"So have I."

Kaylee put a hand to her hair and sighed. She wasn't used to having to do it so often, but no one in Riviand knew how to do box braids. "Is there anyone at the castle who knows how to do hair really well?" she asked.

"Peora does my hair most days. She's good. Would you like me to ask her to do something for you?"

"I don't want to be a bother."

"She loves doing it. She wouldn't mind at all. It gets her out of doing other chores."

Later that day, Kaylee sat in her room with Peora. Kaylee guessed her to be about twenty. Her long brown hair was pulled back into a fancy braid and she wore a neat dress and apron, just like the rest of the staff. Kaylee was trying to draw a picture to explain what she wanted her to do.

Peora tapped her lip as she looked at Kaylee's drawing. "So you want the braids to go back from your face and fall down your back?"

"Yes. Well, it's too short to go down my back and braiding will make it shorter, but I want them all pulled back so they don't get in my face. They need to be really tight so they stay in for a long time."

"I think I can do it," she said, opening her bag.

"I usually have fake hair braided into it to make it longer, but that doesn't seem to be a thing here."

Peora pulled out a comb and frowned. "I've never heard of that before. Where are you from?"

"About as far as you can get," Kaylee said. "What about you?"

"I grew up in Tyran."

"How long have you worked at the castle?"

"Sit here," Peora said, pointing at the chair. "I've worked here for two years. It's the job my family always wanted for me."

Kaylee sat down, and Peora began combing through her hair. "Is it the job you wanted?"

Peora smiled. "None of us get that, do we?"

"What job would you want?"

Peora began parting Kaylee's hair. "Hmm. That's a hard one. It would be ideal to not have to work for someone. Not farming, though. That's what my family does. Working for the queen is a lot better. She's kind and she pays well. Farming is stressful. There's a lot to worry about. In my dreams, a handsome man rides into my life and carries me into the sunset and we go on all types of adventures together. Of course that's never going to happen."

Kaylee grimaced as Peora pulled on her hair. "It might."

"Nah. That only happens in fairy stories. It's all right, though. I'm happy and content, but it doesn't hurt to dream every once in a while, does it?"

Claret sat on her throne and watched a short man enter the room. His eyes scanned the room as if looking for a trap. There was something familiar about him. He held a straw hat and bowed when he approached her.

She motioned for him to rise. "What can I do for you?"

"You don't remember me?" he asked.

She squinted and thought for a moment. "Korum?"

He gave her a half smile. "Yes."

Claret felt her stomach tighten. Korum had worked for the witch. "Did Isadora send you?"

Korum turned his hat in his hands. "No, Your Highness, although she found me after you set us free. I told her it wasn't my choice. I hope you won't hold that against me. She would be angry if she knew I left. I'm working for her again."

Claret frowned. "I can hide you."

"No, she would find me. I've come to tell you she has added to her collection."

Claret's frown deepened. Isadora collected animals and people that she showed off to her friends. She had tried to keep Claret, Kaylee, and Durdessa, but they'd escaped and freed most of the others.

"She was angry with you before, but now that you've stolen her mermaid, she wants more than revenge. If you tell her where you have hidden Jayah, she will let the others go."

Claret's eyes narrowed. "What others?"

"They are people who mean something to your friend."

"Kaylee?"

"Yes. With the help of the goblins, Isadora took some people from the world Kaylee is from. She has also put spells around the dungeon, so you cannot use magic around them to set them free."

"Do you know who they are?"

"No. Two of them speak with an accent so deep I cannot understand them."

"How many are there?"

"Three."

"And you can understand the third?"

"Yes, but he's ignoring me and won't talk. He doesn't seem to know the other two."

"Does Isadora know you're here?"

He shook his head. "She sent me on a different task. I just stopped here on my way. If you act fast, there shouldn't be any resistance. Isadora left me in charge, and she is spending all her time with the goblins. She didn't leave me the keys. I think she distrusts me since you all escaped."

Claret tapped her fingers against the arm of the throne. "Can you tell me where Isadora lives? I don't think I can find it again."

Korum blew into his hand, and a map appeared. He handed it to Claret. "The circled area is where you can find her house. Be careful. I wish I could help more, but I fear her."

"Thank you," Claret said.

He bowed and left the room.

Claret placed the map on her lap and rubbed her temples. If she told Kaylee, she would want to go immediately. So many things could go wrong, and they had promised to stay at the castle until the others returned. If she didn't tell her, she would find out eventually and be angry. She was going to have to tell.

Claret told the guard standing outside the door that she couldn't see any more people today. She hurried through the halls and knocked on Kaylee's door.

"Come in!" Kaylee called.

Claret opened the door and found Peora braiding Kaylee's hair. From the looks of it, she was almost done.

"Is something wrong?" Kaylee asked.

Claret looked from Kaylee to Peora. She couldn't decide whether to ask Peora to leave. She trusted her, and they might need an extra hand if Kaylee went searching for Isadora's house.

"Korum was just here."

Kaylee's eyes widened. "Isadora's servant?"

"Yes. He said Isadora went to your world and captured some people that mean something to you. She thinks we might give Jayah back in exchange for them."

Peora finished Kaylee's hair and stepped off to the side. She stood looking at the floor, waiting for instructions.

Kaylee's brows came together. "Who are they?"

"He didn't know, but there are three of them. He said no one can do magic down in Isadora's basement anymore."

"Great," Kaylee muttered. "I wonder if he has my mom and stepdad. I'm going to have to go for them."

"Not yet. We promised we would stay here. We should wait for Dovin. He's good at this kind of thing."

Kaylee shook her head. "I can't wait and leave them in danger. I'll go alone."

Claret threw her hands in the air. "And do what? How are you going to get them out?"

"I don't know."

"You can't go alone."

"I'll ask Coach Williams to go with me."

"He doesn't have magic."

Kaylee sighed. "That doesn't matter if no one can do magic down there."

"I can help," Peora said. "I don't know exactly what you are talking about, but I'm strong and not too bad with magic."

Kaylee shook her head. "Isadora is a powerful witch. I can't put you in danger."

"If you aren't even from this world, which shouldn't be able to happen, and you can't do magic, then I could be an asset to you."

"Why would you do that? You don't even know me that well."

Peora shrugged. "I told you I dream about adventure." She grinned. "I prefer a handsome man to be involved, but any adventure would be welcome."

Kaylee and Claret shared a look.

"All right," Kaylee said. "Come to my room tomorrow morning and we'll go."

— · —

CHAPTER 3

Mateo sat on a blue cushion in a library in Akkron and read a fictional book about dragon shifters. He'd never seen a library like this one. Shelves went from the floor to the ceiling, and the ceiling was at least thirty feet high. The one in the castle was bigger, but this one felt more comfortable. There were tables and chairs, but Mateo preferred the large cushions.

"I don't think that book will be helpful," Odie said from a green cushion next to him. "Fiction can mean anything goes."

"I know, but those other books the librarian got for us look so boring." Mateo didn't enjoy reading, and non-fiction had always felt painful.

Odie held up the book he was looking through. "This one doesn't seem useful. It only mentioned shifters for one paragraph. I'm going to go find the outhouse."

"Right!" Mateo said, dropping the book and jumping to his feet. "I promised to show you a real bathroom. It will change your life." Mateo led Odie around the library until they found two doors. One said "Men" and the other said

"Women." They entered the one that said men and Mateo led him to a stall.

Odie looked in and narrowed his eyes. "So it's like an indoor outhouse?"

"Yep. That thing is called a toilet. After you do your business, you push this here." Mateo pushed the button and the toilet loudly flushed. Odie jumped back and stared in shock. "And no more mess."

Odie took a step forward and stared into the bowl. "That was amazing. Where does it go?"

Mateo thought for a minute. "I have no idea, but it's gone, so yay."

Odie got down on his hands and knees and began looking around the toilet. "I have to figure out how this works."

"You probably don't want to go crawling around the floor in here. Some people aren't the best aims."

"I'm going to learn how to make one of these."

"If you like that, come see this."

Odie stood and Mateo showed him the sink. He turned it on and Odie's eyes widened as water poured out.

"It's like a pump, but you don't have to pump it?" Odie asked.

"Yep. Akkron is pretty advanced."

"I wonder how hard all of this would be to recreate."

"Pretty hard. Everything is connected to pipes and stuff."

"I bet people would pay a lot for it."

"Probably."

Odie grinned. "I think I've just found a new purpose in life. Do you think there are books about how to make these things?"

Mateo frowned. "Probably not in the library. No one really wants to learn how to make a toilet, so it's probably not going to be easy to find."

"But someone knows how. I need to find them."

"Well, I'm going to go back to reading. You can use the toilet and see how awesome it is yourself." Mateo went out to his cushion and tried to read. He got bored after a few minutes and fell into a light sleep.

"Mateo?" Dovin said, kicking his boot.

Mateo opened his eyes and yawned. "Hmm?"

"Where's Odie?"

"Probably still in the bathroom. He's trying to figure out how the toilet works."

Dovin chuckled. "I think we are wasting our time here. I've had an idea. You remember Tal?"

Mateo frowned. How could he forget the guy Kaylee called cute? "Yes."

"He can communicate with animals. He might be able to tell us something."

Mateo forgot about his uncalled for hatred for Tal for a minute. "Really? I didn't know anyone could do that."

"Let's go talk to him and see what he knows."

"Sounds better than reading a billion books."

"Go get Odie and we can go. Durdessa will meet us later."

"She doesn't want to come?"

Dovin frowned. "She's going to visit our daughter."

"Don't you want to go?"

"She won't see me. I just hope she'll see Durdessa."

Mateo frowned. "Why wouldn't she?"

"Her life has been full of poor decisions. It would be easier if she were sorry about them, but she isn't. She's caused a lot of problems in Akkron. Let's not dwell on that now. It's a problem for Durdessa and me to deal with."

Mateo nodded and ran to get Odie. Tal's house wasn't far, so Dovin had them walk. Odie talked about the possibility of bringing flushing toilets to Riviand the entire way. Mateo tuned him out but made the occasional noise to pretend he was listening.

An enormous house came into view. It had large pillars and an impressive staircase leading up to the door. There were two balconies in the front and at least ten windows going across on all three floors. Mateo stopped to stare. Odie didn't seem impressed, but he grew up in a castle.

"Let's go in," Dovin said, entering the gate. Mateo and Odie followed. A long pathway led up to the front door and was surrounded by perfectly trimmed grass.

"How many people live here?" Mateo asked.

"I'm not sure," Dovin said. "I think Tal has a few staff members who live here."

"Wait, this is Tal's house?"

"Yes."

"I didn't know he lived in a mansion. Sen never told me he had rich friends." Tal was Mateo's brother Sen's friend, but Mateo had only met him a couple of times.

"Didn't you know Tal's father used to be the governor of Akkron?" Dovin asked.

"I knew that, but I guess I didn't realize he was rich."

"The house Tal grew up in was bigger than this one."

They climbed the stairs to the front door, and Dovin knocked. A man Mateo assumed was the butler opened the door. He wore a nice suit and had a neatly trimmed brown mustache.

"May I help you?" the man asked.

"We're here to see Tal," Dovin said. "Is he home?"

"Yes, but I believe he is busy."

"He will see us if you tell him we are here," Dovin said confidently.

The butler sighed. "I was told he was not to be disturbed. He has friends over."

"Well, tell me where they are and I'll disturb them. You can tell him it was my fault."

"He is out back."

"Thank you," Dovin said. They walked around the large house, and before they turned the corner to the backyard, Mateo could hear what sounded like a basketball.

"They don't have basketball in this world," he said. When they came into the backyard, Mateo was surprised to see a half-sized basketball court. Tal and several others were in the middle of a game.

"What are they doing?" Odie asked.

"It's called basketball," Mateo told him. "It's a really popular sport on Earth."

"Kaylee's cousin Graham is a talented basketball player," Dovin said, pointing at Graham. "Tal built this so they could play. Of course they got the hoop on Earth and brought it through a portal."

A short girl with a long black ponytail stopped and stared at them. She looked at Dovin and waved. "Hey, Professor Dovin!" She came jogging toward them.

"Ming Li, how are you?" Dovin asked, catching the girl in a hug.

"Great. You guys are just in time. We could use some more players. I'm guessing you're Sen's brother," she said, looking at Mateo.

"Yes, I'm Mateo."

"And this is Odie," Dovin said.

"Can any of you play basketball?" Most of the other people who had been playing were walking over. Mateo recognized Graham, Tal, and Graham's girlfriend, Wren. There were two more people still bouncing the basketball, but Mateo didn't know them.

"I play," Mateo said.

"I've never seen it before," Odie admitted.

"Well, Mateo should be on my team," Ming Li said. "The teams are already too uneven, and if Mateo is as competitive as Sen, it might even things out a little."

"I'm more competitive than Sen," Mateo said. "I'm in."

"I'm not sure they came to play basketball," Graham said. "If Dovin shows up unannounced, there must be a problem somewhere."

"That's true," Dovin said, "but a quick game wouldn't hurt."

"How's Kaylee?"

"She's safe."

"Good. Then let's play!"

"There's no way to make the teams even," Tal said. "Not with those two on the same team." He pointed over at the man and woman who were still playing.

Ming Li shook her head. "They refuse to be on opposite teams and they both stink. They just got married last month, so I'll give them a pass this time. So I get Mateo, and you get Odie," Ming Li said to Graham.

Graham nodded. "Even with Odie and Wren, my team is going to beat you."

"Hey!" said Wren. "I've gotten way better over the last few years, and I'm better than Jazz." She pushed a stray strand of red hair behind her ear.

They all looked at the two people. The guy threw the ball toward the hoop and missed by three feet.

"Air ball!" Tal called. "Nice, Jazz!"

"I'm not so sure about this," Odie said. "It looks complicated."

"It'll be fun," Mateo said. "You might be a natural."

Mateo took his cape off and threw it on the ground. Odie reluctantly did the same.

"Let's not do teams," Wren said. "Let's play an easier game like Horse. That's easier for someone when they've never played before."

"Sounds good," Graham said, putting his arm over Wren's shoulder. They all walked toward the court. Mateo smiled. It was time to show these people what he could do.

Odie sat on the grass in Tal's backyard and took a tall glass of water from one of Tal's staff. "Thank you." He took a long drink. Basketball wasn't as bad as he had imagined. Once he'd caught on, he wasn't too bad. Mateo drank his water with a scowl. Odie hid a smile. Mateo was better than him and most of the others, but he'd been no match for Graham or Ming Li.

Jazz and his wife had already gone home, but it still felt like there were a lot of people he didn't know. Dovin was sitting next to him. He'd patiently waited for the game to end.

"So why are you here?" Ming Li asked, sitting down. "You don't just come to watch me trounce these people at basketball. I hope you aren't planning on taking anyone back down to Riviand. It sounds unsafe to be under the ocean. I couldn't believe it when Graham and Tal told us about it."

"We came to talk to Tal," Dovin said. "We need his expertise."

Tal shot him a crooked grin. "This is a first. You usually come looking for Graham."

"Can you really talk to animals?" Mateo asked.

Tal nodded. "In a way. It's not exactly talking, it's more like we can read each other's minds."

"That sounds a little creepy."

He laughed. "It is."

"Even dragons?" Odie asked.

"Yep," Tal said, taking a sip of water.

"Do you need us?" Wren asked. "Graham and I are sup-posed to meet my dad."

"No, go ahead."

They all said goodbye and then went back to dragons.

"Do you know anything about dragon shifters?" Mateo asked.

Tal's smile slipped away. "A little. Why? Please tell me you don't have one in Riviand."

"Not only do we have one, but he is trying to start a war," Dovin said. "Anything you can tell us would be appreciated."

Everyone turned to look at Tal. He put his glass on the ground and sighed. "Dragon shifters are born, not made. They are really rare, but there are several families that are suspected of being shifters. They can talk to dragons in ways even I can't. Dragons gravitate toward them. That's one thing that makes them dangerous."

"Can they control the other dragons?" Mateo asked.

"No, but they're very persuasive."

"Are they usually bad?" Odie asked.

"They're like anyone," Tal said. "They can be bad or good. A lot of them let themselves get corrupted because they know how powerful they are. Most of them keep it a secret because it makes people uneasy."

"That's stupid," Ming Li said. "It's going to make more people uneasy if they don't know who the shifters are."

"People don't talk about it a lot," Tal said. "I think most people assume there aren't any left anymore."

"Do you know any?" Dovin asked.

"I met one once. It wasn't too long ago. He seemed all right. I don't know how to contact him or anything."

"Do you want me to go get Sheba?" Ming Li asked.

"I already called for her," Tal said, touching the side of his head.

Sheba was Tal's dragon. Mateo and Odie had ridden her once when Tal flew them over to Mermaid's Demise.

"I understand why people don't want others to know they're shifters," Tal said. "There are lots of stories about evil shifters, so people would automatically judge them."

Odie looked up and saw an orange dragon flying toward them.

"There she is," Tal said. The dragon landed and sat down next to Tal. "Hello, girl." He stood and ran a hand over her head. Sheba nuzzled her head into Tal.

"How did you get her to like you?" Odie asked. "We have a dragon at Claret's castle and she doesn't trust me."

"It wasn't too much work," Tal said. "I just spent five minutes a day gaining her trust. Once she tolerated that, I added more time. After about two months, we were besties."

Ming Li rolled her eyes.

"Did I say it wrong?" Tal asked.

Ming Li grinned. "No. 'Besties' just sounds funny when you say it."

"Ming Li is from Earth," Tal told them.

"Oh, yeah?" Mateo asked. "What part?"

"California."

"Do you have family here?" Mateo found it strange so many people from Earth had ended up here.

"My mom lives here. She owns the bakery. She's originally from Taiwan, but she likes it here, so I'm sure we'll stay forever."

Tal raised one brow. "Staying for your mom, huh?"

She grinned and punched him in the arm. "You know it." They smiled at each other, and Mateo and Odie shared a look. There was definitely something going on between those two.

Dovin cleared his throat. "So back to shifters."

"Right," Tal said. "Let me talk to Sheba for a minute." Tal rested his hand on the dragon's head and leaned his head into hers. They all sat quietly for a few minutes. He looked up at Dovin. "Do you know the shifter's name?"

"Garin."

He nodded and went quiet again. The dragon reared back and snorted. Tal stroked her head and whispered something to her.

"She knows of Garin," Tal finally said. "All the dragons here hate him. That's kind of odd because most dragons like shifters. They try to stay out of his way. That could be bad or good. If the dragons in Riviand dislike him, then they might not listen to him. If they're too scared of him, they might follow him. I could see it going either way."

Tal glanced at Ming Li, and she frowned.

She stood and brushed off her pants. "I know that look, Talon. You want to go back to Riviand to talk to dragons."

He gave her a crooked smile. "It wouldn't be long. I just need to give them a warning."

"Can anyone learn to talk to animals?" Mateo asked.

Tal shrugged. "I got the power when I went into Padmire's cave. Hundreds of years ago, it was a common enough thing, but I've never met anyone else who can do it the same as I can."

Ming Li crossed her arms and glared at Tal. "If you go, I'm coming."

"I don't think that's a good idea," he said.

"We still have a few things we need to do before we leave," Dovin said. "You two can take time and talk and see what you want to do, and we will come back before we return to Riviand."

Tal nodded. "Sounds good."

Mind Li smiled. "We'll be ready."

4

— · —

CHAPTER 4

K aylee held up a saw with a thin blade. "This will saw through metal bars?"

Trio, the blacksmith, nodded. "It will take some time, but it will get the job done."

She sighed. "Does it make a lot of noise?"

He rubbed his beard. "You won't go unnoticed, if that's what you mean. If you're trying to be discreet, you aren't going to have any easy time. Cutting through metal isn't a stealthy job. If you tell me more about what you are trying to accomplish, I might be able to give better solutions."

"Everything is hypothetical right now," Kaylee said. "I just like to be prepared."

Trio nodded. "If you're trying to break out of a prison, you would want to cut through in one place, then push the bar down with your foot or something like that. Once it's cut, it won't be as strong."

Kaylee nodded and handed him some money. "Thank you."

He nodded. "Let me know if there's anything else I can help with."

Kaylee nodded and hurried back to the castle. Without Dovin and Durdessa, they were going to have to get to Isadora's house without teleporting. That left flying. With luck, Peora would be better at reading a map than she was.

Claret smiled. She had teleported from one end of the hall to the other and back again, and then to her bedroom. She had it down. That would save time, and now she could take Kaylee and Peora to Isadora's.

Teleporting had taken her a while to get down, but now that she could do it, she could rule her kingdom a lot better. She could also go to the upper continent if something happened and Odie and the others didn't return. She couldn't think of a reason that would happen, but it felt nice to have a plan.

She grabbed Odie's ring from the nightstand. Falling back onto her bed, she placed it on her finger and stared at it. She had put it on her ring finger but not on her left hand. She didn't want anyone jumping to conclusions and her ring fingers were the only fingers the ring fit on. The ring was made of something really hard and black. She had studied it more times than she wanted to admit. On the inside, someone had scratched A + N. She wondered if those were the letters of Odie's real parents' names.

She sat up when someone knocked on the door. "Come in."

Kaylee entered and shut the door behind her. "I think I'm about ready to go."

Claret smiled. "Just in time. I figured out teleporting."

Kaylee grinned. "Really? That will save so much time."

"Yes, but how will I know when to come back for you?"

"Getting back isn't as urgent. I really wish I knew who Isadora had trapped in there. It's annoying she's teamed up with the goblins. They must have helped her get to Earth, or they went themselves and got the people for her."

"What if Isadora catches you?"

"You said she's with the goblins. With luck, no one else will care. I'm sure the mermaids will tell her, eventually. I don't get their loyalty to her."

"You should leave soon. The sooner it's done, the better."

"I'll get Peora and come back."

Kaylee left the room, and Claret sighed. All her friends were going into potential danger and she just sat here. Well, the boys probably weren't in danger, but it was hard to know since they were in a place unknown to her.

A few minutes went by and then Kaylee and Peora came in. They were both dressed in black tunics and pants and had black cloaks. They wore high black boots and Kaylee had a bag going across her body.

"Ready?" Claret asked.

Peora's smile looked like it might crack her face. "I can't believe I get to teleport!"

"Can I see the map again?"

Kaylee pulled it from her bag and showed it to her.

"All right, hold on to me." Kaylee grabbed one of her hands and Peora grabbed the other.

Claret closed her eyes and felt... absolutely nothing. "Something is wrong."

"You can't do it?" Kaylee asked.

Claret dropped their hands and tried to bring up an orb of light. That was something she could do in her sleep. Nothing happened. "I can't do magic."

"None?" Kaylee asked.

She tried again. "None. I can't even feel it."

Kaylee frowned and stared at Claret's raised hand. "Is that Odie's ring?"

Claret blushed. "Yes. I'm... keeping it safe for him."

"Take it off and try."

Claret took the ring off and handed it to Kaylee. She raised her hand and a ball of light appeared.

Kaylee handed the ring back, and Claret placed it on her finger. She held up her hand and tried to do magic. Nothing.

"Odie's ring blocks magic," Claret said with wide eyes. "Do you think he knows?"

Kaylee shrugged. "Does that mean he can do magic, and he just doesn't know it?"

"I've never seen him without it, so it's possible. He said he had the ring when the goblins found him." Claret returned the ring to her nightstand. "Let's try now." They all grabbed hands and Claret took them to the backyard of Isadora's large manor.

"I'll figure out a way back. Don't worry about us," Kaylee said.

Claret nodded and teleported herself back to the castle. If they weren't back in a few days, she would send Captain

Nerman for them. She grabbed Odie's ring and turned it in her hand. Why would he have a magic-restricting ring?

Kaylee and Peora walked quietly down the steps to Isadora's dungeon. If Korum was right, Isadora wasn't here, and they had nothing to worry about. When they got to the bottom, they paused. Cells lined the hallway. They shouldn't be as full as they had been, since they had freed a lot of the creatures Isadora had put in here.

Peora glanced into the first cell. It had a tree growing from the floor and monkeys happily playing. "How odd. I wonder how she captured them."

"She used to have a troll and giant in those cells, but we got them out," Kaylee said.

Isadora might be a witch, but she kept her captives well cared for. Each cell was designed for the creature inside and they were all clean and comfortable. When they came to the mermaid tanks, they paused.

Peora's mouth hung open. "Mermaids! I never would have believed they were real!" The three mermaids glared at them.

"Great," Havva said, pushing her long black hair away from her face. "Did you come to cause more trouble?"

"We aren't the ones causing the trouble," Kaylee said. "That's all Isadora."

The mermaid with a long brown braid frowned. "When you took Jayah, it almost broke Isadora. You need to leave."

"Jayah is safe and happy," Kaylee said. She didn't really know about the happy part because she hadn't seen her in a while, so she was guessing.

"I suppose you've come for the humans?" Havva asked. "I hope you have. All they do is argue. At least I assume that is what they are doing. When they speak, it's impossible to understand."

The mermaid with red hair swam to the back.

"Don't hide, Bryn. These people will think you're unhappy and try to take you away."

"I'm happy," Bryn said. "I just don't like people gaping at me."

Peora looked the other way. "Sorry."

"We aren't here to bother you," Kaylee said.

"Kaylee?" someone called from the cell next to the mermaids.

Kaylee hurried to the cell and saw her best friend from Earth holding on to the bars. "Mia! Don't worry, I'm going to get you out of here."

"Thank goodness," said a voice from the shadows. "I thought we'd be here forever."

"Chad?" Kaylee rolled her eyes. Isadora was crazy if she thought Chad was a person Kaylee wanted to see.

Mia shook her head, her short, red hair bouncing. "You didn't come a minute too soon. If I have to stay in here with Chad for one more minute, I'm going to go full Mateo on his face."

Kaylee giggled. "I hope not."

"He got in a lucky punch," Chad muttered, pushing his brown hair from his eyes.

Peora frowned. "Is it strange that I can't understand a word you're saying? Well, maybe one or two."

"No, they're from a different world." Kaylee grabbed her bag and pulled out the hacksaw. She turned to Mia. "This is all I have to get you out of here, so I better start." She got to her knees and began sawing. The high-pitched sound made the hairs on her arms stand up.

"You're going to wake up the hot, grumpy guy," Mia whispered.

Kaylee looked around the cell. There were three beds and a small table. On the bed closest to the far wall, a man was lying with his back to them. Kaylee began sawing again, and the man sat up. Kaylee frowned. He wasn't anyone she knew. He appeared to be around twenty and had black hair and brown skin. She frowned. He looked a bit like Mateo.

"Who are you?" she asked.

He just frowned.

"He doesn't speak English," Chad said. "I tried talking to him in Spanish, but all he did was glare at me."

Mia rolled her eyes. "You don't speak Spanish."

"Sure I do. I took two semesters in middle school."

"He can talk to the woman who put us here," Mia said.

Kaylee changed to Akkronese. "Who are you?"

He glared at her.

She raised her brow. "You have a glare that looks just like Mateo."

He stood and sauntered to the bars. "You know Mateo?"

"Yes."

"My mom said she let him go to Riviand."

"He's been in Riviand, but he's on the upper continents right now. He'll be back. Are you his brother?"

He nodded. "I'm Miguel."

"How did you get here?"

"I was on campus working on a research paper. A bunch of goblins jumped out and grabbed me before I had time to think. They knocked me out and when I woke up, I was here. The witch told me she was keeping me here to get something she wants and then she would let me go. The word of a witch means nothing to me."

"Well, let me try to cut through this," Kaylee said. "I'm Kaylee."

"The girl who came with Mateo? Graham's cousin?"

"Yes." She began sawing at the bar again. "This might take a while."

"We can take turns. What's your name?" he asked.

Kaylee looked up. He was looking at Peora.

"Peora."

"Are you from Riviand?"

"Yes."

Kaylee kept sawing. Her arm was getting tired fast, and the sound was really annoying.

"Can't you move faster?" Chad asked.

Kaylee glared up at him. "It's not easy. You could do it."

"I could do it faster."

Kaylee handed him the saw and stood. "Fine, go for it."

Miguel and Peora had moved down to the other end of the cell and they were talking quietly.

"Where are we?" Mia asked. "I woke up and couldn't figure out how I got here."

Chad looked up from his sawing. "A woman came to the school, and I heard her asking questions about Kaylee. I told her I knew more about her than anyone else, unless you count Mia. I pointed Mia out to her. She told me she wanted to show me something and the next thing I knew, I was here."

Kaylee rolled her eyes. "Why would you tell her you know me well? You don't know that much about me."

"Sure I do."

Mia shook her head. "Give it up, Chad. So are you going to tell me where we are?"

Kaylee rubbed her lips together. "You won't believe me even if I do."

"Try me."

"A witch captured you and she brought you to a different world."

Chad stopped sawing and shared a look with Mia.

"The weird thing is, I'm telling the truth."

"Okay," Chad said. "So how do we defeat a witch?" He went back to sawing.

"We don't. We escape and get as far from here as we can. When Mateo comes back, he can take you back to Earth."

Mia glared at her. "That's really not funny. Mateo's around here?"

"Sort of. We're actually under the ocean. This place is magical. Mateo is in the same world, but up above."

Mia and Chad stared at her like she'd grown horns.

"You don't have to believe me, but you're in danger and we have to get you out of here."

"I thought you were studying abroad," Mia said.

"Well, this is about as abroad as it gets."

"We heard Mateo was sent back to Mexico."

"He was. It's because he was suspended for punching me," Chad said, dropping the saw and rubbing his hand. "This is hard."

"He wasn't suspended. Dovin brought us here. Coach Williams is here as well." She reached through the bars and grabbed the saw and began sawing again.

"Dovin gave his notice, but Coach William just disappeared," Mia said.

"They're both from this world," Kaylee explained. "Once you get out, you'll both believe me. There are mermaids right next to you."

Mia sighed. "I don't think you're all right. The people next to us are jerks. They keep yelling at us. I can't tell exactly what they are saying, but it doesn't sound nice."

Miguel came over and held out his hand. "Let me take a turn." Kaylee handed over the saw, and he got to work.

"How can you understand him and talk like that?" Chad asked.

"Dovin taught me. And Miguel is Mateo's brother."

Miguel looked at Chad and frowned. "Do you know this guy? I can't understand most of what he says, but he's annoying."

"We went to school together."

"Is he talking about me?" Chad asked.

"I think he said you're annoying," Mia said. "But it's hard to tell."

Chad crossed his arms.

"I wish I could use magic in here," Peora said. "I've tried and I can't do anything."

Miguel frowned and kept sawing. If she remembered correctly, Mateo had said most of his brothers couldn't do magic.

"Did you say something about mermaids?" Miguel asked.

"Yes, they're right over there," Kaylee said, pointing.

"These two I'm sharing a cell with keep fighting. Whoever is over there keeps yelling at them. They're probably as tired of listening to them as I am." The vein in his forehead was poking out. Sawing through bars wasn't easy. "I think I've almost got it."

5

—·—

CHAPTER 5

Odie, Mateo, and Dovin stood on a small porch and waited for Durdessa to knock. Durdessa wanted to talk to her brother and let him know she was alive. The house looked like it could blow over in a slight wind. Odie wondered if it had more than one room, and the curled roof had seen better days. The white paint had all but peeled off the front door and pieces of the siding were loose.

Durdessa took a deep breath and knocked. She waited patiently for a minute, then knocked again.

"Go away!" came a voice from inside.

Durdessa got a determined gleam in her eye and knocked harder. "Open the door, Arving!"

There was silence for a moment, and then the door opened a crack. A man peeked out and then threw the door open. He was wearing a worn white shirt and britches with a hole in the knee. His messy brown beard hung to the middle of his chest. He stared at Durdessa with his mouth gaping open.

"Dessa? You're alive?"

She stepped forward and wrapped her brother in a hug. "I'm alive."

He clung to her and frowned. "Where were you?"

She pulled back and looked at him. "I got sucked into Mermaid's Demise."

His eyes narrowed. "How did you get back?"

"It's a long story. I've been in Riviand."

"It exists?"

"Yes. What have you been doing, Arving?" She wrinkled her nose. "Why are you living in this dump, and when was the last time you bathed?"

He sighed. "I couldn't stay at my other house anymore. Too many memories. You were the last of my family. Once you were gone, I gave up on everything."

She shook her head. "You can't live like this."

Arving looked over at Odie and Mateo. "Who are these people?"

"I met them in Riviand. I'm going back, but I couldn't without checking on you."

He grabbed her arm. "Going back? You can't do that!"

"Not forever. There are some things I need to do there and then I'll come back."

He shook his head and glared at Dovin. "I blame you. Dessa never had the urge to travel until she met you."

Dovin grinned. "Good to see you again, Arving."

"I'm coming. If you are going back, you have to take me."

Durdessa looked at Dovin. "What do you think?"

"Let him come. It might be good for him."

"Just give me a few minutes to get cleaned up."

"What if we come back in a half hour?" Durdessa asked. "You can bathe and hopefully find something clean."

"All right, but don't forget to come back for me. I missed you, Dessa."

She smiled and put her hand on his arm. "I missed you too."

Durdessa looked around her old home with a huge frown. Mateo grinned. Dovin was going to get it.

"Once I disappeared, you decided to never clean again?" she asked.

Dovin chuckled. "It looks that way, doesn't it?"

Mateo wasn't the neatest person ever, but even he couldn't believe what a mess Dovin's house was. Clothing was thrown over all the furniture and there was garbage strewn across the floor.

"I kept my house on Earth tidy," he said. "I didn't like to spend more time here than I had to."

"Who is taking care of the dragons?"

"I have a boy who comes in and feeds them and cleans up when I'm away."

"Cleans up the dragons? Not inside."

He smiled. "Yes. When we come back from Riviand, I'll clean it all."

Durdessa nodded. "I hope so."

Odie's mouth turned down. "Claret's going to be sad when you leave."

She rubbed her lips together and sighed. "I know. But now that we know how to move back and forth, I can visit her often."

"What's your brother going to do in Riviand?" Mateo asked. "He doesn't look like someone who should be taken out in public."

She moved some books from the couch and sat down. "He wasn't like that before. I hope Riviand will breathe new life into him. I feel bad I did this to him."

"You didn't," Dovin said. "He made his choices."

"Should we go back for Tal?" Mateo asked. "He's waiting for us."

"Why don't you two go get Tal and we can go back and help Arving get ready? We can meet back here."

Odie sighed. "Does that mean I have to teleport with Mateo?"

Dovin laughed. "I can drop you off first."

Dovin took them to the front of Tal's house and then left. They knocked and Tal answered.

"Hey, come in."

They followed him into a large entryway. It made Kaylee's look small, and that was saying something. A large staircase went up. It had a fancy railing that curved down, but it was missing some of its gold paint. Mateo touched a spot where the paint was peeling and looked up at Tal. It didn't fit the rest of the area.

Tal grinned. "I know. I shouldn't slide down the banister, but seriously, look at that thing."

"Are you ready to go?" Odie asked him.

"Ming Li had an idea. She thinks you should go to the cave at Meegore."

Mateo frowned. "Isn't that where Padmire lives?" Mateo didn't dislike Padmire, but he didn't like him either.

"Yes. Padmire can give anyone who goes through magic. He can even choose the type. You could ask him to give you the same thing I got there. Then you could communicate with animals. I would still go with you to Riviand because it takes a while to get the magic figured out."

"I dunno," Mateo said. "If Padmire is in charge, anything could happen."

"But your friend here could get magic as well."

Odie scratched his head. "I've always wanted magic."

"Then let's go," Tal said. "Ming Li went ahead to talk to Padmire. He should be expecting us."

Mateo grabbed onto Tal's cloak, and Odie grabbed the other side. They arrived on an island before Mateo had a chance to think. Tal could teleport fast. The island was covered with trees and weeds. In front of them was a small hill with an enormous rock in front of it. Purple crystals that were at least a foot high grew out of the ground.

"That's the cave," Tal said, pointing at the small hill. "Padmire will need to move the rock."

Odie glanced into the cave opening. His heart was pounding, and he wondered if he would really leave here with magic. Padmire had opened the cave and was standing with them, tapping his webbed foot against the dirt. His blue nose twitched, and he glared at them.

"I knew you would be here eventually," he said. "I thought you'd want my help earlier."

Mateo squatted down to talk to Padmire. "Can you give me magic to talk to animals? Like Tal?"

Padmire scoffed. "Of course I can."

"And give Odie magic?"

The bungle stared up at Odie and smiled with his pointed yellow teeth. "Interesting. The last time we met, you had no magic. Now I see it pulsing through you."

Odie frowned. "What are you talking about?"

"Something has changed in you."

"I don't think so."

Padmire put his little arms against his hips. "You doubt me? Hold out your hand."

Odie stuck out his hand.

"Now think about an orb of light."

Odie pictured an orb of light appearing in his hand. He gasped when it actually appeared.

"How is that even possible?" Mateo asked.

"No idea," Padmire said. "Something must have happened."

Odie's breathing felt funny. He had dreamed of having magic so many times he found this hard to believe.

"You did it fast, too."

Tal frowned. "I've never heard of anyone suddenly getting magic."

"Me neither," Ming Li said.

"It's not normal," Padmire said. "Either something happened or something was blocking it. Well, no reason to waste time wondering. Go ahead and go through."

Ming Li crossed her arms. "I know Padmire can give them magic without making them go all the way through, but he refuses. He says they have to earn it."

"Be careful," Tal said. "I would take the slide to the left. It's an easier path, in my opinion."

Ming Li nodded. "Climbing is easier than swinging on a rope."

Padmire grinned. "I'll see you at the end."

Odie and Mateo stepped into the cave entrance, and Odie cringed when the rock rolled back over the opening. Mateo pulled up an orb of light and Odie did the same.

"I can't believe this," he said. "Why would I suddenly have magic?"

"I dunno. It's weird."

"Since I have magic, why am I even here?"

"To get something cool. After my brother Sen came through here, he could throw fire. He said people get magic that isn't very common or even magic that's been lost."

"Dovin can throw balls of fire."

"Yeah, but most people aren't like Dovin. He knows some crazy stuff."

Odie walked slowly down the stone staircase and tried to ignore the eerie shadows that were bouncing off the cave wall. He wasn't afraid of the dark, but this was a little creepy. He could see his big shadow on one wall and even though he knew it was his, it felt unsettling.

"How long do you think this will take?" Mateo asked. "Dovin and Durdessa are waiting for us."

Odie cringed. "They aren't going to be happy. We should have told them first."

"Yeah, but who knows if they would have let us come if we did?"

"I can't believe I can do magic," Odie said. "I wonder if I can only do it when I'm up here. Maybe Riviand blocks me or something."

"Are you from Riviand?" Mateo asked.

"I don't know where I'm from. The goblins found me when I was three. My goblin family never told me much about it. I don't understand how there's a cave like this. Couldn't people come in and get all the magic they wanted?"

"That's why Padmire guards it," Mateo explained. "No one could come in here for hundreds of years. If someone comes in, they get new magic, and Padmire was tired of people trying to get powerful and take over. That's why he sealed the cave. Now no one can come in unless he lets them. At least that's what my brother told me."

They got to the bottom of the stairs and stepped into a small cavern. Yellow dust covered the cave floor. Odie sighed as the dust clung to the bottom of his pants. He kicked his leg, but it didn't come off.

"We'll just have to wash it off later," Mateo said.

Odie looked around the dim cavern. He hoped he wouldn't regret coming in here.

6

— · —

CHAPTER 6

C laret walked across the large ballroom of the castle with a big leather book in her hands. She wasn't wasting time while her friends were away. If she could learn to teleport, she could learn to do anything. The ballroom was empty and her boots echoed across the shiny gray floor. Large windows on the far wall let in light. There hadn't been a ball in years, so there was no reason for anyone to come in and bother her.

Claret opened the ancient book to the first chapter. It was about shooting fire from your hands. There had been times in the last few months when that would have come in handy. There were very few people who could use magic to make fire, but she was going to do it.

This book had belonged to Claret's father. He had never used it and he told her she shouldn't either. It was kept locked up, but Claret couldn't see any good in that. If no one was ever going to read it, what was the use of keeping it around?

"To make a ball of fire, start in your stomach," Claret read. "Feel the heat of a fiery inferno. The warmth should flow from your stomach to your chest, then travel down the arm and out the hand." Claret wrinkled her nose. That couldn't be all there was to it, but that was all it said.

Claret placed the book on the floor and closed her eyes. She tried to make her stomach feel hot. She frowned when her stomach began rumbling. It felt warm and a little bubbly. It might make her sick. She kept her eyes closed and willed the heat to go up into her chest and down her arm. Her entire body felt like it was burning. She opened her eyes and her hand to see a burning ball of fire.

She laughed. "I did it! And it was easy!" She laughed again, then frowned. "Now what?" She held the burning ball and looked around. This was ridiculous. She couldn't throw it in the castle. Why hadn't she gone outside? She tried to think cold thoughts, but the ball kept burning. She walked carefully to the door, opened it with her free hand, and shut it behind her. She couldn't have anyone wandering in and finding the book.

Captain Nerman came walking down the hall. There was nowhere to hide, so Claret stood tall and put on her most competent face.

"Hello, Captain. Are you looking for me?"

"Yes," he said, looking at the ball of fire in her hand. "We found two more vorcraws around the castle grounds. We've taken care of them."

"Wonderful. Your men are doing a great job."

His eyes hadn't left her hand. "Um... what are you doing, Your Majesty?"

"Just going for a walk." She turned and walked in the opposite direction.

"Is that safe?" he asked.

Claret was panicking. She turned back to the captain. "Perhaps not. I figured out how to make this ball of fire and now I don't know what to do with it. It won't go away." She felt ridiculous admitting it.

Captain Nerman rubbed a finger over his mustache. "I can open the door and you can throw it outside."

"What if it starts a fire?"

"You could throw it in the pond behind the castle."

"Good thinking." Claret followed the captain out the door and around the castle. When they got to the small pond, she dropped the fireball in and watched it sizzle. "Thank you, Captain."

Claret felt a little shaky. She hoped it didn't show. She turned and went back to the castle, leaving the captain to wonder what she was up to.

"Can everyone fit through?" Kaylee asked. They had finally cut through the bars, but it would still be a tight fit. Miguel crawled through the hole and stood. If he could get through, the others could. "Come on, Mia."

Mia scurried through and then Chad.

"Let's get out of here," she said twice so everyone could understand. They all started down the hallway and then Chad stopped.

"What?"

Chad pointed at the mermaids. "Those actually look real."

"Whoa," Mia said.

Miguel looked impressed but not the way the other two did.

"We should hurry," Peora said. "The witch could be back any minute."

Kaylee led them down the hall, up the stairs, and out the window they had come in.

"Now what?" Chad asked.

"We get as far from here as we can."

"We run? Does anyone have a cell phone? We need to call the police."

Kaylee shook her head. "They don't have cell phones here or the police. Let's move fast."

Kaylee hurried away from the house and toward a grove of trees and hoped the others followed. They walked in silence. She didn't stop until she saw Colter's Lake ahead. She'd lost track of the time, but it felt like they'd been in the trees for an hour at least. No one had complained or tried to make conversation.

"Let's stop for a minute," Kaylee said. "We don't want to go to the lake. We want to go that way," she said, pointing.

"What are the chances of finding something to eat?" Miguel asked.

Peora smiled. "That is where I come in." She held out her hand and blew onto it. A loaf of bread appeared in her hand.

"What just happened?" Chad said, his eyes wide.

Kaylee smiled. "Magic."

Peora handed the bread to Miguel and blew into her hand again, this time bringing a chunk of cheese. "I prepared ahead of time. I made sure I had food, and I knew where it was so I would be able to bring it."

Miguel broke the bread into pieces and handed some to everyone.

"My mind can't wrap around everything that's happening," Chad said. "It's also confusing when you switch languages."

"I can't help that," Kaylee said, biting into her bread.

Mia glanced over at Kaylee. "The woman who locked us in her basement. She did it because we know you. Why is that?"

"We freed one of the mermaids, and it made her angry. She took you guys to try to force us to tell her where the mermaid is. I guess she figured we would exchange the mermaid for you."

"Why did she take Chad? That doesn't make any sense." Chad scowled.

Kaylee shrugged. "Chad said he told the witch he knew a lot about me. She must think we're friends."

"All of this is crazy," Chad said. "There's no way I'm going to believe we're in a magical world that's under the ocean."

"You saw Peora do magic, and you saw the mermaids," Kaylee said. "I'm not sure how else to convince you."

"What is he complaining about?" Miguel asked. "I can only understand a few words."

"He doesn't believe we're in another world."

"A mermaid isn't enough? I grew up in Boztoll and I've never seen a mermaid. He should be impressed."

"I have an idea," Peora said. "I've heard that some people can do the reverse of summoning things."

Kaylee tilted her head. "What do you mean?"

"I think I might be able to send something to the castle. We could send a note to the queen and she could come and get us."

"Let's try."

Kaylee pulled a paper and pen from her pocket and wrote a note to Claret, telling her to meet them at Colter's Lake. "I guess we'll go to the lake after all. It's the only place I know of around here that Claret can look at a map and teleport to."

Peora took the paper and held it in her hand. She closed her eyes, and it disappeared. "I hope it went to the queen's pillow."

"Now we need to go over to the lake. With luck, she'll see the note soon and we won't have to wait."

Kaylee quickly explained to Mia and Chad, and they all began walking toward the water.

"So there's a queen?" Mia asked.

"Yes."

"And she's going to come get us. That's the part I'm confused about."

"She can teleport. She can come and take us back to her castle."

Chad frowned. "Teleport? This is getting weirder and weirder."

They walked over to the water, and Kaylee looked around. "I guess this is as good as any other spot to wait. Claret will have to walk around a bit to find us since all she'll have to guide her will be a map."

Miguel tilted his head and frowned. She explained what she'd said to him. Saying everything twice was getting annoying.

Claret hugged the magic book to her and took it to her room. She couldn't believe she'd never studied it before. If making fire was so easy, then the other things in here might be as well. She pulled open her wardrobe door and opened the false bottom. She put the book safely inside and locked it. A book that powerful needed to be kept safe.

A paper on her bed caught her eye. She picked it up and her eyes scanned it. Kaylee needed her to go to Colter's Lake. How had she sent the paper? Claret bit her lip. What if it was a trick? What if Isadora had sent it? She thought of the fireball. No one would expect her to be able to do that.

Finding Captain Nerman again was harder than Claret expected. She'd asked several people before she found him out training with the rest of the soldiers. When he saw her, he came over.

"Captain, I need to leave for a short time."

He frowned. "You're supposed to stay here until we stop all the vorcraws and Dovin returns."

"I have to get Kaylee. It will be fast."

"Get her from where?"

"She's near Colter's Lake."

He tilted his hand. "That isn't close."

She leaned in so no one would hear. "I've learned to teleport."

His eyes widened. "Even if that is true, you need to be careful."

"I will be. I'll just pop over there and be back. It shouldn't take more than a few minutes. I can't leave her there."

"Take a soldier with you."

"No, I don't know how many people I'm going to have to bring back, and I don't want to make it more complicated."

"I don't agree with this."

"That's all right. I just wanted to let you know you are in command until I return."

Claret turned and went back to the castle before he could respond. She didn't have time to waste arguing.

7

CHAPTER 7

Mateo's eyes scanned the small cavern, and he frowned. "Now what? It's a dead end." He held up his light and looked up. "Is that a hole up there?"

Odie looked at the place he pointed. "It looks like it. Do we go up there?"

"I don't see anywhere else. It's not too high, but it's going to be hard to get into. I mean, one of us could boost the other one, but how would the other person get up?"

"Levitating?"

Mateo shook his head. "I can barely lift anything bigger than a rock."

"I could try. What do you do?"

"You point your hands at whatever you want to lift, and you focus, then lift it. I've tried for years, so I don't think you are going to get it in one try."

Odie pushed up his sleeves and pointed his hands at Mateo. Mateo sighed and crossed his arms. He might as well let Odie try so he would realize magic wasn't as easy as it looked. Odie slowly raised his hands and Mateo felt his feet lift off the ground.

"Whoa!" Mateo said, putting his arms out in case he fell. Odie continued to lift him until he went up into the dark hole. Mateo brought up a light and saw that there was a small tunnel in the rock. "Push me to the left!"

Odie gave a quick jerk of his hands and Mateo fell into the tunnel. He sat for a second to get control of his breathing. He had never in a thousand years expected that Odie would be able to do that in one try.

"What's up there?" Odie asked.

"It's a tunnel. It's narrow, so we'll have to crawl."

"All right. I'm going to levitate myself up."

Mateo wanted to tell him it wouldn't work, but who knew what Odie could do? A few moments later, Odie came floating up and into the tunnel. This didn't seem fair. Odie had only known he could do magic for thirty minutes and he was already doing things Mateo couldn't.

"Let's go," Odie said.

Mateo nodded and began crawling through the dark rocky tunnel, but he was having trouble crawling and holding onto his light. "I wish it were light in here," he said. As soon as the words left his mouth, the tunnel lit up with an unnatural dull light. Mateo couldn't see where it was coming from.

"Wow," Odie said.

"Did you do that?"

"No. I think it happened because you said it."

Mateo let his light go out and crawled faster. The longer this took, the angrier Dovin was going to be when they met up. His cape kept getting in the way, so he had to slow down a little.

"Can you see to the end?" Odie asked from behind.

"It looks like it might turn."

Mateo kept going until he came to the turn. "It goes in two directions. Which way do you suppose we should go?"

"Since we don't know where we're going, I guess it doesn't matter."

"All right." Mateo turned right and kept going. "This is killing my knees."

"That's what I was just thinking."

"Tal said something about a slide. I wonder when that will appear." There were several turns, but Mateo didn't waste time asking Odie which way he should go. He just went right every time. That way, they would know which way to go if they came to a dead end or needed to backtrack.

"I'm surprised there aren't any bats or spiders," Odie said.

Mateo came to an abrupt stop, and Odie ran into the back of him. He hadn't thought about what might be in here. So long as there weren't any snakes, he would be fine. He started again.

"I think I see an opening," he said, crawling faster. He stopped when the tunnel ended and braced himself in case Odie ran into him again. He didn't. Mateo looked down. They were a few feet off the ground. He got into a sitting position and dropped to the cave floor below. He heard Odie drop behind him.

"Wow," Odie said.

They stood in a large cavern. The walls shimmered and gave off the appearance of being liquid. Colorful bubbles floated across the room, bouncing off the walls and the floor. In the middle of the cavern was a round platform that was about one foot high and four feet across. Padmire stood next to the platform, his hands on his hips.

"Hey," Mateo said. "What are those bubbles for?"

Padmire scowled. "You cheated."

Mateo and Odie shared a confused glance.

"What do you mean, cheated?" Mateo asked.

"You crawled through my tunnels! You are supposed to go through the challenges."

Mateo's eyes narrowed. "What are you talking about? The tunnels were the only way."

"In all my years of letting people through here, you are the first ones to go the wrong way! You were supposed to find the hidden door in the first cavern, not go up into the tunnels."

Odie chuckled. "If you want people to go a certain way, perhaps you shouldn't have the door hidden."

Mateo nodded in agreement.

"All you had to do was look closely at the walls and you would have seen the hinges. Behind the door are humongous slides that take you to two different areas. Then you climb a wall and go through a lake. You skipped it all by going over the top!"

Mateo shrugged. "How were we supposed to know? Wasn't our way faster?"

"Of course it is, but that isn't the point."

"Well, we're in a hurry. Can you just let us be done? You aren't going to make us go back and do it again, are you?"

"Fine," Padmire huffed. "Pick a bubble, then get out of here."

Mateo watched a floating bubble. "The bubbles are the magic?"

Padmire rolled his eyes. "I'm not going to explain it all now. Just take a bubble, stand on the platform, and get out of here."

Mateo grabbed a green bubble. He had expected it to be hard to hold, but it was solid. He held it up to his eyes. It appeared to have liquid inside. He shook it a few times, then turned to Odie. "Ready?"

Odie held up a red bubble. "Yep."

"Great, get on the platform," Padmire said.

Mateo stepped up and frowned. "What's with the red paint?" he asked, pointing at a red spill on the platform.

Padmire grumbled. "I need to clean that off. There used to be a little poem that told people how to get out. Someone threw a bubble at the poem and I haven't had time to clean it off."

Odie stepped onto the platform and turned to Padmire. "Now what?"

Padmire just frowned. Mateo felt himself being lifted into the air and he was surrounded by rainbow colors that were flying past his face at lightning speed. A cold breeze blew against him and before he could think, he was standing in the forest. Odie was next to him.

"Padmire could have warned us about that," Mateo said.

Odie nodded. "Where did the bubbles go?"

"I don't know. If they were magic, it might have been absorbed into us."

"So now we should have some cool new magic?"

"That's what I understood."

"How do we know what it is?" Odie asked.

"I don't know, but I should be able to talk to animals, right? I mean, that's why we came here."

Odie shrugged. "We better go meet Dovin. He won't be happy we kept him."

Dovin stared at Odie. "You could do magic before the cave opened?"

He nodded and sat on Dovin's sofa. It was actually clean. "Padmire told me I could, and he was right."

"And he can already levitate better than I can," Mateo grumbled.

"I've never heard of anyone getting magic without something happening to them," Dovin said. "There has to be something more to it."

"I thought we were going to get a lecture," Mateo said.

Dovin glared at him. "I think I'll give that lecture to Tal later."

Tal grinned. "I'll take it. But don't you think it'll be worth it? If Mateo can communicate with animals, it'll be helpful. I don't know how I got through life before I could do it."

"Be that as it may, we've been waiting for longer than we planned. I was about to come looking for you. Durdessa already had time to clean this room, and it was a disaster."

Tal grinned. "I'm surprised she didn't make you do it."

Dovin frowned, but his eyes sparkled. "She made me clean the kitchen."

"Where is she now?" Mateo asked. "Shouldn't we be going?"

"She's in the kitchen, making sandwiches with Arving. Did Ming Li decide to stay behind?"

Tal nodded. "She said I have two days and then she's coming for me, so we better make the most of it. With luck, I can give Mateo enough pointers to get him through. I'll also talk to any dragons I can find and let them know Garin is bad news."

"That won't be easy," Odie said. "Dragons aren't a common thing to see. They stay in Dragon's Cove most of the time. We have a little one at the castle, but I don't know how much help that will be."

"I'll talk to it and see what it knows," Tal said. "Or Mateo can try."

"I'm still confused about Odie's sudden magic," Dovin said. "Did anything strange happen before you went into the cave?"

"No," Odie said. "Maybe I could just do it up here."

"I don't know. It seems odd. I've studied magic for years and my family passed on a lot of knowledge others don't have, and there's nothing about getting magic from nothing."

"I can't explain it."

"Well, let's grab the others and get back to Tyran. I don't trust those girls to keep to the castle and I won't relax until we know they aren't out trying to fight vorcraws."

"They said they would stay," Mateo said. "I'm not too worried."

Kaylee grinned when she saw Claret appear a few paces from them. She'd worried she might go to the other side of the lake to look for them.

Chad pointed. "Did you see that? She appeared out of nowhere!"

"I think I'm beginning to believe in the whole magic thing," Mia said. "This is crazy! And it's not like we can tell anyone when we get home. Who would believe us?"

Claret rushed toward them. "Are you ready? There's no reason to stick around here."

"We're ready," Kaylee said. "Come on, you guys. Grab a piece of Claret's cloak. We can do introductions later." She said it again for Miguel's and Peora's benefit. They all squished together and picked up a piece of Claret's burgundy cloak. Without any warning, she teleported them to her throne room.

Chad fell to his knees. "That was crazy."

Mia grinned. "Crazy awesome."

"Now what?" Chad asked. "Are you going to take us home?"

"We can't," Kaylee said. "Once our friends get back, they can."

"Why can't the queen?"

"Teleporting only works if you know the place you're teleporting to. Claret's never been out of Riviand, so she can't take you."

The door opened and Dovin peeked inside, then looked behind him. "They're in here." He came in and Odie, Mateo, and Graham's friend Tal followed him.

"Miguel!" Mateo exclaimed, hugging his brother. "What are you doing here?"

Dovin frowned when he looked at Mia and Chad, then at Miguel. "Do we want to know?"

"Hi, Mr. Dovin," Mia said.

"Can you take us home?" Chad asked. "Some woman locked us in her basement, but Kaylee got us out."

Dovin looked at Kaylee. "Did you leave the castle?"

"I had to save them."

"Why are you talking like that?" Chad asked. "I can't understand you."

"I will take you home," Dovin said, in English. "But it will have to wait until tomorrow. Was it Isadora?"

Kaylee nodded. "She thought she could trade them for Jayah."

"Why would she take Chad? I'm surprised you didn't leave him there."

"Hey!" Chad said.

Dovin ignored him. "You should have waited for us to get back."

Kaylee crossed her arms. "I knew Isadora wasn't home, so I needed to jump on that."

"Did you find the information you were looking for?" Claret asked. "And where is Durdessa?"

"Tal can talk to dragons, and with luck, Mateo will be able to as well," Dovin said.

Claret's mouth turned down. "Why Mateo?"

"He and Odie went through a cave… it's a long story. Odie can do magic now, too."

Kaylee frowned. That meant she was the only one in the group who couldn't do magic.

"And Durdessa?" Claret asked.

"She brought her brother back with her. She's finding him a room."

"Why can't you take Chad and Mia back right now?" Kaylee asked. "It would only take you a minute now that you know where the cave is."

"I want to talk to them first. I need to know what Isadora told them."

"They couldn't understand her. Miguel could."

"Then I should probably talk to him first."

8

— · —

CHAPTER 8

Odie sat on his bed and took off his tall boots. He threw them to the floor and sighed. Claret wasn't wearing his ring. He hoped she hadn't lost it or decided he wasn't worth it. She'd barely glanced at him when they were in the throne room, and what was even worse was that she had barely looked away from that boy they called Chad.

He let out a breath. Hopefully, Dovin would have Kaylee's friends back to Earth today. He couldn't compete with a person from a different world. Kaylee's two friends and Mateo's brother had been dressed strangely. Maybe that was why she'd stared at him.

He looked up when there was a knock at the door. "Come in."

Claret entered and closed the door behind her. She came over and settled next to him on the bed, her blue dress puffing up when she sat. She opened her hand. Odie's ring rested in her palm. Odie swallowed. She was giving it back.

"How often do you wear this ring?" she asked.

"I never take it off unless I'm washing it."

"I can't do magic when I'm wearing it."

Odie raised his brows. "Really?" He held out his hand and made a ball of light.

"It's exciting that you can do magic now."

"It is, and I think I'm good at it. I haven't tried a lot of things, but the things I tried felt easy." He let the light go out, then took the ring from Claret. He pulled up another light.

"Maybe you have to put it on your finger."

He pushed the ring over his pinky and tried to make a light. Nothing happened. He let out a long breath. "That means I've spent my entire life thinking I couldn't do magic, and it was just the ring?"

"At least you know now."

He frowned. "King Ummi said I had the ring when they found me. What if they actually gave me the ring so I couldn't do magic?"

"It's possible. Do you know what the inscription means?"

Odie pulled the ring off and looked inside. "A + N. I always wondered if that was a clue about who my parents were."

"It might be."

"Well, I won't wear it now. I can't believe this. All this time, I could have been doing magic."

"I don't know if it's a bad thing," Claret said.

Odie looked at her and raised his brows. "Oh?"

"What makes you the person you are? You learned how to make so many things, potions and things like that. Why did you do that?"

"Because I couldn't do magic and I felt like I had to prove myself."

"Your experiments are useful and so clever. If you had magic, you might not have made them."

Odie felt his face go warm. "I suppose that's true."

"And now that you have magic, you can probably add that to your experiments and do even greater things."

Odie grinned. "You're right. It also gives me an advantage with Garin. He doesn't know I can do magic. I'm going to get rid of the ring. I shouldn't have kept it all these years."

Claret took the ring from his hand. "No, let me keep it. I'll put it on a necklace. If you can hold it and still do magic, then I should be able to wear it on a chain."

Odie nodded, trying not to look too pleased. "What do you think about Kaylee's friends?"

"I'm not sure yet. Their clothing is so odd. Did you see what the boy was wearing? It was like a cape with sleeves. Kaylee told me it's called a hoodie, not a cape, but I find it strange."

Odie smiled. Claret had been staring at Chad's clothing.

"I'm glad you're back," Claret said. "There's still an hour until supper. Do you want to play a game?"

Odie shrugged. "What kind of game?"

"Kaylee taught me one called Checkers. Since we don't have it here, she made one with painted rocks. I can teach you. It's easy."

He nodded. "Sounds good."

"What do you know about Peora?" Miguel asked as he sat backward on a chair in Mateo's room.

Mateo sat on his bed and took off his boot. "Peora? I've never heard of that."

Miguel rolled his eyes. "She's a person. She helped Kaylee rescue us."

"Ohhhh. The girl with the brown hair? I think she's Claret's maid or something like that."

"She's smart. And really pretty."

"I guess."

"What do you mean, you guess? She's gorgeous."

"I don't pay attention to older women," Mateo said, grinning.

"Older women? She can't be older than twenty."

Mateo shrugged. "It's older to me. I don't really know anything about her."

"It's been a long time since I had someone besides family I could talk to in our language. I've missed it."

"You speak Spanish well."

"Yeah, but that didn't come easy, and I still get lost occasionally. Not all of us got to learn it just by jumping through a portal. I'm thinking of staying here for a while."

"Won't you miss your college classes?"

"Yeah, but now that I'm here, I'm not sure I care. I might want to move back. Maybe go back to our farm in Boztoll."

"Do you think it's still there?"

"Sure. We left suddenly, but I doubt anyone would take it over. Or I could ask Grandma if I can stay with them for a while."

"You know everyone up there can do magic now, right? You would be the only one who can't."

"Who cares? I've missed the people in Basura. I'm going to give it some thought." He looked at Mateo and shook his head. "I can't believe you haven't noticed Peora."

Mateo laughed. "Well, I can tell you have."

"Sen had his adventures, and now here you are. I don't want to miss out on everything."

There were three taps on the door, then Kaylee poked her head in. "Hey, can I come in?"

"Sure," Mateo said, standing.

Kaylee came in carrying the little orange dragon. "I thought you might want to practice on this little one. I know Tal is going to help you later, but I don't think you've spent a lot of time around her."

Mateo sighed and took a step toward the dragon.

Miguel grinned. "Watch out for germs."

Mateo shot his brother a dirty look. Animal germs had always bothered him. He was getting better but not completely. You never knew what gross thing an animal had been into.

"Odie needs to name her," she said, holding her close to Mateo.

He reached out his hand and placed it on the dragon. "I wonder what I should do. Try to read his mind like Tal said?"

Kaylee shrugged and placed the dragon on his bed. Mateo sat down and tried to connect his mind to the dragon, but nothing happened.

"Is something going to happen?" Miguel asked.

"I dunno. It doesn't seem like it. I'm not feeling any-thing."

"Maybe it takes time," Kaylee said.

"Put your heads together," Miguel said, grinning.

Mateo rolled his eyes. "You just want to make me look like an idiot."

"Maybe."

Kaylee laughed. "It might work."

"I don't think so. I'll wait for Tal to give me some point-ers."

"You can't do magic, can you?" Miguel asked, looking at Kaylee. "That's why Peora summoned the food."

"I can't."

"But you like it here?"

"Well enough."

"Do you think you'll stay here?"

Kaylee shook her head. "No. I belong on Earth."

"What makes you say that?"

Kaylee scrunched her nose. "I don't know. I've always lived there."

Miguel looked at Mateo. "That's how I feel about this world."

"Me too," Mateo said. "You know I've been trying to get Mom to let me come back since we left. I thought you liked Earth, since you don't have magic and all."

"I've missed Basura since we left. Every time we visit Sen, I think about staying."

Kaylee sat on the bed on the other side of the dragon and patted her head. The dragon rubbed her head into her hand and made a sound like a cat purring.

"She likes you," Mateo said.

"I don't know why she likes me and not Odie. Odie's been trying a lot harder than I have."

"Probably because you smell like vanilla and not like something Odie blew up."

"Is that it?" Kaylee asked the dragon. "Does Odie smell like an explosion?" The dragon stepped onto her lap and placed her head on Kaylee's shoulder. Kaylee ran her hand over the dragon's back and it licked her face. She laughed. "Dragon kisses. That was gross and smelly."

"Lucky dragon." Mateo clamped his mouth shut. Kaylee's eyes narrowed and Miguel's brow came together. "I'm kidding. Anyway, we should probably take the dragon to Tal. I'm sure he'll be able to help me."

"I'll go look for him," Kaylee said, jumping up. She rushed out the door and slammed it behind her.

"What was that?" Miguel asked.

Mateo put his hands over his face. "Ugh. It was another thing that will play through my head at night, haunting me when I'm trying to sleep."

Miguel laughed. "I bet. That was pathetic. I know you've been antisocial since we moved to Earth, but, man, you need some practice when it comes to talking to girls."

"I'm fine. I don't know how that slipped out."

"Now I see why you didn't notice Peora. You're too busy noticing Kaylee."

"It doesn't matter. She doesn't like me."

"Well, maybe she would if you didn't say things like you just did."

Mateo shook his head. "I swear, every time I talk to her, I lose sleep at night thinking about whatever stupid thing I said to her that day."

"I bet."

"It's stupid anyway. I need to get it through my head that she doesn't like me. It wouldn't matter if she did. She wants to live on Earth, and I don't."

"You know you don't have to make all your life's decisions when you're sixteen, right?"

"I know."

"And I'm here if you need to talk."

Mateo arched his eyebrow. Miguel wasn't really the brother people went to for advice. "You've never had a girlfriend. What makes you think you can give me advice about girls? That would be worse than giving myself advice."

Miguel shrugged. "Just because I've never had a serious girlfriend doesn't mean I don't know anything. I've been on plenty of dates."

"Well, once you get a girl who actually wants to date you more than twice, we can talk."

Miguel grabbed a pillow from the bed and threw it at his face. "Have you ever been on a date, little brother?"

Mateo scowled.

"That's what I thought. You were too busy playing video games, lifting weights, and feeling bad for yourself."

"You weren't a lot different."

"I guess not. I've gotten better."

"Maybe we were just meant to live here."

Miguel smiled. "Maybe."

"Why are you grinning like that?"
"The dragon just did its business all over your bed."
Mateo sighed. "That figures. It's that kind of day."

9

— · —

CHAPTER 9

"This is all so crazy," Mia said, flopping down on Kaylee's bed. "I can't believe all this magic stuff exists, and I'm in a castle."

"You should have let Dovin take you home," Kaylee said. Dovin had talked to Mia and Chad and found out everything they knew about Isadora, which wasn't much. He'd offered to take them home, and they had both refused.

Dovin had gone to Earth and told both of their parents that they had won a week-long trip and surprisingly none of their parents had found it odd that they didn't even come home to collect anything. Isadora must have told them something as well because they hadn't been concerned that their children hadn't been home in a few days.

"I haven't been on vacation in forever and last night I slept in a castle. If I can stay here longer, then I'm gonna do it."

"It's good to see you. It feels like it's been forever. I wish Chad had gone home, though."

Mia nodded. "He doesn't know when he isn't wanted. I think he's spending all his time eating."

Kaylee grinned. "You have to admit, the food here is good."

"It is. This is so much better than the cruise my parents took me on two years ago. It was full of old people who kept telling us to be quiet."

"I'm actually surprised Dovin didn't force you to leave. Things are dangerous around here."

"Why force us to leave and not you?"

"Well, because... Dovin has been training me for this for years. All the self-defense and language lessons."

"It was so strange the way you disappeared. It was like we all got put on teams, you left with Mateo, we had those crazy tornado clouds, and then you never came back. I thought it was odd you didn't tell me you were going away. Your mom seemed so excited when she told me about it that I forgot to think about how weird it was."

"It was more strange for us, believe me. Mateo and I found a sword in the orchard we were in. When the green clouds appeared, we started for the school and goblins chased us. We found Coach Williams and Dovin, and then we ended up here."

"That does sound weird. So now you're trying to find a dragon? It's so confusing when everyone talks. I only catch a few words."

"There's a dragon shifter. It's a long story."

"Is he hot? A dragon shifter should be hot."

"He's evil."

"But hot?"

"I guess, in a way."

"It's funny you ended up here with Mateo. Has he grown on you, or does he still drive you crazy?"

Kaylee smiled. "Both."

Mateo stood in the kitchen and watched Chad eat another piece of Cook's cake. For not being able to communicate, Chad and Cook were sure becoming friends fast. He liked her food, and she liked that. The food wasn't actually Cook's. The kitchen staff did the baking and Cook took credit for it.

Mateo crossed his arms and leaned against the wall. "You should go home," he said slowly, hoping Chad understood.

Chad smirked. "I like it here."

"A dragon might eat you."

"What?"

Mateo wasn't going to repeat himself. Chad could pretend Mateo was the one who couldn't speak correctly, but here it was Chad that no one could understand. Mateo was already feeling testy because he'd spent hours with Tal the night before trying to understand the dragon. Mateo didn't get any feelings or thoughts coming from her. Tal had finally decided that communicating with animals wasn't the power Mateo had gotten.

Chad took another bite of cake. "You don't think I'm gonna leave Kaylee here when there's so much danger, do you? I'll go home when she does."

Mateo frowned. "I'll take care of Kaylee."

"By punching anyone who talks to her?"

"Anyone who bothers her."

Chad said something else Mateo couldn't understand, so Mateo just glared at him. Chad reached out to grab a knife, probably to cut more cake. Mateo's hand shot forward, and the knife flew into his hand. Chad's eyes went wide, and so did Mateo's. He'd never been able to do that before.

He grinned like it was nothing and tossed the knife onto the table. "Later." He turned and left the kitchen, forcing himself to walk normally. Once he got in the hallway, he ran to Odie's room and pounded on the door. He opened it, not waiting for an invitation. Odie and Claret were sitting at his small table, playing a game that might be checkers. It had a drawn grid and painted red and black rocks.

"Hey," he said. "Do you guys want to see what I can do? Watch."

Mateo held out his hand, and one of the red rocks flew into it. "Awesome, right? I think my magic from the cave gave me that ability. It's like levitating and bringing things to me super fast. I wonder if I can throw them fast as well." He opened his hand, and the rock sped from his hand across the room and broke a hole in Odie's wardrobe.

"Oops. Sorry."

"Wow," Claret said, staring at the hole. "That was fast! I've never seen anyone do that before. Levitate yes, even throw things, but not with that speed."

"I've never been good at levitating, so that is going to be awesome. Have you figured out what you can do, Odie?"

Odie picked up a rock and jumped it over one of Claret's pieces. "Um... Not really, but something strange happened last night. I felt like one of the plants in the hall wanted water. I looked in the pot and it was dry."

Mateo laughed. "Are you saying you can talk to plants?"

Odie grinned. "I don't know. If I could, it might be helpful for my experiments. What if they could tell me what they're capable of?"

"That's an interesting thought," Claret said. "I've never heard of anything like that."

There was a tap on the door, and Tal entered. "Hey, you people are hard to find. I talked to your little dragon. She doesn't know anything about shifters. Bantams don't run in the same group as bigger dragons, so it makes sense that she isn't aware of them. I warned her just in case."

"Okay, thanks," Mateo said. "Are you leaving, then?"

"I am, unless you can find me a bigger dragon to talk to."

"Hey, have you ever heard of anyone who can talk to plants?" Mateo asked, shooting Odie a teasing smile. "Odie thinks he heard a plant tell him it was thirsty." Mateo let a small laugh escape.

Odie sighed. "I said I wasn't sure."

Tal gave them a half smile. "Let's all take a field trip outside."

The three of them got up and followed Tal to the back of the castle where the flower garden grew. Odie was looking at all the flowers and concentrating.

"I don't feel like they're talking to me, but I feel like... I don't know how to describe it."

"You know you sound a little crazy, right?" Mateo asked.

Tal's eyes danced. He waved his hand through the air and a vine burst from the dirt and wrapped around Mateo's ankle, knocking him to the ground. Claret screamed. Mateo sat up and tried to rip the vine off. Tal raised his hand, and another vine busted out and wrapped around his other foot.

"Wow," Odie said. "Can I do that?"

Tal grinned. "Probably with a little practice. Padmire mixed up the magic, it seems. When I went through the cave, I got magic to control plants and talk to animals. You must have gotten the same thing."

"That's amazing," Odie said. "There weren't any vines here. How did you make them grow?"

"I don't really know. I can always make vines spring up. Maybe there are seeds in the ground and I call to them? I don't know, but it's come in handy a lot."

Controlling plants was cool, but Mateo was happy with his own magic. Levitating and pulling things in and throwing them seemed a lot more useful. Mateo hadn't been thrilled about talking to animals, either. They made him a little nervous and knowing what they thought was terrifying.

"Let's go try to talk to the dragon," Tal said. "If you can do it, I'll stay for a few more hours."

"I didn't notice anything when I was around Gregor," Odie said. "Shouldn't I have heard his thoughts?"

"It came on slowly for me," Tal said. "It's also different around different animals. Some I have to really work with before I understand them. Others throw their thoughts at me."

Odie sat on his bedroom floor and placed one hand on the dragon. Images filled his brain. They flashed so fast he couldn't make them out. The dragon pulled away, but the images kept flashing through Odie's mind.

"She said you're thinking too fast, and it's scaring her," Tal said.

Odie scowled. "I'm thinking too fast? Her thoughts are flashing so much I can't even tell what they are."

Tal grinned. "You have to focus on one of them. It takes some getting used to. You need to make sure you're only focusing on one thought when you try to talk to her. Most animals will put their attention on whatever you're thinking if you're focused. It narrows their thoughts and makes it easier to interpret."

"I don't know what to think."

"Ask her what she wants her name to be."

"In my mind?"

"Yes. Or out loud. It works both ways."

Odie gazed at the dragon. "Do you have a name?" He concentrated on the question and repeated it over and over in her mind.

"Keep your focus," Tal said. *"Don't think about whether it's going to work, only think of the question."*

Odie's eyes flew to Tal. "You just spoke in my head."

Tal smiled. "I wasn't sure it would work. That's awesome. I've never been around another person who could talk to animals. I always wondered if it would work."

"Can you talk to other people like that? I mean, people are animals, right?"

"No, I can't. There are ways to communicate telepathically, but this is different. Now, try again."

Odie focused on the dragon, but she was ignoring him.

"Try a different question," Tal said. "Dragons don't like to waste time on things like names. Ask if she likes a specific name."

"Do you want me to call you Apalla?"

She snorted and crawled under the bed.

"How about Midnight?"

The dragon poked her orange head out from under the bed and stared at him. Her thoughts were still confusing but felt peaceful. That was the only word Odie could use to describe it.

Tal sat on the floor and rubbed the dragon's head. "I think she likes it."

Odie smiled. "Great. Midnight is a perfect name."

Tal raised his eyebrow. "I'd say she's a little too orange for the name, but if she likes it, then go with it."

Gregor flew in from the crack in the window and landed on Odie's table. He rushed over and scooped him up. He didn't want Gregor to become Midnight's dinner. The dragon crawled out from under the bed and her eyes became glued to the puffin.

"Friend," Odie thought over and over.

An image of Midnight and Gregor popped into Odie's head. They were flying together over a lake.

"She accepts what you said," Tal said. "She's willing to be friends."

Next, a picture of Gregor eating fish came vividly to him. Odie grinned. "And that means Gregor is hungry."

Tal laughed. "I think so."

Midnight walked over and sniffed Gregor. Odie froze and watched the two creatures study each other. Gregor was still thinking about fish.

The squeaking of the window caused Odie to turn. A hand from the outside was pushing the window open. Odie frowned. It was too high for someone to climb.

"What the—" Tal went to the window right as a vorcraw pushed his way in. Tal took a few steps back. "What is that?"

The vorcraw growled and held his sword in the air. Odie cursed himself for not replacing the glass of water that had been on his table. Gregor had spilled it and he forgot. Another vorcraw flew up and into the window, landing on the floor with a thud. Odie's sword was in his wardrobe, which one of the monsters blocked.

Tal levitated a chair and threw it at the first creature. It fell back a few steps and roared. Odie's brain sprang to life and he began levitating anything he could see and throwing it all at a vorcraw. He wasn't finding anything big enough because the first vorcraw was ignoring the items and walking toward him.

Midnight and Gregor had gone under the bed. Tal jumped over the bed and grabbed the fallen chair. He smashed it over one of the vorcraws' heads, then kicked it in the chest. Odie jumped on his bed then landed next to Tal. Tal threw his arm in the air, causing a lantern on the table to rocket across the room and smash into the vorcraw's head.

The other vorcraw was trying to step onto the bed but was having trouble. Odie levitated the chair at it and it fell back onto the stone floor. Odie threw open the wardrobe and grabbed his sword. He jumped back over the bed and plunged the sword into the fallen creature. It disappeared, leaving wisps of smoke in its place.

Tal kicked the remaining monster again, then punched it in the chest. It took three steps backward and growled. Tal grinned and turned to Odie. "You wanna throw me that sword?"

Odie tossed the sword, and Tal caught it. In one smooth motion, he stabbed it through the vorcraw's chest. It turned to smoke and Tal shook his head.

"I haven't had anything like that happen in a long time. What was that?"

Odie wiped sweat from his brow. "A vorcraw. A witch keeps sending them after us."

"I'm a little out of practice. I shouldn't have paused to see if I could communicate with them."

"Could you?"

"No."

"They die if you throw water on them."

Tal arched his eyebrow. "And you don't keep any on you?"

Odie shrugged. "I had a cup on the table, but Gregor spilled it."

"If I kept getting chased by those things, I'd keep some with me at all times. And close the window."

"Gregor can't get out, and my room will be a mess from his droppings if I shut it."

Tal chuckled. "I guess you have to choose what you hate more. Monsters or bird droppings."

10

—·—

Chapter 10

"You have to take Mia and Chad back home," Kaylee told Dovin.

Dovin sat on a kitchen chair and peeled a banana. "They don't want to go back yet."

"Why do they get to decide? Mia is going to want to help, and I love Mia, but she isn't going to be helpful. Chad is just—Chad. He's annoying."

"We can't make choices for other people, Kaylee. You know that."

"Do you see anything in their auras? Are they supposed to be here?"

"Auras don't work like that. I haven't seen anything about either of them."

"Shouldn't that mean they should go home?"

"I don't see auras around most people. It doesn't mean anything."

The kitchen door opened, and Odie and Tal came in.

"Some vorcraws came into my room," Odie said. "We took care of them, but if they can get into the castle, we need to be careful."

Dovin took a bite of his banana. "We need to deal with Isadora. The vorcraws won't stop until we do."

Tal grabbed a banana from the table and sat in a chair. "On the plus side, Odie can communicate with animals. Padmire must have mixed up the magic when he tried to give it to Mateo."

"Nice," Kaylee said. "If I had magic, that's what I would want."

"I need to leave soon," Tal said. "I can bring back the others if you need help."

"I think we're fine," Dovin said. "I'll come get you if we need reinforcements."

"Who counts as *the others*?" Kaylee asked.

"Graham and the rest of my friends." Tal took a big bite from his banana and turned to Odie. "Come see me if you need any help. I'm going to get my stuff and I'll see you all later." He tossed his peel in the garbage and left.

"We need to go to Dragon's Cove," Odie said. "I can try to talk to a dragon there."

Kaylee leaned against the table. "I thought you only saw one dragon last time, and it was Garin. Maybe they don't live there anymore."

"We didn't search. They have to be somewhere."

"I wonder how Garin knew you were there." She found it hard to believe that it had been a coincidence he'd found Odie and Claret, unless he spent a lot of time there.

"We should go soon. Like tomorrow," Odie said. "We don't know what the goblins and Garin have been up to in the last few weeks, and the sooner we see what the dragons think about everything, the better."

"Tomorrow is rather fast to plan," Dovin said.

"What is there to plan?" Odie asked. "Since we don't know what to expect, we don't know what to prepare for. If we take food and a few weapons, we should be good."

"Dragon's Cove is surrounded by desert," Dovin said. "Make sure you have water."

"There was fresh water once we were out of the desert. It was boiling hot, so we probably want to dress appropriately."

"So no dark colors?" Kaylee asked, smiling. She couldn't remember ever seeing Odie in anything but black.

"Probably not."

"And no long sleeves and dark feathered capes?"

Odie grinned. "I don't have anything to wear."

"Mateo might let you borrow something."

Odie shook his head. "I can run to a shop before dinner. I'll go tell the others so they can prepare."

"By others you mean Mateo and Claret, right?" Kaylee asked. "I don't want to see Mia and Chad tagging along tomorrow."

Odie nodded. "Mateo and Claret. I can't talk to your friends, so I've been steering clear of them to avoid the awkwardness."

"If you're going to a shop, I'll accompany you," Dovin said, standing. "I don't want any of you out alone until the vorcraws are dealt with. Are you ready?"

Odie nodded and the two of them left.

Kaylee wasn't sure what to do. Getting ready for tomorrow would only take a few minutes. Claret was busy meeting with people and she hadn't seen Mateo in a while.

A cook came in and began searching through cupboards, so Kaylee left. She didn't want to be in the way.

"Hey, Kaylee, where are you headed?"

She turned and frowned when she saw Chad. He was wearing a tunic and cape. He really needed to go home before he got too attached.

"To my room."

"You wanna hang out?"

"No."

"Why not? I don't get you."

"No, you don't. See you around." She walked in the opposite direction.

He walked beside her. "You know I'm staying here for you, right?"

She sighed. "Well, don't. Go home."

"What if I do? What if I tell your mom where you really are?"

Kaylee laughed. "She'll think you're nuts. Besides, she's in the Bahamas. There's no reason for you to be here. I have things to do, and you're only going to get in the way."

"I can help."

"Oh yeah? Can you do magic?"

"No, but neither can you."

"But I have the Blade of the Phoenix. It's kind of like having magic." Kaylee should take the sword to Dragon's Cove. The sword and water, in case any vorcraw showed up.

"What's the Blade of the Phoenix?"

"It doesn't matter. Could you stop following me?"

He let out a long breath and threw his hands into the air. "What is it you don't like about me? Just tell it to me straight."

Kaylee bit the inside of her cheek. Telling Chad she thought he was conceited, rude, and pushy seemed mean.

He glowered at her. "I mean, if you had someone else you were interested in, I'd get it, but you don't."

"How do you know?"

"Mia told me."

"That was a long time ago. Things change."

"So you met someone here?"

"It's Mateo. We're pretty much dating," she lied.

He narrowed his eyes. "You're just saying that to get me to go away. If you liked him, you'd spend more time with him, and I've only seen you in the same room a few times. Fine. I'll go find Mia. She doesn't like me, but at least she isn't a liar." He turned and went the other way.

Kaylee shook her head. She wasn't a very good friend. She didn't even know where Mia was and what if he asked Mia about Mateo? If Kaylee was dating someone, Chad knew Mia would know, and now she was going to have to pretend to like Mateo, without Mateo thinking she liked him. Being a liar was such a stupid thing to be.

Claret watched Odie mix something in a vial and shake it up. "What are you doing?"

He looked up. "I'm making something we can use so we don't get sunburned tomorrow. I already made a balm that should work well." He got up from the table in his room and grabbed a box from the top of his bed. He took out a small round tube and handed it to her. She unscrewed it and looked at the gooey stuff inside.

"This will help our lips not get burned?"

"Hopefully. Last time we were there, mine got so chapped they hurt for days."

Claret smelled it. It didn't have an odor. "Mine did as well. I'm glad you're doing this."

Odie looked confused. "Oh?"

Claret handed back the small tube. "I worried that once you got magic, you wouldn't make things anymore."

"I'll always make things. It's part of who I am."

Claret smiled and touched Odie's ring that was hanging from her necklace. "Do you really think it's a good idea for all four of us to go?"

He sat on the edge of the table and crossed his arms. "You don't want to go?"

"I do. And Durdessa and Dovin are here to make sure the kingdom is safe. I just feel like we all run into trouble a lot and we might want to have backup people just in case."

"Dovin will come for us if we have trouble."

"I still haven't met Durdessa's brother."

"He's a little odd."

"She said he needs time to rest and slowly see Riviand. She worries about him being overwhelmed after spending so many years alone."

"Miguel is here as well. If we really need help, he might come. Mateo said he does martial arts, which means he can do fancy fighting or something like that."

"He doesn't have magic."

"No, but neither did I, and that didn't stop me."

Claret smiled. "Peora has been late twice to help me with my hair. She's never done that. I think she's been spending time with Miguel."

"Do you think he'll stay here?"

"Perhaps. Or she might leave. She wants adventure and I'm sure life here is dull for her."

Odie nodded. "I think I'm finished. Do you want to play checkers?"

Claret sat at the table. "I'm surprised you like to play it so much. I think you've won two of the past ten games we played."

"It's not about the game. It's about the company."

Claret blushed and waited while Odie cleaned off the table. He placed the game on the table and Claret collected the red stones. Claret didn't really enjoy checkers, but she did like talking to Odie. She paid little attention to her moves, so he was letting her win, or he was terrible at the game.

Claret smiled and decided to lose the next game. She moved her first checker. After putting her piece in jeopardy at every possible chance and watching Odie avoid jumping over the pieces, she had her answer.

She narrowed her eyes. "You're trying to let me win."

Odie's eyes went wide. "What are you talking about?"

"I grew up a princess. I know when people are letting me win, it happens all the time."

Odie grinned. "Being a princess must be a lot different from being a goblin prince. I had to try my hardest to win and then everyone cheats."

"I would imagine growing up with goblins would be difficult."

"I didn't mind it much until recently."

"Let's start over, and this time, no cheating." Claret pulled her rocks over to her side of the paper. Gregor pecked at her shoe, but she was getting used to him. "You try your hardest, and I'll try mine."

11

—·—

CHAPTER 11

"A re you all ready?" Dovin asked. Mateo placed his bag over his shoulder and nodded. "If anything goes wrong, teleport back. If Garin appears, come back immediately. Do you all understand?"

"Yep," Mateo said. "Don't worry. Now that Claret can teleport, that makes two of us, so it will be easier if we get split up or something."

"I think I should get to go," Chad said, standing against the wall with his arms folded.

Everyone ignored him.

Odie pulled a container from his bag and unscrewed the lid. "Everyone, put some of this on. It will prevent sunburn... at least I hope it will. I haven't had time to test it." Everyone stuck their fingers in and rubbed it on their faces and arms. "Then I have this," he said, pulling out four tubes. "It's for your lips."

Mateo wrinkled his nose. "I'm not walking around with shiny lips."

"You'll regret it," Kaylee said, taking one and putting it in her bag. "Have you ever burned your lips? It's miserable."

"People who use lip balm are addicted to it. If you never use it, you never need it."

Kaylee just shook her head. She'd taken out her braids and pulled her hair back in a ponytail. "I'll take Mateo's so we have it when he wants it later."

Odie handed it to her, and she put it in her bag.

Claret took the lip balm and rubbed some on her lips. "Last time we were there, mine got really painful."

Mateo was glad she'd dressed responsibly. She wore a tunic and britches and not a dress. She'd pulled her hair into a long braid.

"So we're ready?" Mateo asked. "Do you want me to take us there?"

Kaylee shook her head. "Claret should take us. She's already been there and no offense, but it's smoother."

Mateo wouldn't argue. She was right. Kaylee stepped up next to him and took his hand. Mateo might be imagining it, but it seemed like she was standing closer than she needed to. She grabbed Claret's hand and Claret took Odie's.

"Ready?" Claret asked. "Here we go."

The next thing Mateo saw was Chad running across the room. He flinched when Chad smacked into him. He went flying and did a roll. When he opened his eyes, he was in a red sandy desert.

Chad was a few feet away from him, and Kaylee was on the other side. Odie and Claret were nowhere to be seen.

Kaylee jumped up and brushed off her pants. "What the heck, Chad? Why did you do that?"

Chad and Mateo got up, and Mateo made a fist. Kaylee shot him a look.

Chad crossed his arms. "I don't think Mr. Dovin should get to tell me where I can go. I might be helpful to you."

"Where are Odie and Claret? This is all your fault! If we have to spend time looking for them, we aren't ever going to accomplish anything."

Kaylee said some more things, but the angrier she got, the less Mateo could understand since she was speaking to Chad. Chad said some things back, and Mateo was still lost. They argued back and forth for a minute.

"Should we go back to the castle?" Mateo asked, breaking into their fight. "Do you think Claret and Odie will?"

Kaylee frowned. "Unless they're separated. Odie can't teleport."

"Well, let's go back and see and leave Chad."

"I heard my name," Chad said. "What are you two saying?"

"We need to go back to the castle," Kaylee told him. "To find our other friends."

Chad shook his head. "I'm not going." He started walking across the sand.

Mateo shrugged. "Let's leave him."

Kaylee tilted her head. "We can't. He'll die out here."

"I wish I could teleport normally. Then I could grab him and take him. If I have to run, I probably can't force him to do that."

"Then I guess we follow him and hope we reach Drag-on's Cove." She frowned and looked at the sun. "Dragon's Cove should be south. He's actually going in the right direction. That's irritating."

They began following Chad, and Mateo was already regretting not taking the lip balm. It was hot out here and he could feel his lips drying out.

Kaylee took a deep breath. "Chad was bugging me yesterday, and I sort of told him you and I were dating."

Mateo stopped dead in his tracks. "Oh, yeah?"

"I feel like a terrible liar, but I thought it might get him to leave me alone."

Mateo grinned. "I am totally willing to play along with this."

Her mouth turned down. "Don't overdo it."

"Me? Overdo? Never. I would hold your hand right now, but I'm sweating so much it would just slip."

She laughed, and they started walking again. Chad looked over his shoulder to make sure they were following.

"This sand is hard to walk through," she said. "I'm nervous about Claret and Odie. Why aren't they here?"

"Maybe when Chad barged into us, we teleported and they didn't."

"But Claret was the one doing it. Wouldn't she have to be here?"

He shrugged. "I don't know. Maybe it caused her to let go of your hand once we'd already started. Maybe that threw us out early or something."

"That makes sense. I wonder how big this desert is."

"It looked small on the map."

"So did everything."

"I guess. If I could teleport to the castle and back here, I would. I don't think I could come back to the same place, though, since I don't know where in the desert we are."

"Can you teleport us the rest of the way to Dragon's Cove?"

Mateo shook his head. "If I had the map."

"It's pretty hot out here. Chad might get too hot and let us take him back. He doesn't have any supplies. I give him thirty minutes."

Kaylee wanted to scream. Chad wasn't giving up, and it had been over an hour. Kaylee's throat was getting dry, but she'd been trying not to drink her water. They brought extra water in case vorcraws found them, and she didn't want to get stuck without any. They all had two pouches, but they didn't know how long they would be here, and Chad didn't have any. She had the Blade of the Phoenix at her side, so she might have to rely on that if the vorcraws found them.

Chad stopped and turned. He was getting sunburned. He hadn't put any of Odie's salve on it. "Someone want to give me a little water?"

Kaylee frowned and unhooked one from her belt. "This is all we have. You can take this one, but make it last."

He grabbed it and took a big gulp. "Thanks." He hooked it onto his own belt. Kaylee and Mateo both took a small sip from their water.

"This is ridiculous, Chad," Kaylee said. "You're already sunburned and we don't know how much farther it is. Let us take you back to the castle."

"Nope. Can I use your lip balm?"

Kaylee wrinkled her nose, but saying no would be rude. His lips looked a little puffy. She searched through her bag until she found the small tube. She opened it and held it out to him. He stuck his finger in and rubbed it over his lips.

"Try putting some on your face," Kaylee said. "It's going to be really bad if you don't."

He scowled but rubbed some on his face, then took a little more for his arms.

Kaylee was glad she'd taken Mateo's lip balm as well, since Chad had used so much of hers, and her lips already needed more. She stuck her finger in and applied some to her lips. "You should use some, Mateo. Your lips are looking dry."

"I'm good."

"He's stubborn," Chad said. "I don't know why you're even trying. You won't win."

She turned to Mateo and stepped up to him. "Oh, I can get him to wear it," she said.

Mateo crossed his arms and grinned. "Go ahead and try it."

Kaylee stuck her finger in the lip balm and took out a healthy amount. She held it in front of his face. He stepped back, and she stepped forward. She raised her hand toward his lips, and he grabbed her wrist and pushed it back into her own face. He made her rub it on her lips and around her mouth.

Mateo grinned. "I win."

Kaylee scowled.

Chad shook his head. "Told you."

Kaylee narrowed her eyes and wondered what the sun was doing to her brain. She took another step forward, grabbed Mateo's tunic in one hand, and pulled him toward her. His eyes widened, and before she could talk sense into herself, she pressed her lips against his and smeared the lip balm dramatically across them. It wasn't a kiss. It was just her wiping her lips on his. Even she knew that was a lame excuse.

She pulled away and tried to smile. "I win."

Mateo shook his head. "I think I did."

"You two are so immature," Chad said. "We're wasting time. Let's go." He turned and trudged off through the sand.

Kaylee started after him, and Mateo followed. Kaylee had a feeling she was going to regret this moment for a long time. She sighed and tried to tell herself it was the sun's fault. If she wasn't so hot, she never would have done it.

Mateo grabbed her hand. He was right. It was sweaty, but so was hers. "I think he bought it," he said.

Kaylee swallowed. She wanted to laugh it all off, but now she just felt embarrassed.

"It wasn't really what I expected my first kiss to be like."

She turned to look at him. "That was your first kiss?"

Mateo frowned. "No, of course not... I meant my first kiss with you." His face was slightly red, and Kaylee decided not to push it.

"It wasn't actually a kiss," Kaylee protested. "All I did was wipe the lip balm on you."

"With your lips... on my lips."

"So it was a little unconventional."

"And you can do it again anytime you want."

Kaylee rolled her eyes. "I think you should learn to put your own lip balm on."

He grinned. "I'll remember that the next time you apply it."

She narrowed her eyes and opened her mouth to tell him he better not, but he cut her off.

"So how many guys have you kissed?"

Kaylee pressed her lips together and tried to think of a way out of this conversation.

He tilted his head. "That many, huh?"

She let out a breath. "None, all right? I don't think it's a good practice to go around kissing everyone. It should mean something and be... I dunno. Special, I guess."

"Wow, so I'm your first kiss?"

She rolled her eyes again. "I told you. It wasn't a kiss."

Mateo shrugged. "If you say so."

Claret's legs were getting tired from scurrying around Dragon's Cove looking for her friends. When she'd teleported here, something odd had happened. Something had jerked them right as she teleported and when she had opened herself up, she was alone on Dragon's Cove. She'd called for her friends, but they were nowhere to be found. She hadn't seen any dragons, either.

She had teleported back to the castle to see if she had somehow left them behind, but Dovin said they had all disappeared, and that the boy Chad had run into them and gone as well. He must have made her lose her hold on her friends. She worried they might be lost in the darkness of teleporting, but Dovin told her that wasn't possible.

She had come back with instructions to go back for Dovin if she didn't find them in an hour. "Are there any fairies here?" she asked, hoping a helpful fairy might respond. None appeared. She walked around the pond and remembered the last time she had been here with Odie. That was the first time vorcraws had attacked them.

Claret touched the sword at her side, just to make herself feel better. She thought about how different Odie had looked this morning in his blue tunic and tan pants. It was the first time she'd ever seen him wear something that wasn't black. Claret walked over to the twenty-foot-tall mound of rocks that the waterfall came out of. She'd jumped off those rocks and into the pond when they were here last.

"Claret!"

She turned to see Odie running toward her. She sighed with relief and waited for him.

"What happened? Where are the others?" he asked, stopping in front of her.

"I don't know. Chad ran into us and he must have messed things up. I've been walking all around looking for you all."

"I haven't seen anyone else. I ended up in the desert, but I could see Dragon's Cove from where I was. It was still a walk but manageable."

"So now what?" Claret asked. "I don't see any dragons here, and I don't see the others. I wonder if the stories about Dragon's Cove were all made up and there aren't any dragons."

"It looks like there might be a cave behind the waterfall," Odie said, walking closer to the flowing water. "Look, there is," he said, pointing. "Do you want to look inside?"

Claret frowned. "Not really. I think we should keep looking for the others."

"But we might find something."

Claret had been in enough dark places this year to last her a lifetime. Still, Odie was right. What if they found something?

"All right, but let's hurry."

They moved closer to the waterfall and water droplets pelted them. It felt good after being in the scorching sun. Claret followed Odie as he went behind the waterfall and into the dark cave. They both made lights appear in their hands and walked over the rock floor. The cave was narrow but large enough to fit a dragon. And it was tall. Claret hoped they didn't stumble upon anything scary.

The cave turned to the left and they could see a dim light coming from somewhere down below. The cave floor sloped and Claret had to concentrate on not slipping.

"What do you suppose is down there?" she asked, grabbing Odie's arm when her foot slipped.

He put a hand on her lower back. "I don't know, but get ready for anything."

When they reached the bottom, they stopped, and Claret's mouth hung open. "It looks like a miniature town," she said in awe. There were rows and rows of tiny streets with tiny houses. They were all covered in a yellowish-brown substance that was thick but slightly see-through. Some houses had been crushed.

Odie kneeled down and inspected the closest house. He ran his hand over the roof. "It reminds me of amber."

"How would everything get covered in amber?"

"It's probably something else, but that's what it puts me in mind of."

Claret couldn't see the end of the houses. They seemed to go on forever. She glanced up to inspect the ceiling. It was high and gold-colored. How did this place exist?

"Look!" Claret said, pointing into the distance. A red dragon ran, stomping houses as it went. It jumped into the air and flew up close to the ceiling.

"I can't believe there's enough room here for that," Odie said. "Do you suppose all the dragons are down here?"

"They might be. Perhaps that is the reason for all the crushed houses."

"So they live under Dragon's Cove, not above."

"But what of the houses? The dragons didn't make those."

Odie ran his hand over the house again. "Fairies."

"Fairies?"

"I would almost bet on it. Fairies live underground. Maybe the dragons got into the fairy village and messed it up."

"Fairies are powerful. Would they allow that?"

"Dragons are also powerful."

"But not magical?"

Odie stood and tilted his head as he studied the flying red dragon. "I'm not sure."

The dragon came closer. Claret gritted her teeth and hoped it didn't fly into them.

"She's friendly," Odie said. "I can sense it."

The dragon landed ten feet in front of them, crushing a house in the process. She studied them for a moment, then lifted his head into the air and released a blood-curdling roar. Claret covered her ears and took a step back.

"She's calling to others," Odie said. "She's telling them to come."

Claret shivered. "So a bunch of dragons are going to appear? I wish we weren't in a cave for this. I feel trapped."

"You can go back. I'm going to stay and try to figure out what's going on."

Claret swallowed. "I'll stay."

Odie took her hand, and she gasped as she saw several dragons flying toward them. This was either exactly what they were looking for or their doom.

12

CHAPTER 12

Odie had never imagined this many dragons in one place. There were at least thirty, in all colors, standing in front of them. His heart pounded with excitement and he had to concentrate hard not to be overwhelmed with the feelings they were projecting to him. With that many, he would never separate their thoughts or feelings. The biggest feeling he was getting was curiosity. The dragons were wondering who they were and why they were here.

Claret was trembling slightly but standing tall. He squeezed her hand. "They're only curious."

"There are so many."

"I'm Odie," he said to the dragons. "This is Claret. We are friends."

Some dragons paced, crushing what was left of the nearby houses, but most of them watched Odie. They must sense he could connect with them. He wished he'd had more practice.

"Why are you down here?"

The red dragon roared, and the others all began moving around nervously. Images of Garin came into Odie's head, and the dragons' feelings all made Odie feel cold and terrified. He turned to Claret. "They fear Garin."

"Do you think they trust us?"

Odie nodded. "I don't know how to explain it, but I can feel it. I can also feel that they don't mean any harm, so you don't need to worry."

Claret nodded, but she didn't release his hand.

"I'm going to let them know we're here to help, and we don't like Garin either." He closed his eyes and tried to send them flashes of his memories of Garin. They all began growling, so he stopped.

Claret rubbed her lips together nervously. "Do you think we can get them to go up above?"

"I can try." He closed his eyes again and thought about going above ground. All he could sense from them was confusion. "Let's go up and see if any follow."

Claret nodded and released his hand. She rushed up the slope and Odie was close behind. He looked behind him and saw the dragons staring at them. The red dragon took a step forward, then launched into the air and followed them.

"Duck!" Odie said, grabbing Claret's arm and pulling her down. The dragon flew over their heads and around the corner of the cave.

"I can't believe he could do that!" Claret exclaimed. "I didn't think there was enough space for that."

Odie looked at all the dragons behind them. He could sense that they were all going to fly through. "Get down flat and cover your head." Claret didn't ask questions. She went to her stomach and put her hands over her head. Odie did the same, right before he felt the breeze from the dragons flying over them. He felt something hit his back and he heard Claret let out a surprised gasp.

"What just hit me?" Claret whispered as the breeze from the dragons stopped. Odie got to his feet and felt something fall from his back. He looked down to see a mixture of brown and white goop.

Odie grinned and held his hand out to her. She let him help her up. "You don't want to know. It's all over your braid and your back. It got me too."

Claret's eyes went wide. "Wait, are you saying..."

Odie laughed. "I'm saying it's a good thing there's a lake up there so we can clean up."

"Oh gross," Claret said, hurrying up the slope. Odie knew he should be disgusted, but the look on Claret's face was priceless. He followed behind her and squinted when they left the cave and came out from behind the waterfall.

Dragons flew through the sky, making Dragon's Cove look the way Odie had always pictured it. Claret dove into the lake and Odie panicked for a moment, worried she might hit her head. The water must be deeper by the waterfall because she surfaced and began vigorously scrubbing at her hair. The water came to her shoulders. When he'd been in the pond before, it had been shallow, but that was on the other side. Claret took out her braid and kept dunking her head and rubbing her hair. Odie stood there, grinning at her.

Claret scowled at him. "Are you going to stand there with a silly grin on your face or clean the dragon dung from your back?"

Odie laughed and jumped in. The water was warm. He surfaced and tried to wipe anything off his back he could reach.

"I wish I had some soap," she said. "I can't believe they got it in my hair. Can't you tell them not to do that to people?"

Odie laughed. "Dragons are like birds. They just let it go when they need to. They didn't do it on purpose."

"How can you laugh after something like that?"

He grinned. "Sorry, but you should have seen the look on your face."

She frowned and pushed water into his face. "I'm surprised you aren't collecting the dung for one of your experiments."

Odie's eyes lit up. "I didn't think of that. I wonder if I have anything I can put it in." He frowned. He'd jumped into the water with his pack over his shoulder. Everything he had was wet.

"I lost my sword," Claret said. "I jumped in without thinking."

"I'll get it." Odie swam under the water and quickly spotted the sword. He scooped it up and surfaced. He held it up and handed it to Claret.

"Thanks." She shifted awkwardly in the water as she tried to put the sword back in its sheath.

Odie looked up at the flying dragons. "You have to admit, they look amazing."

Claret looked up and nodded. "I suppose. All I know is that I'm going to avoid walking under them."

"Hey, there's something up ahead!" Chad called.

Mateo squinted and nodded. "I think he's right." He could see trees and a whole lot of green. They still had a ways to go. There were things flying around the area, but they were too far away to make out.

"Are you beginning to understand English better?" Kaylee asked. "You seem to know what Chad says most of the time."

Mateo shrugged. "No more than I always could. I think I understand it better than Claret and Odie do because I grew up watching a lot of English cartoons. I get lost when people talk too fast or mumble, but Chad isn't too hard to understand."

Kaylee sighed. "I should be excited that we can see something that isn't desert, but it looks so far."

"I can teleport us now because I can see it."

"That would be great. Hey, Chad!"

Chad turned.

"Mateo can teleport us over there."

Chad frowned. "How do I know you won't take me back to the castle instead?"

"He won't," Kaylee said. "We need to get over there to find Claret and Odie."

"Fine," he said as they reached him.

"We have to hold on to Mateo and run."

"Why run?"

"Because that's the way it works when he teleports."

Chad crossed his arms. "I'm not holding his hand."

Mateo rolled his eyes. "Hold Kaylee's." He didn't want Chad holding Kaylee's hand, but he didn't want to hold Chad's hand any more than Chad wanted to hold his. "All right, ready? Run." They ran three steps through the sand, then Mateo took them to Dragon's Cove. He smiled when they didn't fall over but came to a graceful stop.

"Look at the dragons," Kaylee breathed. "They are so… majestic."

Mateo nodded as he watched them fly overhead. "Drink some water, then we can look for the others. Odie said there's fresh water here, so we'll be able to refill."

Mateo unlatched the water from his belt and took a long drink. It felt good going down his parched throat. He forced himself to leave some, just in case they ran into a vorcraw before they found more.

Chad was draining his water, and Kaylee was taking one swallow at a time and pausing between. She had more self-control than he ever would. Mateo touched his lips as he thought about their non-kiss. He didn't care what she said. He was counting it as a kiss. Sure, it was a bit slimy with lip balm, but it was more than he'd ever thought he would get from her.

She looked at him, and her eyes narrowed. Mateo grinned at her and she rolled her eyes.

"I think I hear water," he said, glancing around. "Let's go that way." He started into the trees and they followed him. A large pond or a small lake, he wasn't sure which, appeared in front of them. A waterfall poured out of a rock formation and not too far from it, he could see people in the water.

"Is that Odie and Claret?" Kaylee asked.

"I hope so, but I can't tell. Should we head over there?"

"I say we swim over. It would feel so good right now, and it would wash off the sand."

"Sounds good to me."

Chad frowned. "What are you saying? You want to swim?"

Kaylee turned to him. "Yes, it will wash us off."

"I'd rather walk around."

Mateo grinned. Chad couldn't swim. He wouldn't tease him, though. That would annoy Kaylee.

"All right, we can just wash off," Kaylee said, dropping her pack and wading into the water. She turned to Mateo. "It feels so nice."

He took off his boots and tossed them next to her bag and put his pack by it, then followed her in. He wasn't walking around in soggy boots all day. Getting the rest of his clothing wet would feel good and keep him cool. He kept his sword, just in case.

Chad crossed his arms. "What if there's some type of creature in there?"

Mateo grinned. Maybe he could swim, and he was just scared. He heard someone yell and looked over to see the two people waving. It must be Odie and Claret.

"Are you sure you don't want to swim across?" Kaylee asked Chad.

"No, I'll walk over there and meet you. I'll take your stuff." Chad grabbed Mateo's boots and their packs and began jogging around the lake.

"That seems oddly nice of him," Kaylee said.

"Wanna race?" Mateo asked. He didn't want Kaylee to think of Chad as a nice guy. He obviously had an ulterior motive.

"No, the sword feels really heavy right now. I'm going to pace myself so I don't drown. I should have had Chad take it, but I don't trust him."

Mateo's sword was a lot lighter than the Blade of the Phoenix, so when he started swimming, it didn't bother him much. Kaylee was doing a backstroke, and she looked like she was focused.

By the time they reached the other side, Claret and Odie had gotten out of the water and were standing on the shore, dripping. Mateo climbed out, and Kaylee was right behind him.

"We're so glad we found you," Claret said. "I was so worried."

Kaylee squeezed water from her ponytail. "We were too. We've been walking through the desert. Chad's coming. This is all his fault."

"We found a cave," Odie said. "The dragons were all down there. And there's a small village. I bet it once belonged to the fairies."

Kaylee's eyes sparkled. "Can we see it?"

Claret's mouth turned down. "It's probably safer now that the dragons are out."

Odie laughed. "I'm sure it is."

Claret threw her wet hair over her shoulder and glared at him. "Odie thinks getting splatted by dragon dung is hilarious."

Mateo snorted. "It kind of is. Wait, is that why you two were in the water?"

Odie nodded. "Yep. One of them got us good."

"It wasn't funny," Claret said. "I hope I got it all out of my hair."

Mateo laughed. "Well, here comes Chad, then we can go into the cave." Chad was walking toward them, a slight smile on his face.

"Why is Chad here?" Odie asked.

"He ran into us when we were teleporting," Kaylee said. "That's why we all ended up in different places."

"Here you go," he said, handing Kaylee her bag. He tossed Mateo's at his feet and handed him his boots.

"Thanks," Mateo said, sitting on the ground. Everyone else was going to be walking around with soggy boots. He pulled on one and then, when he almost had the second on, his foot touched something. He pulled it off and held it upside down. A small brown snake fell to the ground.

Mateo dropped the boot and rolled away from the snake. He jumped to his feet and turned, his fist clenched.

Chad laughed. "I wonder how that got in there."

Mateo's eyes narrowed, and he took a step toward Chad.

Kaylee put a hand on Mateo's chest and shook her head. "Don't."

Mateo's heart was racing. He didn't know why snakes scared him so much. Kaylee picked up the snake and walked it over to some tall grass, then released it. Chad was still laughing and leaning over, resting his hands on his knees.

"You should have seen your face!" he said, laughing some more. Mateo clenched and unclenched his fists. This reminded him of the first day he met Chad and had wanted to punch him. He would have if Kaylee hadn't intervened. He probably shouldn't get credit since he ended up punching him later.

Kaylee walked calmly over to Chad, and before Mateo had time to wonder what she was doing, she jumped up and had him in a headlock. "Don't ever do that again. Do you hear me?" she said through gritted teeth.

Chad tried to break free, but Kaylee had a firm grip. Mateo grinned.

"Let me go. I don't want to have to hurt you," Chad said.

"Go ahead and try. What do you think would have happened if Mateo had stepped down on the snake? It would have been seriously injured and possibly killed."

"It's just a snake," Chad protested.

Kaylee frowned and tightened her grip. "Don't do it again. How stupid are you? Don't you remember the last time Mateo punched you?"

"It was a lucky hit."

Kaylee released him and pushed him over. He sat on the ground and glared up at her.

"I've stopped him from punching you twice now. I'm not going to next time."

Chad stood up and brushed off his pants. "Whatever, I'm sick of you people. Take me back to the castle."

Claret stepped forward. "I'll do it." She grabbed him and disappeared. Less than twenty seconds later, she was back. "I wasn't going to give him the chance to change his mind. Come on. We'll show you the cave." Odie and Claret began walking, and Mateo and Kaylee fell in behind.

Mateo glanced at Kaylee and grinned. "I thought you were defending me for a minute back there. I should have known you were worried about the snake."

Kaylee raised her brow. "But you know I was bluffing, right? I'm not going to let you punch him."

"But you know he deserves it." He wouldn't mention that she'd just thrown him to the ground.

"Yeah, but you're better than that."

"Am I?"

"I know you are."

13

CHAPTER 13

"Wow," Kaylee said as she looked around the small village. "Why is so much of it crushed?"

Mateo squatted down to try to see in one of the house's windows. "Yeah, it looks like Godzilla came through here."

"The dragons trampled some of it," Odie said.

Kaylee picked up a broken piece of a roof. It was covered in something hard and see-through. "What's all over everything?"

Odie shrugged. "It reminds me of amber, but I don't see any way it could have gotten on everything."

"If this is a fairy village, where are the fairies?"

"I don't know, but there are more dragons down here," Odie said. "I can sense them."

Claret rubbed her arms and looked around. "Where are they?"

"I'm not sure, but there are a lot."

Kaylee stepped over a broken house and ignored the squish of her wet boot. "Do we go farther and risk meeting fairies or leave?"

"Fairies don't want people in their space," Odie said. "And when they punish you, it's horrible."

Mateo grinned. "Are you ever going to tell us what the fairies did to you?"

Odie shook his head. "Never. It was bad enough when it happened. I don't want to relive it."

"The fairies might tell us things," Kaylee said. "Like why the dragons are down here."

"I think they're hiding from Garin. They're all scared of him."

"Hmm. Do you think the fairies are helping the dragons?"

Claret frowned. "We know the fairies are helping Isadora. That makes them the enemy in my mind."

"What about Arelia?" Mateo asked. "She helped us more than once, and she said fairies helped us when we were trying to save the continent from rising. Why would they do that if they're bad?"

Odie ran a hand through his wet hair. "Perhaps they helped us then because they were in as much danger as anyone if the continent rose. Now that it isn't a threat, they've moved on and are helping the witch."

Kaylee sighed. "It just seems weird they would help us so many times, then turn and help our enemies."

Mateo shrugged. "They might be like goblins. On your side one day, then fighting you the next. Selling out to the highest bidder."

Odie clenched his jaw, then shook his head.

"Sorry, Odie."

"No, you're right. It's just hard to hear since I considered myself a goblin for most of my life. It is true, though. Goblins will flip sides faster than anything. Maybe fairies are the same."

"But they didn't take the Blade of the Phoenix when we offered it to them," Kaylee said. "They could have taken it and given it to Isadora. She wanted it, after all."

Claret was still looking around like something might pop up and grab her any second. "But perhaps they hadn't teamed up with Isadora yet. This might be a recent development."

"Should we be talking about fairies in a place they might hear us?" Mateo asked. "It sounds like they have good hearing."

"Probably not, but do you really think there are any down here?" Kaylee asked. "It looks like all their homes have been frozen in this stuff and lots of them are stepped on. Maybe this was an abandoned village, and the dragons took it over."

"That's probably right," Odie said. "A fairy would have the power to block the dragons if it wanted to. It doesn't seem like anyone has tried to block the cave."

"Let's go back up," Mateo said. "I don't see a reason to stay here. Not unless we're looking for more dragons."

They turned and began walking back up into the cave. "I'm going to warn all the dragons about Garin," Odie said. "It shouldn't be hard, since they already fear him. If they know we aren't like him, they'll trust us more. That's what we need to do. Build trust."

Kaylee shaded her eyes when she came out from behind the waterfall. "How do we get them to come down so we can build trust?"

Odie looked into the sky. "I might be able to get them to come." He kept staring up without blinking.

"Vorcraw," Claret said, pointing into the trees.

Kaylee grabbed at her water, then remembered she'd forgotten to refill it. The monster was still a good distance away, but she didn't want to be caught bending over. She grabbed the Blade of the Phoenix and held it in front of her.

Mateo and Odie both took out their swords, and Claret unstopped her water.

"We could jump in the water," Mateo suggested.

"We could also teleport," Claret said, "but that is only a temporary fix."

The vorcraw walked toward them, and Kaylee saw two more come out from behind the trees. Their tiger eyes were all fixated on Claret, who had walked in front of the others. When the first one was close enough, Claret flung her water at him. The water splashed into his face and ran down his fur, but he didn't turn to smoke, or even slow down.

Mateo grabbed Claret's arm and pulled her back behind them. Kaylee held her sword, ready to attack. She could hear Claret's sword scrape against the sheath as she pulled it out. A growl at her side caused her to turn her head. Three were coming from that direction as well. That made it six to four.

Kaylee shook her head. "If water isn't killing these guys anymore, I don't think we can handle this many."

"Run to the left," Odie said. "We don't want to get surrounded, especially if we can't jump in the water for protection."

They all ran, and Kaylee could hear the roars of the vorcraws as they pursued them.

"Do we stay together or split up?" Claret called. She spun around and stopped.

"Don't stop," Kaylee called over her shoulder.

Claret held up her hand, and a ball of burning fire appeared. She threw it at the closest vorcraw and it roared as the fire hit it in the chest. Odie and Mateo stopped and changed direction, going back to Claret. She brought up another fireball and threw it at the next monster, but she missed and it hit the ground.

The first vorcraw was growling and batting at its singed fur. Mateo ran forward and stabbed it.

"How fast can you throw fire?" Kaylee asked.

"I don't know," Claret said, throwing another ball and hitting one in the face. It fell to its knees and Odie stabbed it.

Claret began throwing fireballs one after the other. The vorcraws were backing up even though Claret was missing more than she was connecting with them.

Kaylee didn't want to go after any of them for fear of being hit by Claret. She ran off to one side and hoped one would follow her. When she turned, she saw one walking toward her. She ran forward and raised her sword in the air.

She swung it and the vorcraw raised his sword, deflecting her blow.

A ball of fire whizzed past her face, and she pulled back. "Don't help me, Claret," she muttered too quietly for her friend to hear.

The vorcraw swung at her, and she fell to the ground and did the most ungraceful roll in history. She swung the blade at its legs, knocking it to the ground. She jumped up and pointed the sword at the creature. Blue light shot out and hit it in the chest. Before it could recover, she ran forward and thrust her sword through it. Smoke rose as it roared and disappeared.

She took a deep breath, then ran back to the others. They must have taken care of them because there wasn't a vorcraw in sight.

"You should have shot the lightning from the sword before you attacked," Odie said.

Kaylee shrugged and secured the sword at her side. "I still don't know how it works. Sometimes it shoots something out and sometimes it doesn't."

Mateo sheathed his sword. "All I've got to say is, thank goodness Claret can make fireballs. When did that happen?"

Claret pushed a stray hair from her face. "I learned it from a book. It's actually quite easy."

"Well, I think it saved us," Odie said.

Mateo grinned. "Even if you throw like a girl."

Claret just grinned.

Kaylee reached into her bag. "What does a girl throw like?"

"Claret."

Kaylee pulled the lip balm from the bag and threw it at Mateo with everything in her, hitting him square in the chest. He grabbed it before it fell.

"Ouch! Dang it, Kaylee! I'm going to have a bruise."

She smiled. "Probably."

He raised his eyebrow, then smiled. He held up the lip balm. "I'm going to keep this. There are good memories tied to this."

Odie's forehead furrowed. "I thought you didn't want any."

Kaylee could feel heat running up her neck and onto her face.

Mateo tossed it into the air and caught it. "That was before I realized lip balm can be quite pleasant when applied in the right way."

Kaylee grabbed the other lip balm from her bag and threw it. Mateo was ready this time and caught it. He laughed and Kaylee growled. She knew it was her fault this conversation was happening, but did Mateo really have to hint about it around the others?

Claret looked confused, and Odie had a small smile. Kaylee shot Mateo one last dirty look.

"Why didn't the water work on the vorcraws?" she asked, changing the subject.

Odie rubbed his chin. "I bet Isadora did something to them. There are some easy ways to make water repelled from something. If the right mixture was rubbed on the fur, the water wouldn't actually touch them."

Claret folded her arms. "It's a good thing they aren't very threatening. I mean, they look terrifying, but they don't seem overly hard to defeat."

"It might get tricky if she sends a lot at once," Odie said. "Six was harder."

Mateo looked up at the sky. "And what if she makes them stronger or more coordinated?"

The red dragon landed by them and curled up, looking at Odie.

"She seems to be the only red one," Odie said, rubbing her nose.

"It would have been nice of her to come by and blow fire on the monsters," Mateo said.

Odie patted the dragon. "I'm going to tell her to stay away from Garin and I'm going to show her where the castle is so she can find us if she needs to. It might take a while and it might be easier if you all aren't here to distract me."

"We can't leave you here," Claret said. "You don't know how to teleport."

"I'm already wet, so I think I'll swim around for a while," Mateo said. "You two want to join me?"

"No," Kaylee said. "I'm too tired. I think I'll sit and put my feet in the water."

"Me too," Claret said.

They left Odie with the dragon and went to the lake. Mateo put his bag near the lake and placed his sword on top. He took off his shirt and boots and tossed them to the side, then entered the water. Kaylee and Claret walked around until they found a large rock that wasn't too far out in the water. They took off their boots and placed their bags nearby, then waded to the rock.

Kaylee climbed up and sat with her feet dangling in the water. Her sword was still at her side. She wasn't leaving that behind. Claret sat next to her and sighed.

"Anything wrong?" Kaylee asked.

"No," she said, moving her feet around. "I just feel like I'm never going to be as useful as the rest of you."

Kaylee bumped her with her shoulder. "That's ridiculous. You saved the day back there. Without those fireballs, we would have been a lot worse off."

"But my aim is atrocious."

Kaylee smiled. "It could use some work, but you took the pressure off. We couldn't have done it without you. Just ignore Mateo. He thinks he's funny." Kaylee watched Mateo swim across the lake.

"What did he mean about the lip balm?"

Kaylee moved her lips to the side and blew out a breath. "He's a dork."

Claret tilted her head. "What do you mean?"

"Nothing. His lips were dry and I couldn't get him to put the lip balm on, so I put it on for him."

Claret's eyes went wide. "So you actually ran your finger over his lips? No wonder he was acting like that. He must have been thrilled."

Kaylee placed her hands on top of her head and closed her eyes. "I might not have used my finger."

"What do you mean?"

"I might have used my… lips."

There was a moment of silence, then Claret giggled.

Kaylee opened her eyes and frowned. "I can't tell you how long I'm going to regret it. I blame the sun. It was frying my head, and I wasn't thinking right."

"Perhaps you should stop being in denial and realize you actually care about Mateo."

She shook her head. "No. Mateo is... not... I don't know. He doesn't know when to be serious, he solves problems with his fists, and he doesn't want to live on Earth. That's three strikes."

Claret drummed her fingers on the rock. "But you still like him."

Kaylee's heart started pounding, and she realized she was still watching him. "I... ugh." She ran a hand over her face. Was Claret right? Did she?

"You can't tell me you kissed him and you don't like him. I've gotten to know you and that isn't you."

"It wasn't a kiss. I just wiped my lips across his."

Claret patted Kaylee's hand. "If your lips touched his, then it was a kiss."

Kaylee felt like she'd swallowed a rock.

"And you keep talking about Mateo using his fists, but you threw that lip balm at him pretty hard. You also put Chad in a headlock and pushed him over. Perhaps you aren't as different as you want to think."

Kaylee bit her lip. "You're right. I need to apologize. For all of it. It's going to be incredibly embarrassing." If she thought her heart was beating hard before, it was nothing compared to now. Her hands were shaking slightly, and she thought she might puke.

"You don't have to do it right now," Claret said. "Wait until we get back to the castle."

Kaylee took a deep breath. "If I don't do it now, I'll talk myself out of it." She stood and jumped into the water and walked to the shore. She pulled on her boots and looked out at Mateo.

"Mateo!" she yelled. "Mateo!" He stopped swimming and looked around until he saw her. She motioned to him with her hand, and he swam over and got out of the lake. He walked toward her and she frowned when she saw the red mark on his chest. It was going to be a huge bruise by tomorrow.

"What's up?" he asked.

"Can we talk for a minute?"

His mouth turned down. "Sure. Let me grab my stuff." He jogged over to his pile of things and pulled on his tunic and boots. She walked slowly over to him. "What is it?"

Kaylee bit her lip. "Can we go where Claret won't see us?"

"Um... okay." He followed her into some trees.

She hugged herself and tried to think of how to begin.

"I know," he said. "I'm sorry I teased you in front of everyone."

She shook her head. "No. I'm sorry. I shouldn't have thrown things at you."

He grinned. "It's all right. I deserved it."

"I'm also sorry about the other thing."

He arched his brow. "What other thing?"

"The other lip balm thing. In the desert."

He shrugged and smiled. "It's fine. I told you. I'm keeping the gloss. Don't worry. I know you did it for Chad's sake."

Kaylee closed her eyes and shook her head. "That isn't entirely true." She looked up at him and tried to read his expression, but she couldn't.

"It isn't?" he asked, his brown eyes probing hers.

"No. I was also trying to beat you at your own game... and... I wanted to." Kaylee waited for a laugh or a teasing smile, but Mateo just kept his eyes locked on hers. "And I shouldn't have done it."

"Why?"

"I'm not ready for a relationship and we're too different." He looked so serious she wanted to fidget, but she didn't. She took a deep breath and blew it out. "And like I said before. First kisses should be special, not a joke."

"It's like you said. It wasn't really a kiss," he said, running his finger over her cheek. She held her breath and told herself to walk away. Her legs didn't listen. "I get that you aren't ready for a relationship. I respect that. But let me be your first real kiss, then we'll never talk about it again. What do you say?"

Kaylee wondered if her heart could actually break out of her chest. She swallowed and felt herself nod. She hoped he didn't notice the way her hands were shaking when she put them on his shoulders. He put his hands around her waist and gave her a small smile. It wasn't a typical teasing Mateo smile. He looked slightly nervous.

He leaned down and touched her lips with his, and butterflies rampaged across her stomach. She leaned in closer and wrapped her arms around his neck. This had been a terrible idea. She could do this forever. At least she could if she didn't forget to breathe and pass out. Her stomach was a mess of flutters. She broke the kiss and her eyes gazed into Mateo's. She kissed him quickly, one more time, then turned and ran.

Mateo watched Kaylee disappear around a corner. He touched his tingling lips and frowned. It was a perfect first kiss. At least in his mind. And now it was over. He'd told her they wouldn't ever talk about it again, and he had to honor that. He let out a breath and leaned against the nearest tree and put a hand over his pounding heart.

Everything inside of him felt different. He'd liked Kaylee since the day he met her, but until today, he had thought she didn't feel the same. When she rubbed the lip gloss on him, he thought it was to get Chad off her back, but right here, right now, he'd seen something in her eyes. She was conflicted but not indifferent to him.

It should have made him happy, but it stressed him. She liked him against what she thought was her better judgment. Now she was going to put up an even bigger wall between them and probably end up hating him. He frowned. Maybe he should put up his own wall. He didn't need to get hurt.

He stood up straight when he heard something coming toward him. He put a hand to his side, but he didn't have his sword. Kaylee burst through the trees and looked at him. Her mouth turned down, and she ran toward him. His eyes widened as she jumped into his arms, hugging him tightly. He hugged her back and wondered if his heart could take this.

She pulled back and looked at him, her eyes glistening. "If we're never going to talk about it again, then I want it to be worth it." She pressed her lips to his, and he forgot about everything else. He'd give her time and space, but he wouldn't give up.

14

— · —

Chapter 14

Claret sat in her throne room the next day and watched everyone argue about who should take Mia and Chad home. Dovin thought he should do it, but Mateo thought it should be him. He said there were some things he wanted to grab from Earth. Dovin didn't trust him to be able to teleport between worlds. He said going between worlds was more difficult and required different concentration.

Kaylee had been quiet since she'd had her conversation with Mateo, and she stared out the window, unaware of what was going on in the room. Odie didn't see any reason to be here, so he was in his room, experimenting with something.

Claret tapped her fingers against the throne and sighed. There were far better things they could be doing than arguing over this. "Why don't Dovin and Mateo go?"

Dovin frowned. "More people create more problems."

The door opened and Miguel and Peora came in. Claret's eyes widened. They were holding hands.

Miguel went up to Dovin. "Peora and I want to go to Earth as well."

Mateo grinned. "I thought you wanted to stay here."

"We might be back. I want Peora to meet Mom. The two of them will love each other."

Peora smiled and hugged Miguel's arm. "I hope that's all right, Your Highness."

Claret smiled. "Of course. I wish you happiness."

"What if you just tell me what you need, and I'll get it?" Dovin said to Mateo.

"If you have to take Miguel to Mexico, couldn't I go and see my family for an hour or so?" Mateo asked.

Dovin sighed. "I suppose it has been a while. Kaylee, do you want to go visit your mom?"

Kaylee rubbed her lips together. "I suppose. Do you think they're still on vacation?"

"No. She said it was a one-month cruise. It's probably good for you all to go back. It will assure your parents you're all right."

"How long are we going to stay?"

Dovin rubbed his chin. "How about two days? I'll return Mia and Chad and drop Kaylee off with her mom. After that, I'll take the three of you to Mexico," he said, looking at Mateo.

"If I give you some gold, will you buy a real game of checkers?" Claret asked. "I would like to see what they actually look like."

"You don't need to give me gold," Dovin said. "I'll get you one."

"Thank you."

"All right, everyone, hold on to me."

They all gathered around and grabbed a piece of Dovin's cloak. Chad made sure he wasn't anywhere near Mateo or Kaylee. They all disappeared and left Claret sitting on her throne. She sighed. She would go talk to Durdessa, but her aunt was spending all of her time going on walks with her brother. Claret had only seen the man twice, and he had paid no attention to her.

Standing, she brushed the wrinkles from her pink dress and headed for Odie's room. She knocked on the door and waited.

"Come in."

She entered and smiled when she saw Odie holding a dropper over a mixing bowl with his tongue sticking out. He put two drops of something into the bowl, then looked up.

"Hi."

"Hello."

"Did the others leave?"

"Yes. All of them. Even Mateo's brother. And my maid."

He tilted his head. "Your maid?"

She giggled. "I guess she's going to meet Miguel's family."

Odie smirked. "That was fast."

"What are you making?" she asked, walking around Gregor. Midnight was cuddled up on Odie's bed, sleeping.

"I'm trying to make a sleeping potion that doesn't have to be on fire to work. It's really inconvenient to have to break the vial and start the fire."

She looked in the bowl and wrinkled her nose as the smell of old fish assaulted her. "It seems like most of the things you make smell bad."

He flashed his white teeth. "It does, doesn't it? Perhaps someday I'll figure out a way to make everything smell like roses."

She frowned. "Please don't. I hate the smell of roses."

"Really? I thought everyone liked the smell."

"Not me. It makes my head ache and my nose itch."

"Well, I'm hoping this works. If we end up fighting the goblins, it would be nice to throw the potion in and knock them all out. Will you hand me that vial with the green liquid on the middle shelf there?"

Claret went over to his shelf and picked up the only thing that had something green in it. She handed it to him and he pulled out the stopper. He put in three drops and stirred.

"I think this should work, but if it doesn't, it might with a bit of talmin oil. It's on the top shelf. I don't think you can reach. Can you stir this while I get it? Stir fast and don't stop."

Claret grabbed the spoon and stirred while Odie looked at the shelf. She wrinkled her nose and tried to ignore the smell. She blinked a few times and yawned. Odie turned, holding a vial in his hand.

"Oh no," he said, putting it down. "Stop stirring and get out of here."

Claret yawned again and dropped the spoon. Why would he tell her to get out? He took a deep breath and held it, rushing toward her. She closed her eyes and felt herself slip from the chair.

Odie caught Claret right before she hit the floor. He scooped her up and carried her into the hall and took a deep breath. He was such an idiot. Durdessa was standing in the hallway, talking to her brother. Arving looked different from when they had met. His hair was neatly trimmed and so was his beard. Durdessa looked at Odie and frowned. She rushed toward him, her blue dress billowing behind her. All Odie could do was stand there looking guilty.

"What happened?" Durdessa demanded.

Arving came up beside her.

"She's just asleep," Odie assured her.

Durdessa's eyes narrowed.

"We were making a sleeping potion."

"And you tested it on her?"

"Well, not on purpose." Odie steadied himself for a lecture, but to his surprise, Durdessa laughed.

"My goodness, Odie. You really don't let things get dull around here. Take her to her room. I'll open the door."

Odie followed her down the hall and prayed he wouldn't drop Claret. Her dead weight was hard to manage, and her head kept trying to flop to the wrong side. Durdessa opened the door and Odie rushed in and laid her onto the bed. It was a bit more clumsy than he would like, but it was all he could manage.

"It's a good thing she doesn't have anything scheduled today," Durdessa said. She pulled off Claret's shoes and draped a blanket over her. They left the room and shut the door behind them. Arving was waiting for them.

"I can't believe you let this boy test things like that," Arving said. "He should be monitored."

"Odie is good at what he does."

"He's the boy who blows things up. I've heard it from the servants."

Durdessa smiled. "He does occasionally, but he's made some clever things."

Odie was surprised she was sticking up for him. Arving muttered something about young people.

"And what kind of name is Odie?" Arving asked.

Odie frowned. He didn't like this man. "It's Odious, actually."

"Who names their kid Odious? Ridiculous."

"Knock it off, Arving," Durdessa said.

"I was raised by goblins."

Arving's eyes widened in surprise. "And you have him in the castle?"

"It's not your concern. He's been very helpful."

Odie had never dreamed he would have an ally in Durdessa.

"I'm going to air out my room. I probably put Gregor and Midnight to sleep as well."

Durdessa laughed again, and Arving shook his head.

Odie took a deep breath and held it, then opened his bedroom door. He hurried in and threw open the window, then ran back to the hall for a breath of air. Another deep breath and he went back and grabbed Gregor, who was sleeping peacefully on the floor. He took him into the hall and looked around, unsure of what to do.

He went back to Claret's room and peeked in. Claret was sleeping soundly, so he went in and placed Gregor next to her. He hoped she wouldn't mind, but he didn't want to leave the puffin in the hall where he might get stepped on.

One more trip had Midnight at the foot of Claret's bed. He looked at the three of them sleeping on the bed and scratched his head. With luck, Claret would be forgiving.

Claret tried to open her eyes, but she was so tired. The sun was shining in, so she must have overslept. She tried to roll over, but something was on her leg. Prying her eyes open, she gasped. Gregor was sleeping on the pillow beside her. She sat up and frowned. Midnight was sleeping on her legs. Odie was sitting at her table, reading a book.

"Odie?"

He jumped up and dropped his book.

She motioned to the dragon. "What's going on?"

"I'm sorry. The sleeping potion I was working on... well, it works."

She put a hand to her head. "And I fell asleep?"

"Yes. Sorry."

She licked her dry lips. She must have been sleeping with her mouth open. "I think I remember falling."

"I caught you before you hit the floor, so no injury."

She pulled her foot out from under the dragon. She didn't want to know how she got into her room.

"The sleeping potion works, but I don't know how to mix it and contain it before falling asleep."

She yawned. "I'm sure you'll think of something."

"I hope it's all right that I stayed here. I wasn't sure how you would react when you woke up with Gregor and Midnight in your bed."

She smiled and pushed back a piece of hair. "I was a little surprised to open my eyes and see Gregor on my pillow. How long have I been asleep?"

"About two hours."

Claret nodded. "That's pretty good. If we can knock out our enemies for that long, we might have a tremendous advantage."

"True. I'm hopeful."

"Has anyone come looking for me?"

"No, but Durdessa and her brother saw me run out carrying you, so I'm sure she's taking care of things."

Claret frowned. Durdessa didn't like Odie, so that probably hadn't helped. "Was she angry?"

Odie grinned. "I thought she would be, but she actually laughed and defended me to her brother. I can already tell I'm not going to get along with him."

"He's not friendly?"

"Not from what I've seen."

"That's disappointing. Durdessa is the best person I know. I'm glad she's been able to reconnect with her family, though. That's an important thing." Claret sighed and tried to rid herself of unwelcome thoughts.

"What's wrong?"

"It's nothing important."

"I can tell it's bothering you, whatever it is. Can I help?"

Claret twisted her blanket in her hands. "It's just, well, my parents were good people. They weren't overly available to me, but they cared. When Durdessa came, everything changed. She played with me and encouraged me to be me. In some ways, I feel like she cared about me more than my parents did. Now she's found Dovin and Arving, and I'm happy for her."

"But you're worried about losing her?"

Claret nodded. "I think she's going to leave Riviand when this is all over. Then I won't have anyone who cares about me. I know that sounds selfish. I'm the queen and I have everything, but I don't know. I really hope she decides to stay, and Dovin as well. It's nice to have parental figures in my life."

Odie nodded and came to sit on her bed. Claret was so self-absorbed. Here she was complaining to Odie about her need for parents and he had been raised by goblins. He didn't even know who his parents were.

"I know what you mean," he said. "Dovin is great. He's supportive and helpful. Durdessa, I don't know as well. Just remember. Even if they leave, there are still people here who care about you."

She looked down at her blanket. "But will they stay around when all this business with the goblins and witches is over?"

Odie put his hand over hers. "They will if you want them to."

15

— · —

CHAPTER 15

Kaylee stood in front of her house and waved as Dovin and the others teleported. They had already dropped off Mia and Chad with strict instructions from Dovin to never go anywhere alone. Kaylee opened the door and entered the large entryway. It felt strange to be home, but Kaylee needed this.

She knew she could talk to Claret or Mia about Mateo, but she wanted to talk to her mom. Kaylee wasn't an emotional person, and she never cried, but she kept feeling close to it, and that seemed like a time to be with your mom. She couldn't believe she wanted to cry over a boy. She hadn't, but it was taking effort. Her feeling didn't even make sense. Why cry because you discover you like a guy?

"Mom? Are you here?" she called.

"Kaylee? I'm in the kitchen."

She rushed through the hallway and into the black-and-white kitchen. Black and white were the only colors allowed in this room. "Hi, Mom," Kaylee said, running up to her. Temperance might not be the best mom,

144

but Kaylee had missed her. Her mom hugged her, then held her at arm's length, studying her.

"You haven't called once," she said. "Dovin told me cell service was spotty, but I expected something."

"Sorry. I've missed you."

"I'll have to show you pictures of our cruise. It was amazing. Are you back for good?"

"No, only two days."

"Wonderful. This is a good experience for you. Don't they have anyone who can do hair where you are?"

Kaylee touched her ponytail and frowned. "I can do my own hair."

Her mom frowned. "A ponytail? Let me text Saundra and see if she can come do your braids. What color do you want?"

Kaylee sat on a stool at the island and sighed. "I don't know."

Her mom pulled out her phone and began texting.

"I don't have a lot of time. I thought we could just hang out and talk."

Temperance tilted her head. "You know I don't have time for that. I only have about an hour today. In fact, you might want to see if you can sleep at Mia's house because I have things I can't cancel."

"I'm only going to be here for two days!"

"And you expect me to drop everything? You didn't call ahead."

"I didn't know I needed to be scheduled in."

"Well, what did you want to talk about?" she asked, sitting next to her.

Kaylee debated telling her mom, but she needed an adult's opinion. "I met a boy."

Temperance raised her eyebrow and smiled. "Oh? What do his parents do?"

Kaylee rolled her eyes. "They have a farm in Mexico."

Temperance's smile fell from her face. "No, Kaylee. Don't get yourself tangled up with someone like that. Farming is well and good but not usually very profitable."

"He's not a farmer. His dad is."

She tossed her braids over her shoulder. "Children often follow in their parents' footsteps."

"I'm not trying to marry him. Come on, Mom. I'm sixteen!"

"Yes, and I won't have you getting attached to anyone until you're finished with college."

"So I'm not allowed to date until I'm twenty-four?"

Temperance looked down at her perfectly manicured nails. "Of course you can, but nothing serious."

"I don't know why I thought I could talk to you about this."

"You can talk to me about anything. What did you want to say about him?"

"Nothing, it doesn't matter."

"You should think hard before making any type of relationship. Being from Mexico is also an issue. Dating someone from a different country can cause problems. People are too different."

Kaylee narrowed her eyes. "Kamal is from India and Dad was from Ireland."

"Yes, so I should know."

Kaylee wanted to argue, but she didn't remember her dad. He died when she was young. "This guy isn't actually from Mexico. His family moved there six years ago."

"From where?"

"A different world."

Temperance glared at her. "Very funny, Kaylee." Her phone pinged, and she glanced at it. Saundra can come right now. That's convenient. I told her to do purple on the ends of your braids.

Kaylee scowled. "Fine."

"I hope you've been applying yourself. It was good of Mr. Dovin to help you secure this opportunity."

"Yeah, it's been great. A lot of work, though."

"That's good for you."

Kaylee wondered what her mom would think if she knew she'd only done three days of schoolwork. "I saw Graham."

Temperance froze. "Where?"

"I got sick, and he's kind of like a doctor now."

Her eyes narrowed. "He's too young to be a doctor."

Kaylee shrugged.

"Maybe you shouldn't go back."

"I only saw him once. I don't even know where he lives."

Temperance shook her head. "I don't want you seeking him out. He got involved with a strange group. Remember when he came back, and he was wearing a cape? Who knows what he's into. Did he say anything?"

"Nothing significant. He has a girlfriend." Kaylee was glad she changed into her regular clothing before coming here. Her mom would have freaked out if she'd come in with a cape.

"Hmm." Temperance stood. "I think I'm going to call Mr. Dovin and see if he can get you tomorrow if you don't want to stay with friends."

"Just tell him to come once my braids are finished."

"You don't want to spend the night?"

"I don't see the point."

Mateo piled potatoes on his plate. His mom made the best food on the planet. His younger brothers were at school, so it was just him, his parents, Miguel, and Peora. He didn't have to worry about carrying on a conversation because his mom was busy trying to get to know Peora.

It was nice to be in the small, cramped kitchen after being in the huge rooms in the castle. This was a lot more cozy. He'd even missed the ruffly red curtains at the window.

"I hope Mateo has been behaving," his mom said, drawing his attention.

Mateo frowned. "You're asking Miguel? He was in Riviand only for a few days."

Miguel laughed. "He's doing fine, Mom."

"I helped save Riviand, but does anyone want to hear about that?" he mumbled.

Kraya rubbed his head and grinned. "You know I'm teasing you. I'm proud of you. Dovin told me about everything you've been doing, and I'm impressed."

"I belong there. You know that, right?"

His mom frowned. "I know. I could tell when you came in. You look... different. We'll talk about it later, all right?"

Mateo nodded and drowned his potatoes in gravy.

Dovin teleported into the room, and they all jumped. "Sorry," he said with a grin. "I forget you aren't used to magic anymore."

Kraya smiled. "And we didn't even know teleporting was a thing until recently. Do you want to eat?"

"No, I was just wondering if you might have room for Kaylee. Her mom is busy, and she needs somewhere to stay while we're here."

Mateo frowned. After months of not seeing her daughter, she couldn't make time?

"Of course," Kraya said. "We would love to have her."

"She wanted me to make sure before I brought her. I'll be back." Dovin disappeared.

"Kaylee is the girl who went with you and Dovin, right?" Kraya asked.

Mateo swallowed his food. "Yeah, she was at the school you sent me to in Missouri."

"It's too bad her family is busy."

Mateo nodded. He knew his parents would drop everything if they only had two days to spend with him. He wondered how Kaylee was feeling.

Dovin popped back in with Kaylee at his side. She was wearing a T-shirt and jeans, and her hair was in small black-and-purple braids that went down to the middle of her back. She looked beautiful—and sad, even though she was smiling.

Kraya stood and hugged Kaylee. "Welcome. I'm Kraya. You must be Kaylee."

Kaylee's eyes were wide at the unexpected hug, and Mateo hid a smile. His mom was a hugger.

"Yes, I'm Kaylee," she said. "Thanks for having me."

"Are you hungry?"

"No, thank you."

"Why don't you eat anyway?"

Mateo's father smiled behind his mustache. "There's no use arguing when Kraya is serving food."

"That's my husband, Rosendo," his mom said, guiding Kaylee to a chair and getting her to sit next to Mateo.

Mateo smiled at her. "Don't worry. If you can't eat it, I'll finish it for you."

Kaylee smiled, but it didn't reach her eyes. They hadn't talked more than a few words since Dragon's Cove and he didn't know what she was thinking.

"You too, Dovin. Sit and eat."

Dovin laughed. "Thanks, Kraya." He sat down and began talking to Mateo's dad. Peora and Miguel were talking quietly in their seats, and Mateo was pretty sure Peora wasn't going back to Tyran.

Mateo handed the bowl of potatoes to Kaylee, and she blinked a few times. There were tears in her eyes she was trying to hold back. Mateo panicked. He didn't know what to say or do. He looked at his mom, who was also watching Kaylee.

"Hey, Kaylee?" Kraya said. "Can you come out back with me for a minute?"

Kaylee nodded and followed his mom out the back door. Mateo debated staying or following. What was his mom going to say?

Dovin put a hand on Mateo's shoulder. "Let your mom talk to her," he said quietly. "She's good at that sort of thing, and I think Kaylee needs a motherly figure at the moment."

Kaylee walked with Kraya toward a large, neatly painted brown barn. She wondered what Mateo's mother wanted with her. She was talking about Mateo's brothers and Kaylee was having a hard time paying attention. Mateo had his mom's eyes, but that was where the resemblance ended. Kraya had shoulder-length blond hair and was shorter than Kaylee. If she remembered correctly, Kraya was from Basura and Mateo's father had been born in Mexico.

Kraya led her around the barn to a small fenced area. "I want to show you the baby lambs."

Kaylee perked up. She loved baby animals. She looked over the fence and saw two small lambs.

"Do you want to hold one?" Kraya asked.

"Yes!" Kaylee exclaimed.

"They're a little spoiled, so they like people." She opened the gate, and they entered. "Sit down and I'll get her on your lap."

Kaylee found a spot that wasn't too messy and sat. Kraya picked up one lamb and put it on Kaylee.

"It's so sweet," she said, rubbing its wool. "I can't believe Mateo is nervous around animals when he grew up with them."

Kraya laughed. "He's not too bad with them. He just doesn't like germs. We only make the boys help on the farm as much as they want. We prefer they focus on their schoolwork. I probably let Mateo get away with playing too many video games. This lamb is Peppa."

"She's so soft."

Kraya sat next to her. "I know you don't know me, but I thought you looked like you might need someone to talk to. I'm a great listener, if you want to talk."

Kaylee pursed her lips and kept her eyes on the lamb. She did a fake laugh. "I pride myself on not being emotional, but it's been a crazy week. I was hoping to have time to talk to my mom, but she's always too busy for me."

"I'm sorry. That must be hard."

Kaylee shrugged and wondered why she wanted to spill her soul to this stranger. "It's usually okay, but I really needed her today." She swallowed a lump in her throat.

"Is there something I can help with?"

"It's fine. Just boy drama, which I've never had before. I'm not dealing with it very well. I don't know why it's affecting me this way."

Kraya patted the other lamb and pulled it onto her lap. "I have six boys, so I might not be the best for advice, but I have been there. When I first met Rosendo, he didn't speak my language and all he wanted was to get back to Earth. We had some serious ups and downs, but we got through them. You can unload on me if you like."

"Do you like it here?"

Kraya looked around. "Yes and no. I miss Boztoll and magic, but I love Rosendo, and I'm happier here than I would be there without him."

"He didn't like it there?"

"No. He spent a lot of time trying to get back to Earth. He is happier here, and that makes me happy. I'm more content about things than he is, so it's easier for me to adjust."

Kaylee nodded. "I met a boy, and I really didn't like him at first."

"And he's grown on you?"

"Yes. It happened gradually and when I finally realized how much I care about him, it scared me. We're too different. I mean, we're both competitive, but that's where it ends."

"I don't think people need to be the same to get along. Rosendo and I are complete opposites. I think that works for us. Someone the same as me would bore me."

"I get that, but I'm pretty serious and he thinks everything is a joke. Unless he's angry, then I'm telling him he can't punch people."

She frowned. "He's violent?"

"I wouldn't say violent. He punched one guy who was bothering me and another one that he thought... Well, it was a misunderstanding. He thought it was all justified. I think he's getting better."

"Does he like you?"

Kaylee nodded. "He liked me first."

"So the problem is that you don't think it will work?"

Kaylee frowned down at Peppa. "I don't know. I feel confused and guilty."

"Why guilty?"

"I told him more than once that I didn't like him, then I kissed him. Sort of."

"Sort of?"

Kaylee ducked her head. "I rubbed lip balm on his lips. With mine."

Kraya laughed. "I knew I was going to like you."

"Then I apologized later. I shouldn't have done anything to lead him on. This is so embarrassing. I can't believe I'm telling a stranger."

"Sometimes that's easier."

"I guess."

"What did he say when you apologized?"

"He asked if he could give me my first kiss."

Kraya's eyes sparkled. "And did you let him?"

"Yes. And then I ran back and kissed him again. I've been trying to avoid him since."

"Why?"

She let out a long breath. "For one thing, I'm embarrassed. I told him over and over I wasn't into him and then not only did I kiss him, but I ran back for more? It's humiliating."

"You don't want a relationship?"

"I didn't think so, but I might have changed my mind. I feel like a strong person, but sometimes I just want someone to hold me and let me be weak, just for a minute. What if I only want to be with him because I know he'd give that to me?"

Kraya ran her hand over the lamb's back. "That's a hard one. Do you like spending time with him?"

"Yes, but he bugged me so much at first, it makes me wonder about my motives."

"So he's cute?"

Kaylee smiled. "Very."

Kraya laughed. "I'm not sure I have expert advice, but I would say, be patient with yourself. Spend more time with him and see how you feel. You're young and you don't need to rush anything. If he's worth it, he'll wait while you work it out."

"How do I spend time around him without being embarrassed about the way I acted?"

"I don't think you did anything embarrassing. In fact, you probably gave him hope."

"But is that a good thing?"

"It's hard to tell. If he's worth it, then it is."

16

CHAPTER 16

Mateo sat at the breakfast table, ready to get his fill. This would be his last meal with his family, and he felt a little sad about it. His mom was frying bacon and his dad was scrambling eggs with peppers.

"Morning everyone," he said, yawning. He'd stayed up too late playing video games with his brother Juan.

"Don't just sit there, set the table," his mom said. "Set a place for Dovin. He's coming."

He stood and went to the cupboard. "I bet you missed bossing me around while I was gone," he teased.

Kraya smiled as she flipped the bacon. "You bet I did. You seem happier. I'm glad."

"I've made some good friends."

"I knew you could if you ever stopped being so angry about everything."

He sighed. "I know. I'm sorry." He grabbed some plates and placed them on the table. He wondered what his mom had said to Kaylee yesterday. Kaylee had seemed happier when they returned, but she still seemed to be avoiding him.

"What do you think about Peora?" his mom asked.

Mateo shrugged as he searched the utensils drawer for forks. "She's all right."

Rosendo laughed. "Your mom has taken to her. If Miguel doesn't marry her, I think Mom will adopt her."

Kraya laughed. "It's true. I like her."

Kaylee came in, her long braids pulled back into a ponytail. She must be ready to leave because she had on her tunic and cape.

"Good morning, Kaylee," Kraya said. "How did you sleep?"

"Great, thanks."

"Are you ready to go after breakfast?"

"I think so."

Mateo grinned and looked over at Kaylee. He pulled the lip balm from his pocket and held it up. "I have some lip balm if you forgot yours."

Kaylee's eyes widened, and she looked at Mateo's mom, then away. Kraya spun around and looked at Mateo, then at Kaylee. Kaylee sat down and seemed really interested in her plate. A huge grin broke out across his mom's face. He wasn't sure what had just happened, but he was sure he'd missed something.

Rosendo looked out the window and frowned. "One of the lambs escaped again."

"I'll go get her," Kaylee said, jumping up and charging through the back door.

"She loves animals," Mateo said, placing the forks on the table. "Even snakes. It's crazy."

Kraya turned down the griddle and came and put her hand on Mateo's arm. "Kaylee needs a friend right now. Why don't you go help her?"

"Did she tell you what was wrong? She's been acting weird."

"Maybe a little. I think she's a bit hurt by her mom's indifference."

"I get that," he said, giving his mom a hug. "You know I appreciate you, right?"

She smiled. "I do, but it's nice to hear every once in a while. Go help her."

Mateo walked to the back door and opened it.

"And, Mateo?" she said. "Sometimes a girl just needs a hug and a shoulder to cry on. Not lip balm."

Mateo narrowed his eyes and frowned. "Okay."

He went out back and saw Kaylee trying to catch the sheep. What did his mom know about lip balm? There was no way Kaylee told her. He ran toward the lamb from the other side, causing it to turn and run into Kaylee. She scooped it up and rubbed its head.

"We better make sure there isn't a hole in the fence," he said, walking out around the barn with her. "Sheep can be escape artists."

"They're so adorable. It looks like the gate was open." She placed the little lamb in the enclosure with her sibling and shut it.

"Hey, Kaylee?"

She didn't look away from the lamb. "Hmm?"

"Are you all right?"

She bit her cheek and blinked a few times. "Sure."

"Liar."

She turned and shook her head, but he could see tears in her eyes.

"I'm sorry your mom couldn't spend more time with you."

A tear ran over her cheek, and she wiped it away. "It's fine. She's got her life." She covered her face and started sobbing. Mateo looked around for help but knew no one was there. He stepped up and wrapped her in a hug. "She's never there for me. I don't understand it. She expects so much from me and gives me nothing. Great. Now I can't go back in the house because I'll have puffy eyes."

"No one will care."

"I never cry," she said into his shoulder.

"Everyone cries."

She looked up. "Even you?"

He grinned. "Sure, but I'll never admit it to anyone else." He wiped a smudge of mascara from her cheek. "Just cry. You might feel better."

Fresh tears rolled down her face, and she clung to him. He rubbed her back and stood there until she was able to compose herself. He thought about the lip balm in his pocket and shook his head.

"You didn't, by chance, tell my mom about the lip balm, did you?"

She looked up and wrinkled her nose. "I'm sorry. I didn't tell her it was you."

He shrugged. "I'm the one who opened my big mouth and tried to be funny."

"She knows, doesn't she?"

"I'm pretty sure."

She hid her face against him. "I don't know what came over me. Your mom is so nice. I just spilled my guts out to her."

He rubbed his hand over her braids. "She has that effect on people."

"Can this be another thing we never talk about again?"

"If you want it to be."

"Thanks, Mateo. I'm feeling a lot better. I still don't want to go inside like this. Can you tell Dovin to come out here when it's time to leave? I'm sure my face will look better by the time everyone eats."

"Won't you be hungry?"

"No, I don't feel like eating. I'll just sit out here with the lambs."

"Are you sure you're okay?"

"Yes."

"All right."

He didn't know what to say, so he returned to the kitchen. His parents, Dovin, Miguel, and Peora were all eating and talking.

"Is Kaylee okay?" his mom asked when he sat at the table.

"Yes. She isn't hungry."

"What's all over your shirt?" Miguel asked, pointing near Mateo's shoulder.

He looked down and frowned. Kaylee's tears had soaked the shoulder and sleeve, and there were black streaks that must be makeup. He just shrugged and his mom patted him on the back. His mom really was too observant.

Odie tore through the castle. He'd seen a goblin, he was sure of it, but every time he turned a corner, the goblin was turning a different one. He was almost positive it was his brother Tipp, but he couldn't get a good enough look. If it was Tipp, he should be able to catch up. Tipp wasn't fast.

He rounded another corner and almost stepped on his brother. He came to a halt. "What are you doing here?" he demanded. "Believe me, you do not want to show your face around here."

Tipp kicked at the floor. "We need to talk."

"This isn't a good place." He grabbed Tipp's arm and pulled him to his room. He shut the door and glared. "What are you doing here?"

Tipp took a peanut from his pocket and tossed it to Gregor. The puffin pushed it around with his beak and went under the bed. "I came to warn you. The goblins are getting uneasy."

"About what?"

"Garin."

"What about him?"

"Did you know he can change into a dragon?"

"Yes."

"Well, we don't like it. Father is impressed by it for some reason. Some of the goblins are talking about rebelling against Father."

Odie sat on the edge of his table. "I'm not surprised."

"Father won't listen to anyone. You need to go talk to him. He listens to you."

Odie shook his head. "If I go back, I'll get arrested. Father isn't going to forgive me twice."

"Well, I'm not staying around to become a slave to a dragon. I'm going to go with the others if they leave."

"Good idea."

"The goblins don't like the witch either. She's always with Garin. I bet they're going to take over the world and rule it together."

"Unless one of them kills the other. I bet they're both planning it. That's the way people like them think."

"I don't know. I think they actually like each other."

"That might be worse. If they tried to kill each other, it would make things easier on everyone."

Tipp shrugged. "So are you going to come talk to Father?"

"No, I already told you."

"It's because of the queen, isn't it? You keep saving her."

"It's not only that. The goblins' motives are all wrong. Gold shouldn't dictate the way you live your life."

"Neither should a female."

"What are you talking about?"

"Your priorities are getting in line with the queen's. You let her influence you because you fancy her. She won't ever care about you. She's using you, probably for your experiments."

Odie rolled his eyes. "Go away, Tipp. You don't even know what I'm doing here. I have friends. I'm not here just for Claret."

"But you fancy her."

"So? Who wouldn't?"

Tipp sighed. "Fine. I can tell you won't listen to reason. I'll be back, though, after you've had time to think."

The door opened and Claret peeked in. "Odie?"

"Oh no, she's on to you!" Tipp said. "We have to escape!" He ripped a hole in the air. "Jump through, Odie."

Odie frowned and looked at Claret. She was glaring at Tipp. She was going to think Odie was working with him.

"I've been listening at the door," she said. "Leave, goblin, and don't come back."

Tipp glowered and jumped through his portal. It sealed itself, and Odie let out a relieved breath.

"I'm not usually happy when people eavesdrop on me, but I am this time."

Claret crossed her arms and smiled. "Really? Even when you admitted you fancy the queen?"

Odie gave her a lopsided smile. "It's all right. She already knows. How often do you listen at my door?"

"This is the first. I saw you running down the hall and watched you drag the goblin in. Dovin and the others are back."

"Oh, good."

"I asked Dovin to get me a real game of checkers and he brought some other games as well."

Odie smiled. "Sounds fun."

"Do you think the goblins will split?"

His smile fell. "Possibly. It might be to our advantage. If they do, they might fight amongst themselves."

"Dovin thinks we should hold a ball. He said the people are getting nervous and they need a distraction. We haven't had one in years and the thought of it makes me anxious."

"Who do you invite? Surely not all of Riviand."

"Dovin said I should invite important families from all the towns and cities. It will help us better prepare for appointing governors in all the different areas. I wanted to wait until we dealt with Garin, but I think we'd be more united this way. If the governors take care of their cities, then report to me, it will help tremendously."

"That's a good idea. So when is this ball?"

"Dovin said we can't let it wait, so in one week. I've already sent messengers out to the different areas, so the people have time to come. Some areas are rather far, so Dovin will teleport some of the messengers."

"I've never been to a ball."

"I haven't since I was young, and I was only allowed to stay for a few minutes. I'm glad we have people to organize these things."

"I don't know how to dance."

Claret smiled. "Neither do I."

Odie raised his brows. "I thought queens had to know things like that."

"My parents gave up on me. I was really bad. I kept hurting myself. That's another reason I'm nervous. I'll be expected to dance with so many people and it's going to be a disaster."

Odie grinned. "It might be fun to watch."

17

—·—

CHAPTER 17

C laret felt like everything was back to the way it should be. She cut her meat and looked around the table. Dovin, Durdessa, Odie, Mateo, Kaylee, and Arving were all sitting around the table. This was the way Claret liked it. Well, she could do without Arving. He just glared at everyone.

"I can't wait to try the new games you brought," Claret told Dovin. "Do you know how to play them?"

"Some of them. They all have a page with rules inside."

"I know how to play them," Kaylee said. "I can teach you."

"Thanks." Claret had been dying to hear what had happened between Kaylee and Mateo at Dragon's Cove, but Kaylee had been quiet and not in the mood to talk to anyone. She was acting a lot more like herself since she came back from Earth, but they hadn't been alone to talk.

"I also brought some books on installing indoor plumbing for Odie," Dovin said. "I think it might be too big of an undertaking, but you can read up on it."

Kaylee and Mateo laughed, but Odie looked excited. "I'm going to figure it out, and if I can't, maybe someone from the upper world can come down and help."

"That's ridiculous," Arving said, taking a bite of food. "One person is not going to be able to bring plumbing to an entire continent."

"I would start small."

"Give up now. It will save time and disappointment." Odie frowned.

Claret twisted Odie's ring on her necklace. "If Odie puts his mind to it, he can do anything."

Arving's eyes focused on her, and he frowned. "Where did you get that?"

Claret didn't know what he was talking about, and she didn't like to be on the other end of his glare. "What?"

"That ring. You shouldn't have it." He stood and walked toward her. Claret put her hand over the ring and Odie jumped up and stood between them.

"Sit down, Arving," Durdessa said.

"No. The queen has my ring."

"It's not your ring," Odie said.

"I think I know my own ring."

"Stop, Arving," Durdessa said. "There are lots of black rings out there."

"But that one is mine. I can tell."

"It's not," Odie said. "Stay away." He put a hand on his sword hilt.

"I had that made special," he said. "It was expensive and I want it back. Look on the inside. It says A + N."

Claret's eyes went wide. She couldn't see the expression on Odie's face because he was standing in front of her.

"Arving…" Durdessa said. "Please don't make me throw you out."

"I'm telling the truth, Dessa. I had that made for Neva. Well, for Pax. You remember, Dessa? Pax was doing crazy magic. Magic no three-year-old should be able to do. It scared Neva, and she begged me to do something. I had someone make that ring. The person wearing it can't do magic. We put it on Pax's little thumb and that solved that. Not that it mattered for long."

The man deflated and sat back in his chair. "I just want it back."

Claret looked up at Odie. He was taking deep breaths. He turned and looked at her. "Please tell me that what I'm thinking isn't true."

Durdessa was covering her mouth and staring at Odie.

Claret stood and took the necklace off. She took the ring from the chain and placed the ring in Odie's hand. She smiled at him and nodded toward Arving.

Odie turned and looked down at the man. "The goblins found me wandering around when I was three. I had this ring on my thumb."

"Whaaaaaat?" Mateo exclaimed.

Kaylee glared at him, and he covered his mouth.

Arving stared at Odie, and his eyes narrowed. "You're saying you're Pax?"

Odie shook his head. "I'm only saying it was on my thumb. I've always had it."

Durdessa stood and rushed over to Odie. "Why did I not see it before? Look at him, Arving. He has Neva's eyes."

"I don't see it."

"Don't be like that, Arving." Durdessa smiled at Odie and gave him a hug. "That makes you my nephew."

Odie looked like he might try to escape. "I don't know what to say."

"You can start with thank you," Arving said. "Now you don't have to go by that ridiculous name."

Durdessa glared at her brother. "You just found out your son you thought was dead is alive, and that's all you can say?"

Arving's lip trembled. "I'm sorry. I just... it doesn't seem possible." He stood. "I'm sorry, son." He hugged Odie and Odie sent a panicked glance at Claret. She gave him an encouraging smile. Arving let go and wiped his eyes. "Neva took you out on the boat. I always told her it was dangerous. You never came back."

Odie swallowed but didn't say anything.

"Don't worry, Pax. We're going to make up for lost time. We'll go fishing and stuff. You can tell me about your life."

Odie nodded but didn't look thrilled.

"I need some time," Arving said. "I need to go sit in my room for a while. Is that all right?"

Odie nodded and Arving rushed from the room.

Durdessa squeezed Odie's arm. "I can't believe this. Do you remember anything? I used to take you for walks. We would go out and pet the alicorns."

Dovin stood and clapped Odie on the back. "We should have recognized you. You've grown, but you have the same look to you."

Odie just shook his head. "I'm sorry, can I go think?"

"Of course," Durdessa said. "Take whatever time you need."

Claret watched him leave. She wanted to follow, but she would give him time.

Durdessa sat back down. "I can't believe he was here all this time. I even thought he had a glare like Arving a few times, but it never crossed my mind that he could be Pax."

Durdessa and Dovin began reminiscing about moments they'd had with Odie.

Claret couldn't take it. She needed to see if Odie was all right. She went to his room, but he wasn't there. It took her fifteen minutes to find him outside, at a fountain in the garden. He was sitting on the gray stone, staring into the water.

"Odie?"

He looked up and smiled slightly.

"Do you want me to leave?"

He patted the space next to him. "No. Come sit."

She went and sat on the cold stone and took his hand in hers. "Are you all right?"

"I've spent my entire life dreaming something like this would happen. But did it have to be Arving? He doesn't even like me."

Claret rubbed her thumb over his hand. "He's been through a lot. Give him another chance."

Odie looked down at their hands. "For you, I will. But I need time. Right now, I need a distraction. Do you want to play one of the games Dovin brought?"

Claret smiled. "Sure." They stood and walked back to the castle, hand in hand. Claret wished she hadn't asked Odie to change anything about their relationship. What they had now was strange. She sometimes wished he'd just kiss her, but she didn't want to bring it up. What if he didn't feel that way anymore?

Odie wondered if Claret would ever redefine their relationship. Here they were, holding hands, but did that mean she trusted him now? He shook his head. There were other things to occupy his mind. He had a father. A father he didn't like. It figured. Why couldn't Dovin have turned out to be his father? At least he was his uncle.

They went into Claret's room and Odie stared at the pile of rectangular, flat boxes on the table. Claret released his hand and grabbed one off the top. "Don't these look fun?"

Odie looked at the game box. "Perfection," he read on the box. "How do you suppose they put this painting on top? They look like real people. And they say Earth doesn't have any magic." He opened the box and pulled out the pieces. "This is amazing. They've invented such interesting things."

"This paper has the rules," Claret said. "I can't under-stand all the words, but most of them are spelled the same as our words, even though they pronounce them differently. You are supposed to take all those little yellow shapes and turn that little circly thing. I don't know exactly what it all means. But it looks like we try to put the shapes into their holes before something pops up. I'm a little confused."

Odie took the big rectangular thing that looked like it was missing puzzle pieces and turned the circle on the front. It began making a terrible sound, and he dropped it on the floor. They both stared down at it with wide eyes.

"Do you think it might explode?" Claret asked.

"Perhaps it's supposed to sound like that." Odie picked it up and turned it again. "I think that's what happens when you wind it up." He wound it until it couldn't wind any more and sat it on the table. "Now put all the pieces in as fast as you can!" They both started sticking the shapes into the correct spaces. They almost had them all in when it popped, throwing the piece out.

Claret shrieked and jumped back. "Oh my goodness!"

It had scared Odie but not as much as Claret. He laughed. "That was amazing! I think I want to go to Earth someday. If they can make this and indoor plumbing, it must be a great place. I wonder how it works. Do you want to do it again?"

"Yes. It's much more exciting than checkers." She gathered up all the shapes and he wound it up again. They put the pieces in faster this time, and even though they were expecting it, it still made Odie jump when they popped.

Claret squealed and jumped up and down, her long blond curls bouncing. "This is so fun!"

Odie smiled as he watched her.

"What?"

"It's just funny to think that the queen of Riviand is jumping up and down over a game."

Her smile disappeared. "Are you saying I'm not conducting myself like I should?"

"No. I was just thinking of the way I used to perceive you, versus now. You always seemed so stiff and proper. I love to see the way you are when no one else is around."

Her smile returned. "We did see each other a lot differently, didn't we? Then you messed up your perfectly slicked back hair, and it changed everything."

Odie laughed. "My hair? What does it have to do with anything?"

Claret stepped up to him and ran her hands through his hair. "Your hair made you seem so... I don't know. Intimidating. Once you stopped putting all that goop in it, it changed the way I viewed you."

Odie narrowed his eyes. "So you're saying I have good hair? You like me for my hair?"

She grinned. "It's one of the reasons."

He raised one eyebrow. "And what are the other reasons?"

"Do you really want a list?"

"No. But the question I have is, do you trust me?"

She nodded. "Completely."

"And should I trust you? What are you doing to my hair?" Odie felt his hair. It was poking straight up in some spots.

Claret giggled as he pushed it back into place. Her smile faded. "Sometimes I hate being the queen. I hate being stiff and formal. At the ball, I'm going to be stiff, formal, and clumsy. I don't see anything good coming of that."

"You can dance with me, then blame me."

"But I can't dance with you for every dance. That would be rude to my guests, wouldn't it?"

Odie sighed. "I guess it would."

"Are you going to start going by Pax?"

Odie hadn't taken time to think about that. "It's a better name than Odious."

"But not Odie. I like Odie."

"And I like you."

Claret smiled. "What is that word Kaylee uses? Cheesy or was it cringy? I think that's where we're headed."

"I think we reached both of those words a while ago."

"Well, I'll stop talking as soon as you decide to kiss me."

Odie grinned. "I've been waiting for an invitation."

18

CHAPTER 18

A gigantic tree stood in front of Kaylee, its branches gently swaying in the breeze. The colors were off. The leaves appeared metallic, and the bark was silver. She went closer and rubbed her hand over it. It felt smooth and cool. A swing appeared on one branch and she sat and began swinging back and forth, her long purple dress flying behind her. She got higher and higher.

"You better stop before you fall," said Isadora.

Kaylee stopped and glared at the witch. Her long brown hair was braided and wrapped around her head, and she wore a long blue dress.

"Get out of my dream," Kaylee said.

"How else am I going to speak with you?"

"I have nothing to talk to you about."

"I noticed you freed your friends."

"You weren't guarding them very well."

She smiled. "No. I don't have time for that kind of thing. But now you know how far my reach goes. I brought them here from your world, and I can bring others. It would have been easier to take people from Riviand, but I need you to know I'm serious. I won't stop until you return Jayah."

"She doesn't want to be trapped by you. She's not like the other mermaids."

"Please. Is she happy now, hiding off somewhere?"

Kaylee shrugged. In reality, Kaylee hadn't thought a lot about Jayah since she left. It was better she didn't know where she was. All she knew was that she was safe with Coach Williams.

"I'm surprised you've joined Garin. I'd think someone like you would be a one-woman show."

"One woman, yes, but I don't mind sharing my triumphs with someone like Garin. I always find the strongest man and allow him to assist me."

"What makes you think he'll assist you? He wants to take over, not work for the person who took over."

"That's how they always start. I'm not worried about Garin or the goblins. You should, though. Now are you going to tell me where my mermaid is, or do I have to capture, say, your mother? I thought about it last time, but I thought I might save her for leverage."

"I'm sure she's too busy to be captured by you."

"Yes, if your dreams are anything like reality, you might be right."

Kaylee's brows came together. "What do you mean?"

"I don't reveal myself in every dream I visit. I've watched you fight with your mother in your dreams. It's sad really. I usually avoid those. Not as much as I avoid the ones with what's his name? Mateo, is it? He seems to be the focus of most of your dreams these days. Perhaps he is the one I should have been after and not his brother.”

“You’re lying. I haven’t dreamed of him.”

She patted her braid. “We don’t remember all our dreams, do we? Believe me when I tell you, you dream of him often.”

Kaylee grabbed a tree branch from the ground and chucked it at Isadora. It went through her and she shook her head.

“Temper, temper. I see I’ve touched a nerve. Maybe I will leave your mother and go after the boy.”

“Just because you see something in a dream, doesn’t make it true. I dreamed I was in the circus and guess what? I hate the circus.”

Kaylee turned and ran. There was no point in wasting time with that woman. She didn’t know where she was expecting to go, but anywhere was better than staying there. She ran through a field of daisies and wildflowers. A figure stood in front of her. He had his back to her, but she recognized Mateo.

“Mateo?”

He turned. “Hey. What’s with all the flowers?”

“Who knows? This is my dream, but it isn’t going too well.”

“Dream?”

“Yes, and Isadora was here.”

“Is that why you were running?”

“Yes. She says she might come after you if I don’t tell her where Jayah is.”

“What else does she say?”

"She said I dream about you a lot. I don't, or I think I would remember."

He looked up at the sky. Pink and orange clouds appeared. "I hope you dream about me. At least sometimes. I sure play that moment at Dragon's Cove over and over in my head at night."

"So do I. But I'll never admit it to you."

"You just did."

"Yes, but you aren't really here."

"Then we could recreate that moment, right? Dreams aren't real."

Kaylee knew there was something she should tell Mateo. Something about Isadora, but that part of her dream was beginning to fade. Did a dream kiss count? Kaylee was sure they didn't. She rushed over to Mateo and threw her arms around him, and smashed her lips to his. It felt real, but it was better in a dream than it had been in real life. In a dream, she didn't have to feel scared or nervous. In a dream, everything could be the way she wanted it to be.

Mateo's eyes popped open, and he touched his lips. That had been the most realistic dream he'd ever had. He sat up and rubbed a hand over his face. That had been the best dream ever. He almost would have sworn it had happened. He threw his legs over the bed and sat for a minute, letting the dream replay in his mind. Standing, he turned to make his bed. A wildflower was crushed on the sheet.

He frowned and picked up the flower. That was impossible. He rushed to the wardrobe and got dressed. He grabbed the crushed flower and hurried down the hall to Kaylee's room. She didn't answer when he knocked, so he went to the dining room. He opened the door and entered to see Claret, Odie, and Kaylee already there. When Kaylee saw him, she smiled slightly and took a drink.

"Did you have a dream about me just now?" he asked her.

She tilted her head and frowned. "Just now?"

"Like fifteen minutes ago."

Kaylee laughed. "I hardly ever remember my dreams. Why would you think I was dreaming about you?"

"We were in a field of wildflowers. You said Isadora had been there. Then we were kissing, and I woke up."

Odie snorted, and Claret lightly smacked his arm. Kaylee stared forward, and her eyes went wide.

"When I woke up, I found this in my bed." He held up the flower.

Kaylee put a hand to her chest. "How is that possible?"

"It must be something to do with Isadora being in your dream. It must have messed something up or something. Do you remember it now?"

Kaylee nodded.

"I'm going to ask Dovin about it."

Kaylee coughed. "You don't have to tell him the details."

Mateo grinned. "No, I'll keep those to myself."

"Too late for that," Odie said. "Has something changed in your relationship that I missed?"

Kaylee rolled her eyes. "It was just a dream."

"But a dream you had together."

Mateo patted him on the back. "Don't be jealous, Odie. I'm sure you can have your own dreams about kissing girls."

Odie just smiled, and Claret blushed.

"I wonder if Isadora has been visiting your dreams as well," Kaylee said. "Maybe that is the reason our dream was connected."

"I bet that's it," Mateo said. "I wish we knew more about this type of thing."

"How do we fight someone who can get into our heads?"

"I don't know, but maybe it's not as bad as we think. Dreams are crazy. Most don't make sense. At least mine don't. Can she really learn any truth from them?"

"It's not good," Odie said. "We need to try to not dream about anything important."

"She really wants to know where Jayah is and none of us know," Kaylee said. "No matter how much she bugs us, we can't tell her."

"True."

"But she said something about going after Mateo. I can't remember exactly what it was."

"Why go after me over anyone else?"

Odie grinned. "Probably because you're kissing Kaylee in her dreams."

Kaylee crossed her arms. "You can't hold my dreams against me. I once dreamed I was married to Danny DeVito."

Mateo laughed, and Odie and Claret shared a confused glance.

"So the only kissing the two of you have ever done is dream kissing?" Odie asked.

Kaylee stabbed her egg with a fork and shoved it in her mouth, and Mateo rubbed his jaw.

Odie smiled. "I see."

Kaylee sighed. "Do we even know what we're trying to do? We want to stop the goblins, we want to stop Isadora and Garin, but are we getting anywhere?"

Odie tossed a piece of fish to Gregor. "I think the dragons will stay away from Garin. I spent a lot of time trying to get them to see the seriousness of it. Since they're all scared of him, it shouldn't be a problem. That's a step in the right direction."

"I have the magic book that helped me learn to make fire," Claret said. "We can all study that. It has things in it that no one has done in thousands of years."

"Where did you get it?" Dovin asked, entering the room.

"It was my father's. I keep it locked up."

"Would you allow me to see it?"

"Of course," Claret said. "Whenever you want."

"What types of things does it have?" Mateo asked.

"I only looked through it once and I can't remember. I just started on the first page and learned to make fire, but I haven't had time to try anything else."

Arving entered the room, and everyone grew quiet. Odie fidgeted in his seat. Arving sat down next to him. "Morning, Pax. I've been thinking, we should do an activity together every day. Just to get to know each other better."

Odie nodded. "All right. I'm pretty busy, though."

"Right. I can help with that as well. I used to be helpful back in my day."

"Is there a way to block dreams?" Kaylee asked Dovin. "Isadora was in my dream again last night, and so was Mateo. Mateo remembers it, so she's doing something crazy powerful."

Dovin frowned. "I'll look into it."

"She also threatened to capture my mom and Mateo."

He rubbed his chin. "We might need to think about some of these things. Perhaps put your mother in hiding. Mateo's family as well, and perhaps Mia and Chad."

Mateo shook his head. "I can't believe Chad had to get himself wrapped up in this."

"I think that might be best. Anyone the four of you are close to needs to go into hiding."

Claret leaned forward. "Even Durdessa?"

"Perhaps," Dovin said. "Isadora already went after her once. I think I'll send her to the upper world. Arving will go too, and Jayah and Williams. I have several houses and some of them are well hidden. Durdessa can take them all and keep them safe."

"Will you bring my mom?" Kaylee asked.

"Yes, and your stepfather."

"She isn't going to be happy about that."

"Probably not. Mateo's family will need to come here as well."

"How big is this house?" Mateo asked.

"Big enough."

"I don't think I have anyone who needs to hide," Odie said. Arving frowned. "She doesn't know Arving is my father," he added. "The rest she would target for me all work with her, and I don't think she'll go after the goblins."

"Is the ball still on?" Claret asked.

Dovin nodded. "Yes. We need to build up the government in Riviand and we need to do it fast. The more organized we are, the better."

19

CHAPTER 19

Kaylee paced across the floor of her living room, waiting for her mom to get home. She hadn't bothered changing her clothes. They were going to have to tell her mom what was going on, so there was no point. She hadn't put on a cape because that would distract her mom from listening to her.

Mateo sat on a recliner, flipping through a sports magazine. He was wearing a green tunic and tan pants. Not exactly normal for Earth but nothing that would stand out. Kaylee touched the sword at her waist. That would stand out.

She walked across the shaggy white rug and shook her head. She'd played a conversation over in her head, but she wanted to get it just right. Her mom wasn't going to be thrilled no matter what she said, so if she could present it well, it would be to her advantage.

"Calm down," Mateo said, looking up at her. "I'm sure it'll be fine."

"You don't know my mom. This is going to throw off her plans."

The front door slammed, and she froze. This was it. Either her mom or Kamal was going to walk around the corner any minute. She heard voices coming down the hallway. Great. Both at once. That was probably better.

Temperance and Kamal rounded the corner. Kamal was in his scrubs and Temperance had her hands full of shopping bags. She frowned when she saw Kaylee and even more when she spotted Mateo.

"Really, Kaylee? Boots off. What are you wearing? Who's this?"

Kaylee sat on the floor and pulled off her knee-high boots. Mateo took his off as well. He looked nervous.

"Mom, I need you to sit down. You too, Kamal."

Temperance sighed. "This must be bad." She put her things down and sat on the couch across from Mateo. Kamal sat next to her.

"I haven't been studying abroad," she said.

Temperance's eyes narrowed. "What do you mean? Mr. Dovin told me you were doing well."

"He lied."

"Kaylee Bascom, please tell me you didn't run off and join a theater group," she said, motioning at Kaylee's outfit. "Or worse, that you ran off with the farmer's son." She glared at Mateo and he smiled.

"No, Mom, don't be ridiculous. Dovin is from a different world."

Temperance put a hand to her head. "This again."

"He's from the same world that Graham was originally from. Dovin's been training me to go there. He taught me to speak the way they do."

Temperance smacked her hand against the couch. "No! Don't go there, Kaylee. You aren't leaving this house again. I need to get you an appointment with a doctor."

"It's a magical world. There's a witch there, and she's threatening people I care about. You two need to go into hiding."

Kamal and Temperance just stared at her.

"We're going to take you to the other world."

Kamal stood and walked to Kaylee. He touched her head. "She doesn't have a fever."

She rolled her eyes. "If I can prove it, will you come? We're going to take you whether you like it or not, but it would be better if you cooperated."

Kamal shook his head. "There's no such thing as witches and magic."

Temperance's knee was bouncing quickly up and down. "I knew taking in Graham was a bad idea. It's haunted me ever since."

"Mateo?" Kaylee said. "Show them."

Mateo held out his hand, and a ball of light appeared.

Kamal squatted down to look at it. "Neat trick."

"It's not a trick," Kaylee said.

Temperance closed her eyes. "When we took in Graham, it was only supposed to be for a short time, but then his parents didn't come back. I saw them through the window. They jumped through a bright, shimmering circle and disappeared. Your dad didn't believe me." She opened her eyes. "I never knew how to explain what I saw."

Kaylee nodded. "So you believe me?"

Temperance shook her head. "My eyes must have been playing tricks on me."

Kaylee let out a frustrated breath. "I need to think for a moment. Excuse me." She turned and stomped up the stairs. She hoped Mateo was okay without her.

Mateo smiled awkwardly at Kaylee's parents. What did she expect him to do?

Temperance glared at him. "What do you have to do with any of this?"

"Kaylee's my friend. We work together."

Her eyes narrowed. "What is your accent? It doesn't sound Spanish."

He shrugged. "I'm from the other world."

"Of course you are."

"Kaylee is only trying to help you."

"Well, Kaylee is young and doesn't know what she's saying."

"Maybe if you listened to her, you would understand her."

"You don't know anything about us."

Mateo stood and clenched his fist. "Maybe not. But Kaylee needs you, and you aren't giving her the love she deserves."

"I can barely understand you."

Mateo repeated himself, making sure he spoke slowly.

Temperance's eyes burned into him. "I give Kaylee love. What do you know about it?"

"I know she was excited to come home and see you, and you didn't make time for her. She ended up spending her time with my family in Mexico."

Temperance crossed her arms. "I was busy."

"You hadn't seen her in months. What kind of mother does that? Kaylee is strong, but she was having a bad week, and she thought her mom might help her through it."

"You don't know what you're talking about."

"I know she cried on my shoulder because she felt like her mom didn't care."

"Kaylee doesn't cry."

"So that should make you feel extra guilty."

Temperance pursed her lips and looked up at the stairs.

"You can reevaluate your life from hiding. You'll have plenty of time to think."

"I can barely understand you." Temperance went off on a rant. She was talking too fast for Mateo to follow. Kaylee came back downstairs, frowning.

"What did you say?" she muttered.

"Nothing she didn't need to hear."

A knock on the door quieted Temperance. Kamal looked like he'd been granted his freedom. He hurried off to get the door and a moment later came back with Dovin.

Dovin looked at everyone's faces. "It appears things aren't going well. No use wasting time." He grabbed Temperance's sleeve and Kamal's wrist.

"You have a lot of explaining to do, Mr. Dovin," Temperance sputtered.

"Later." The three of them teleported away.

Kaylee sighed and looked at Mateo. "It actually went better than I imagined."

"You have a last name?"

Kaylee gave him a half smile. "Of course I have a last name."

"Bascom."

"Yep."

Mateo took her hand. "Do you want me to take us to your parents or to the castle?"

"The castle. I'm not in the mood to deal with whatever freak-out my mom is about to have."

He nodded. "Ready?"

"Yes."

They ran three steps, then three more, when they landed in Mateo's room. "I'm getting better at this."

She nodded. "Maybe we should start taking two steps. If you work up to it, you might be able to do it without moving."

"Maybe."

"Now what? I feel like we have all these things to do, but no proper direction."

"I guess we could be more like Claret and Odie. They're probably playing games."

She shrugged. "I suppose. I told Claret I'd teach her Monopoly. She read the instructions, but she's still confused. I think it's a game that's easier to learn as you go."

"I'm the master of Monopoly."

"Great. Let's go play."

Odie and Claret shared a look. Odie was beginning to think Kaylee and Mateo shouldn't be allowed to play games together. At least not this game. They all sat around the table in Claret's room, and Kaylee and Mateo were engaged in a glaring battle.

Kaylee crossed her arms. "There's no putting money in the middle," she said for at least the third time. "It makes the game take forever, and it's not in the rules."

"My brothers and I always put money in the middle. Then whoever lands on Free Parking gets it all."

"Yeah, and that makes it too long and unbalanced."

"You're just saying that because you're winning."

She grabbed a paper and waved it in his face. "You show me where in the rules it says that you can do that."

He grabbed the paper and tossed it to the floor. "It's a house rule."

"This isn't your house."

"Perhaps we should play something else," Claret said.

"No, it's fine," Mateo said. "We can go with Kaylee's rules."

She shot him a dirty look. "They aren't my rules, they're the game rules."

Odie rolled the dice and moved his hat piece four spaces. He paid for the property and passed the dice to Mateo. Mateo rolled and moved the boat.

"I'm going to buy a house."

Kaylee scowled at him. "You can't buy a house. You don't have a monopoly."

"So?"

"You can only build when you have a monopoly."

"Says who?"

Kaylee pointed at the rules on the floor. "The rules. Have you ever read them?"

"No."

"Obviously."

"So I'm going to build a house."

Kaylee grabbed the board and threw it on Mateo's lap.

He looked up and smiled. "And you say I have a temper."

Kaylee took three deep breaths.

Mateo put the board back on the table and picked up the pieces that had fallen to the floor. His money was a big mess and half of it was on the ground and on his lap.

She pushed a braid over her shoulder. "I'm sorry, but I'm never playing that game with you again, you big cheater."

Mateo grinned. "I thought you were going to be humble there for a minute."

"You don't seem to realize that you are the one in the wrong here."

The door opened and Dovin peeked in. "Oh good, you're all together." He came in and looked at all the game money that was all over the floor. Kaylee crossed her arms and glared at him as if daring him to comment. He just shook his head.

"I've gotten everyone we think might be in danger from Isadora in hiding. Mateo's mother is going to help your parents, Kaylee."

"That's just great," she mumbled. "Mateo's parents are nice."

"Your parents are in a bit of a shock," Dovin said. "They haven't said much. Chad and Mia are staying close to them. I think it's because they can understand each other."

"So now what?" Kaylee asked. "I feel like we should be doing something."

Dovin nodded. "I think Odie should go back to Dragon's Cove for a while. Just to keep watch. See what the dragons are doing and if Garin appears. Someone can go with him."

"I will," Claret offered.

"No, you need to stay here for the ball."

"Odie's going to miss the ball?"

"I suppose he could come back for it. Then I need two of you to go to Colter's Lake to get a needle from the wellers."

Mateo's eyes widened. "You want a needle from a weller? Those things are brutal. How do we get it? Let them shoot one into us?"

"If necessary, yes."

"Why?"

"I've been studying Claret's magic book. There's a mixture that can be used along with a spell that makes the person casting it able to read everyone in the area's minds."

Mateo frowned. "I thought mind reading was impossible."

"So did I. We'll have to see. If we could read our enemies' minds, we would have a bigger advantage. It says it only works for five minutes."

Mateo rubbed his chin. "Does it need the weller's needle to cast the spell?"

"No, that's for a different potion. There are so many things we might be able to learn from this book. I've had Odie mix the potion for mind reading. Are you finished?"

Odie nodded. "It was hard. I'm not sure it'll work."

"Let's try it."

Odie blew into his hand, and the container appeared in his hand. He couldn't believe how easy magic was. He handed it to Dovin.

"Wait, you're going to try it on us?" Kaylee asked. "And read our minds?"

"Yes, so watch what you're thinking. You don't want me seeing any of your secrets."

"This is a bad idea," Kaylee said.

"I have to test it on someone. I thought you'd be happy I warned you. Just think about anything."

Dovin shook the container, then opened the lid. He pulled a piece of paper from his pocket and began reciting a spell. Odie's potion rose into the air and formed a pink cloud. When Dovin stopped speaking, the cloud fell down over their heads and disappeared.

Dovin looked at Mateo. "I can hear your thoughts. This is amazing." He frowned. "Control them better."

Mateo grinned. "I have nothing to hide."

Dovin shook his head. "Just think of something boring, not your daydreams."

"Like math?"

Dovin sighed and turned to Claret. Claret was clenching her teeth and her eyes were bouncing around. "You are trying so hard not to let me hear anything that it's a bit of a jumbled mess. We won't have to worry about that with our enemies because they won't know what we're doing."

Dovin's gaze settled on Odie.

Don't think about Claret, Odie thought over and over.

Dovin raised his brows. "Interesting."

He turned to Kaylee, and Odie sighed with relief.

Kaylee's lips were pressed tightly together, and she hugged herself.

Dovin peered at her. "Mateo is a cheater, and you're never playing a game with him again."

"Oh, come on," Mateo said with a grin.

Dovin kept his eyes on Kaylee and his mouth turned down. "Is that a memory? I see a dragon. Dragon's Cove perhaps?"

Kaylee closed her eyes and shook her head as if trying to knock the thought from her head.

Dovin's eyes widened, and he glanced at Mateo. "Oh my." He stepped up to Mateo and frowned as he looked back at Kaylee. "I had hoped that was a dream or nightmare, but Mateo seems to be having the same memory."

Kaylee grabbed her head with both hands. "Stop!" She ran out of the room, slamming the door behind her.

Odie frowned. He wondered what the memory was. It must have been something that happened while he was connecting with the dragons. Another fight, perhaps?

Dovin sat on the edge of the table. "It's fading. Now I can only hear a few muffled thoughts."

"That was absolutely terrifying," Claret said with a shiver.

Dovin shook his head. "I told you all to watch your thoughts. Not your strong points. Now I'm realizing why nothing gets done around here. I'm always working with teenagers."

20

—·—

CHAPTER 20

Kaylee sat on a step outside of the castle and took a bite of one of Mateo's cookies. They really were good. She frowned when she heard the front doors open and someone come out. Dovin sat on the step next to her.

He rested his elbows on his knees and clasped his hands. "I thought you didn't like Mateo?"

"I like him fine. We've become friends."

"Friends?"

She took another bite. "Is this an inquisition?"

"I'm going to send you to Dragon's Cove with Odie."

"Not to Colter's Lake?"

He shook his head. "I'll send Mateo. I'm not sending the two of you out together."

Kaylee rolled her eyes. "Why? Because of that memory you illegally looked at?"

"Illegally? I warned you."

"Yeah, and that made my mind go to the last memory I'd want you to see."

"Well, it made me realize that things would get done more effectively if I split you into groups with people you won't spark with."

"Spark? It only happened once." It wasn't exactly a lie. The lip balm incident didn't count, and neither did the dream.

"You know Mateo likes you. Everyone knows that. If you aren't interested in him, you can't have that happening. You can't lead him on."

Kaylee leaned her elbow against her knees. "Do you really think I'd kiss someone I didn't have feelings for?"

"Kiss? The memory I saw you were hugging."

Kaylee put her hands over her face. "Great."

"So more is happening than I know."

"Nothing is happening. He knows it. We're from different worlds. Literally."

"Why do you want to go back to Earth? You said you like it here."

"I do. Better than Earth."

"So why not stay?"

"Because it's not where I'm from. It's not in my plan."

"Plans can change."

"Look, I know people don't usually spend their entire life with the person they date in high school. That makes dating in high school weird to me. Why waste time with someone if it's not going to be forever? I know myself pretty well, and I'm not the kind of person who's going to fall in love over and over. I'm going to do it once, and it's going to be wonderful or devastating."

Dovin patted her on the back. "Don't make a choice because of fear. I think you'd do well in this world. You have friends and people who care about you, but you have to make the choice."

Kaylee rubbed her lips together. "Am I the only one getting a lecture?"

Dovin laughed. "It's not a lecture."

"I feel like you're telling me to stay away from Mateo but to stay here for him."

"No. I'm saying you can't go with Mateo because I don't trust you to stick to your assignment if you go with him. And I don't think you should stay here for him, but for you."

"I can focus when I'm with him. That memory you saw happened when we had time, not when we were supposed to be doing something."

"I'd feel better if you were with Odie."

Kaylee nodded. "All right. I'll go with Odie. Dragon's cove is cool."

Dovin stayed and talked for a few minutes, then left. Kaylee brushed some stray crumbs from her lap and stood. She needed to pull herself together. No more tossing games at people and glaring. That wasn't her.

Teleporting one person was so easy. Mateo stood in front of Colter's Lake and tossed off his boots and shirt. He wished Dovin had let Kaylee come. They'd had fun the last time they were here. He kneeled down next to the gelatin-looking water, scooped up a handful, and took a drink. A cool tingle fell over his body, and he waded into the lake.

Once the water was to his chest, he dove down and swam, admiring the brightly colored plants. He took a deep breath, happy to see it was still possible to breathe under this water. When he was far enough, he went to the bottom and walked. His steps felt slow, but last time that feeling had only lasted a few minutes.

Now he needed to find a weller and get it to spit a barb at him. He looked around, but all he could see were plants and a few fish. He didn't want to waste time. Time was funny down here and moved slower than up above. He could miss days if he was here for even a few hours.

Mateo ran and jumped gracefully through the water. The feeling of being weightless made him smile. He would be careful not to damage the plants this time, but if he was already here, he was going to make the most of it. He continued running and jumping until he saw a small school of wellers.

The strange seahorse-like creatures were watching him with their dragon heads. He took a deep breath and blew out water bubbles. Scaring the wellers would cause them to shoot out the tiny needles, and he remembered how much they stung.

"Hey!" he yelled at the small creatures. They began turning red and blue and bobbing quickly up and down. He closed his eyes as they shot sharp, thin needles into him. Last time he'd jumped out of the way and still gotten three in him. This time, it felt like so much more. He stumbled backward and watched the wellers swim away.

Dovin only needed one needle, but Mateo would save all of them, just so he never had to do this again. He pulled a few out, then decided to get the rest out on land. He swam as fast as his body would carry him and climbed onto dry ground.

"Those things are evil," he said, pulling the barbs from his arms, chest, and stomach.

"They really are."

Mateo's head spun to the side. A woman with a long brown braid and a flowing pink dress stood beside him.

"Most people avoid the lake."

Mateo just nodded and pulled a needle from his leg. Where had she come from? She looked dressed too formally to be walking around the fields here.

"I must say, I'm surprised to see you here alone."

"Do I know you?" he asked, getting to his feet.

"No, but I've seen you in your dreams."

Mateo's heart sped. "Isadora."

She smiled. "You've heard of me? I'm flattered."

There was no reason to mess around with a witch. He turned and took one step, ready to teleport, but Isadora grabbed him and yanked on his arm. Everything around him went black, and a moment later, he was falling to the floor of the goblins' dungeon. He recognized it from the time Claret had been here.

Isadora closed the cell he was in and smiled. "You can have the queen's old cell. It even has two beds. What more could you ask for?"

"A shirt? I was just swimming."

She laughed. "We may be able to provide that, although the goblins are quite a bit smaller than you are."

He heard a door open in the distance and footsteps on the stone steps.

"That will be Garin," she said. The footsteps became louder. Garin must be walking down the long hallway. Mateo waited, knowing there was nothing he could do.

Garin walked confidently toward the cell and smiled when he saw Mateo. "Ah, Odie's friend. Welcome back." He tossed his black cape over his shoulder and grinned at Isadora. "Good work."

Garin's blond hair stuck out at odd angles, and his orange eyes flashed. "You know I was losing sleep over why you look so familiar to me. It took a while, but it finally came to me. I had a run-in with someone a few years back. It didn't end as well as I would have liked. His name was Sen. Do you know him?"

Mateo didn't answer. He didn't know what his brother had to do with this man, and he didn't want to do anything that might put Sen in trouble.

"Are you his brother? You look similar."

"I don't think he wants to talk to you," Isadora said.

"I suppose not. I wish you had gotten Odie as well."

Isadora frowned. "I'm not your errand girl. I will get them all in my own time. For now, I hope this one gets me my mermaid back."

Garin scowled. "You are much too focused on the mermaid. You have three. Why do you need another? Once we take over Riviand, you can have all the mermaids we can find."

Isadora frowned.

"I don't even know where Jayah is," Mateo said. "I couldn't tell you if I wanted to."

"But there are those who can. Kaylee will tell me."

"No, she won't. She doesn't even know."

"She'll find out to save you."

"Doubtful."

Isadora smiled. "You forget. I've seen her dreams. I know who she dreams about."

The two of them walked away. Mateo frowned and flopped back on one of the beds. It was surprisingly soft, and now he was getting it wet. He couldn't believe he'd been captured, and so easily. With any luck, Vivi would bring him food and he could talk her into helping him escape.

There was something else they had to consider. Isadora and Garin had some way of finding them. There was no way Garin had accidentally found Odie and Claret and taken them to the goblins, and then Isadora had found him.

Mateo's mind went back to the last thing Isadora had said. She said she knew who Kaylee dreamed about. Mateo was lost when he thought about Kaylee. She obviously had changed the way she felt about him, but he wasn't sure how much. Not that it mattered. Now he might be stuck here forever.

Kaylee stood in Odie's room and put her pack over her shoulder. She was getting sick of this pack. It was starting to smell the way an elementary school lunch box does when the year is almost over. She kept meaning to get a new one, but she only thought about it when she was about to go somewhere.

"I still think we should wait to leave until Mateo gets back."

Dovin shook his head. "We don't know how long it might take. If he's in Colter's Lake for two hours, it will be two days for us. We don't know how long it will take to find the wellers."

Odie stood by her in a blue tunic. It was only the second time she'd seen him in something that wasn't black. His pack was nearly bursting from the seams. He must have a lot of his experiments in there.

Arving entered and frowned. "Are you going to let Pax teleport them?"

"I don't know how," Odie said.

Arving sniffed. "You don't need to know how. You should have seen the things that you could do as a three-year-old. Now that you're seventeen, you should be able to do anything."

"I'm seventeen?"

"Yes. Your birthday was last month."

Odie nodded. "Hmm."

"You really were a wonder," Dovin said. "If you watched someone do magic, you could replicate it without knowing how. It was amazing."

"That's why you had the ring," Arving said. "We worried you would jump through a portal or something and we would never find you. We couldn't get you to eat like a normal person because you would summon things from the pantry and snack all day long."

Kaylee couldn't tell what Odie thought about Arving. He didn't seem overly anxious to try to make a relationship with him. He was polite but didn't seek the man out. She probably wouldn't either. He hadn't been nice to Odie when they met.

"I don't think I'm ready to teleport," Odie said.

Dovin stepped forward, and they grabbed his cape and teleported to Dragon's Cove.

"When should I come back for you?" Dovin asked. "Three days?"

Kaylee wrinkled her nose. She wasn't really in the mood to spend three days at Dragon's Cove with Odie. Not that she had anything against him. It just sounded boring.

Odie nodded. "That should be fine. If we need to teleport, I can probably do it."

Dovin nodded and disappeared.

"Why didn't you try?" Kaylee asked.

Odie shrugged. "I don't want Arving telling me what to do. He wasn't even civil to me until he found out he was my father."

"I get that. So now what?"

"I guess we just sit around and watch everything."

"Thrilling. What if we go back into the cave behind the waterfall and explore it some more?"

"That might be interesting."

"All right. Let's go."

21

CHAPTER 21

"**Y**our dreams bore me more than I can say," Isadora said, scaring Claret from her thoughts. Claret looked around her room and frowned. She was sleeping? Her dreams really were dull. She'd just been sitting here reading a book.

"Leave."

"Your friend's dreams are at least a little exciting, but yours? Who dreams of reading?"

"I enjoy reading."

"Yes, I see that. I just thought you might want to know I have one of your friends. I will trade him for Jayah."

Claret frowned and put the book down. "I don't believe you."

"Oh? I found him by Colter's Lake, pulling weller spines from his skin."

Mateo. She must have Mateo.

"Here is my deal. You bring Jayah to me. I promise I won't punish her for leaving. If you don't, Mateo dies. Do we understand each other?"

Claret ground her teeth.

"I would have gone to Kaylee, but I can't find her dreams tonight."

"How long do I have?"

"Two days. You bring her. Only the two of you will be allowed in the goblins' castle. You will tell no one else."

Claret shook her head. "I don't know where she is. I have to talk to someone."

"I'm sure you'll figure it out. And bring your friend a shirt. He would appreciate it."

Claret sat up in bed and rubbed her eyes. This was just great. She jumped out of bed and got dressed. She didn't know where Jayah was, but she needed to figure it out. Isadora wouldn't hurt Jayah, but she had no doubt she would kill Mateo.

She hurried to the dining room and found Dovin and Durdessa eating breakfast. Durdessa spent most of her time in Basura watching all the people who were in hiding, but she popped down often enough.

"I need to know where Jayah is."

Dovin put down his fork and sighed. "Why?"

"I can't tell you."

"That means someone threatened you and you are going to tell them where Jayah is."

Claret rubbed her lips together. "It's better to return her than to keep putting others in danger. We can save her again later."

"That sounds counterproductive."

Claret crossed her arms. "How many people are we hiding, just so Isadora won't use them? I only have two days, and then she's going to kill Mateo."

"Are you sure she has him?"

Claret frowned. "She said she took him near Colter's Lake."

"I'll be back," Dovin said, teleporting away.

"She might be lying to you," Durdessa said.

"Perhaps, but what if she isn't?"

"I don't want you going alone."

"I have to. She said so."

"And you really think she's going to let you leave after?"

Claret looked at the floor. "Probably not."

Dovin reappeared holding a pair of boots and Mateo's shirt. "It looks like she was telling the truth. I shouldn't have sent him alone."

"She told me to bring him a shirt. That must be why."

"We can talk to Jayah and see what she thinks."

"Fine, but we must hurry."

Dovin handed the slightly damp shirt and boots to Claret and teleported himself and Claret to a small cottage. It was cheery enough, with white shutters and rose bushes under the windows. Dovin knocked on the door and Williams answered.

"Uh-oh. What's going down?"

Dovin shook his head. "Can we talk to Jayah?"

"Sure." He opened the door wider, and they walked into a clean sitting room. There was a blue sofa and a love seat, and Jayah was curled up, reading on the sofa.

"Hello," she said, closing her book. "Is something wrong?"

Claret stepped forward. "Isadora desperately wants you back."

"I'm sure she does," she said, pushing her black hair over her ear.

"She is using everyone we know to get you. Kaylee's and Mateo's families are all in hiding. She isn't going to stop. She has Mateo, and she's going to kill him if she doesn't get you back within two days."

"She's not going back," Williams said.

"You're going to let Mateo die?"

"There has to be another way. Dovin is great at breaking people out of prison."

Dovin frowned. "Two days isn't enough to plan. We will have better luck returning Jayah and saving her again later."

"No," Williams said. "Think of something else."

Jayah sighed. "She won't hurt me, but she will hurt the boy. I'll go."

"I won't let you."

"Oh?" Jayah asked with a small smile. "Let me go, and then you can come save me." She stood and kissed Williams on the cheek. Claret tried not to look surprised.

Dovin shook his head. "Sometimes I wonder if I'm a mentor or a matchmaker. If everyone was more focused on the problems at hand and not romance, we might make some progress."

Williams gave him a half smile. "That's easy for you to say. You're married."

"So are you," Jayah said.

Claret scrunched her forehead. "What?"

Jayah smiled and took his arm. "We got married last week."

Dovin's brow rose. "That's unexpected."

She looked up at Williams. "You know I need to go, Magni."

He frowned. "I'll come find you."

"Perhaps you should wait until things are a little more settled, so we don't have to repeat this. Leave me there until you've defeated her."

He nodded and kissed her.

Jayah pulled away and looked at Claret. "Let me grab my locket. Isadora won't want me without it." She left the room.

"Sorry about this," Claret said. "But we can't let Mateo die."

Williams nodded. "I know."

Jayah came out with the locket. "I'm ready."

Claret grabbed her hand and teleported them directly into the goblins' castle. They ended up right in front of the dungeon doors. The two goblins standing guard jumped and pointed their spears at them. They were both wearing armor. Claret didn't remember that from her last experience here.

"We need to speak with Isadora," Claret said.

The goblins looked at each other, and one of them ran. A few minutes later, Isadora, Garin, and King Ummi came walking down the hallway. Isadora had a smug grin, and Garin and King Ummi wore unreadable expressions.

"Jayah," Isadora said. "Nice to have you back. Shall we?"

Jayah stepped forward and Isadora took her hand and they disappeared.

Claret held Mateo's boots and shirt. She stood tall and glared at King Ummi.

"Back to the dungeon with you," Garin said with a small grin.

The guards opened the door and Claret walked down the stone steps. She should have teleported the moment Isadora did, but she couldn't leave Mateo here alone. Garin followed behind her. She hated that she knew the dungeon so well. The farther they went, the colder it became. She walked down the long hall to the last cell.

Mateo was sitting on one bed with a blanket wrapped around himself. Claret frowned. She had brought him a damp shirt. That wouldn't do him a lot of good down here. It would probably make him catch a chill.

Garin unlocked the cell, and she went in. Mateo was frowning.

Claret put his shirt on the bed and his boots on the floor. Garin locked the cell.

"I'm sorry your shirt is a little wet. We were in a hurry."

"It's all right. Are my socks still in my boots? The floor is freezing."

"I think so."

"You should thank me for allowing you to stay together. There will be no escape this time, as King Ummi has finally realized Odie cannot be trusted."

"Odie can be trusted," Claret said. "You are the problem here."

Garin smiled, flames burning in his orange eyes. "Isadora said you would come. I doubted her."

"You know you can't trust her," Claret said. "She's using you. Once you take over Riviand, she'll probably kill you."

Garin laughed. "You say that like it's something I don't know. She can't kill me if I kill her first."

Mateo glared at him. "Why not get rid of her now?"

"It isn't the time. We work well together. She wants the throne but not as much as I do."

"I thought you were giving it to King Ummi?" Claret said.

"Yes, well, King Ummi and I have an understanding. He helps me get the throne and I let him keep his pathetic little kingdom and a percentage of Riviand's taxes. It works out well for both of us. Claret is the only one who needs to make a decision. Marry me or die here."

Mateo glared. "She isn't going to do either."

"Isadora thinks I should marry the queen, take over Riviand, then kill the queen and marry her. There are too many problems with that. Riviand will accept me without a fight if Claret stays alive. Think about it. A war or a wedding? I can get rid of Isadora right now if you agree."

"What's to keep us from telling her your plan?" Mateo asked. Claret rolled her eyes. Didn't he know when to be quiet?

"Do you really think she's going to be back down here?" Garin asked. "She has her mermaid. She doesn't care much about what happens to you from here. So what do you say?" Garin asked.

Claret narrowed her eyes. "You're too old for me."

He threw back his head and laughed. "There's another option. You marry Odious. He's been a problem, but he still counts as a prince. You marry him, then he appoints me his advisor. I rule through you, and you come and smile at events."

"Why do all these options involve me getting married?"

"They don't. There's still the option of war, but are you going to do that to your kingdom? You aren't. How do I know this? Because you are a good ruler." He grinned. "I'm not saying that as a compliment, but I know what people like you are like."

Claret just stared at him. He was right. She wouldn't let her people go to war if she could stop it.

He turned to leave. "I'll give you two days to think about it."

Claret grabbed Mateo's shirt and placed it outside the cell, as close as she could get it to the fire. The fireplace was in the middle of the back wall of the dungeon.

"What am I going to do?" Claret asked. "I'm not stupid. Even if he keeps me alive, he'll probably keep you and possibly Kaylee locked up so that I don't go against him."

"Does anyone know you're here?" Mateo asked, getting out of bed and grabbing his boots.

"Dovin does."

"He'll get us out."

"Within two days?"

"He said you had to make your choice in two days. That doesn't mean you have to marry someone in two days. Tell him you choose Odie, and we'll work it out somehow. Then if you actually do end up getting married, at least it's to someone you... might not mind."

Claret would have laughed if she wasn't so worried. "I suppose. I'll tell Garin I'll marry Odie, but he has to let you go."

"No. He needs some leverage to keep you in line. If he lets me go, he'll just get someone else."

"If we went to war, Riviand would win, but people would die. I can't live with that if I can stop it."

"Do you think Garin knows we know he's a shifter?"

"It's possible. We saw him change, but I don't know if he knew we were watching."

"Don't worry. We're going to win in the end."

Claret nodded and sat on one of the two chairs in the cell. She thought of how different her life had become in such a short time. So many things had changed for the better, but being here in the dungeon was not one of them. Three times she had ended up here. It was almost ridiculous.

Footsteps came near their cell and Claret stood to meet whoever it might be. A familiar-looking goblin came into view. Claret thought he might be Odie's brother.

"Sorry about all of this," he said. He held a vial in his hand. He threw it to the cell floor, shattering it. She expected smoke to rise, but it didn't. He leaned over so Claret couldn't see what he was doing. The mixture from the floor went up in flames. The goblin turned and ran.

Claret frowned. "Odie's sleeping potion." That was the last thing she remembered thinking.

22

—·—

CHAPTER 22

Odie stepped over broken fairy houses as he and Kaylee explored the underground world. He hoped they would only see dragons and not fairies. Dragons he was beginning to understand, but from everything he knew about fairies, they were unpredictable and often cruel. Dragons flew overhead, barely missing them.

"What do you think the stuff all over the houses is?" Kaylee asked, touching the smooth, amber-like surface of one house.

"I'm not sure. It looks and feels like amber, but where would it have come from? Amber comes from trees and there aren't any down here."

"This place is strange. I always think about fairies jumping around on lily pads or flying through the trees. Down here, there isn't much to see."

Odie nodded. "I wonder if they live underground but spend most of their time up above."

"But where are they now?"

"Whatever messed up their homes must have scared them away." The red dragon landed near them and rubbed its nose on Odie's back. He turned and patted her head. "This is the only red dragon I've seen. I wonder why. It seems there are a lot of all the other colors."

The dragon was tired. Odie didn't know why he knew that, but he did.

"Whoa!" Kaylee exclaimed, jumping back. "Look at the size of that bug!"

A large blue and gold beetle crawled out from one of the small houses. The red dragon roared, then opened its mouth and a brownish-yellow goo poured from its mouth and covered the beetle. Steam rose from the place it fell.

"Gross," Kaylee said. "Did he just vomit on it?"

"It looks like it."

"So all the stuff on the houses that we've been touching is dragon puke? Nasty." She wiped her hand against her britches.

"It might be something else. She did that on command. I wonder if there's a connection to the vomit and the beetle, or perhaps they just vomit on everything."

"I didn't see any on Dragon's Cove, only down here."

"That's because the beetles are only down here," said a tinkling voice near Odie's ear. A fairy with long white hair flew around his head. "The dragons have destroyed this city, but it had to be done. We will come back and claim it once the beetles are completely gone."

"Are they bad?" Kaylee asked.

The fairy landed on the ground and grew to their height. "They eat everything. They were ruining our homes. Of course the dragons ruined them in the process of getting rid of them, but it is necessary."

"How far does this city go?" Kaylee asked.

Odie wanted to leave. He'd had his fill of fairies.

"This city is large. The fairies' villages and cities are all connected underground. If you walked far enough, you would find them all. We're hoping the dragons deal with all the beetles before any other cities are infected."

"Do you know where they're coming from?" Kaylee asked.

The fairy frowned. "Yes, and we cannot stop the source."

"Where are they coming from?"

"From someone we cannot defy."

"Someone?"

"We should leave," Odie said.

The fairy nodded. "Yes. We do not like people coming down here. The dragons we will tolerate until they rid us of our problem. You do not want to be found down here, especially when the beetles change." The fairy shrank down and flew away.

"Change how?" Kaylee called after the fairy, but she didn't turn back.

"Come on," Odie said, walking back toward the cave.

"Fairies don't seem bad to me," Kaylee said. "I've only met two. But they seemed all right."

"That's what they want you to think. Everyone is enchanted by fairies, but it never turns out well for those who get involved with them."

"I'm still curious about what they did to make you dislike them so much."

Odie kept walking. That was a story no one would hear. It still embarrassed him to think about it, and it had been a long time ago.

"So you think they're really working with Isadora? Could she be behind the beetles? Maybe she's threatening the fairies into helping her."

"Most people can't threaten fairies into doing anything."

"But Isadora is a witch. What if they need our help?"

Odie shook his head. "I'm never going to trust a fairy. You didn't grow up here. You don't know the stories."

"But a fairy helped Mateo and me a few times."

Odie turned to her and frowned. "They didn't do it out of the goodness of their hearts. It was because they knew you were trying to save Riviand. They didn't want the continent to rise any more than we did. They would have died with everyone else." Kaylee nodded, but he could tell she didn't completely believe him.

Kaylee sat near the lake with her feet in the water. This was a terrible use of time. Odie had coaxed some dragons out and was trying to communicate with them. He should have come alone, and Kaylee should have gone with Mateo. Odie didn't need help, and Mateo might.

A beetle from the cave scurried over her hand and she shook it off and jumped to her feet. The beetle came closer, and she took a few steps back. The beetle didn't stop coming toward her, so she ran a few paces and turned to see it coming faster. This was why she disliked bugs and preferred snakes.

Kaylee shrieked and ran. This wasn't normal for a bug. "Odie!" she yelled, unsure where he could be. She turned to see the bug behind her. It was growing, and fast. "Odie!" It was difficult to run with no boots and her feet kept stepping on sharp things. She would worry about that later. She gazed back at a beetle the size of a small car.

It was going to catch her. She grabbed the sword at her side and turned to face it. She lifted the sword into the air and the beetle stopped. The metallic colors shimmered in the sunlight, but that didn't make it any less terrifying. She pointed the Blade of the Phoenix at the creature and hoped something would happen. When nothing did, she took a step forward.

The beetle lunged into the air and Kaylee screamed and closed her eyes. The weight of the giant bug slammed into the sword and Kaylee felt a splash as the bug burst and its innards covered her in green goo. She wiped the goop from her face and shivered.

"Kaylee!" Odie yelled, running into view. He skidded to a stop when he saw her. "What is all over you?"

She shook her arms, and big globs dropped to the dirt. "Beetle guts."

He narrowed his eyes. "What?"

"I need to wash off, but now I'm scared to go near the water."

"Like the beetles from the cave?"

"Yes, but it grew until it was humongous. I stabbed it and it... burst."

Odie looked terrified and then smiled.

"What are you grinning about?"

He chuckled. "I'm sorry. You're really covered. Let's teleport back to the castle. I don't see any reason to stay here."

"But you've never teleported before."

"No, but I'm sure I can do it."

"It might be better if I wash it off first. I don't want to get it all over the castle."

Odie grabbed his pack and opened it. "Don't wash it off yet. Let me put some of it in a container. It might be useful for something."

Kaylee sighed. She hoped it didn't harden on her. Odie handed her an open jar, and she scooped some of the goo off her and into the jar.

"Thanks."

She rolled her eyes. "Sure. Anything for science. Now I'm going to go dunk myself. Come stand guard and make sure no bugs come near me."

Odie grinned. "All right."

Odie shook the jar full of beetle innards and smiled. He couldn't wait to experiment with it. It was too bad he didn't have more containers. Kaylee was in the lake, dunking her head and trying to get the beetle out of her braids.

The red dragon came up to him and sat. Odie tried to project an image of the beetle into the dragon's mind. The dragon yawned and put its head down. He sent an image back to Odie. It showed a beetle growing bigger and bigger.

"Are they dangerous?" he asked the dragon.

It showed him a beetle biting a dragon. The dragon's leg turned red and swelled.

"How can I get rid of them?"

His brows furrowed when the dragon showed him an image of a dragon vomiting on the small beetles.

"I don't think I can do that. What do you do when they get bigger?"

The dragon showed him a dragon biting a huge beetle. The beetle burst, spraying its insides all over the dragon.

"So they pop and explode everywhere. Interesting."

Kaylee stepped out of the water and wiped her eyes. "I think I got it."

"Emerald said they vomit on the bugs when they're small if they can. If the beetles grow, they bite them and it pops them."

"Emerald?"

"I thought I would name the dragon."

Kaylee looked at the red dragon and shook her head. "You are the worst dragon namer in history."

"Emerald's a nice name."

"Maybe if she were green. Ruby might be better."

Odie didn't really get Kaylee. Emerald sounded a lot better than Ruby in his mind.

"I shouldn't be surprised. You named an orange dragon Midnight."

"So?"

She shrugged. "It's fine, just weird. I'm curious to see what you name your children."

"I don't think I'm too bad at naming things."

"Gregor the Destroyer?"

Odie smiled. "That was years ago. I should get a pass for that. Do you want to go back?"

Kaylee frowned. "I do, but Dovin might send us back. I don't see any reason for us to be here, though. Did you ask the dragons if Garin's been back?"

"He hasn't. They keep mostly to the cave because they're still scared. I told them not to tell him anything about us, but it's hard to know how much they actually understand."

Kaylee smiled. "What if we ride back on the dragon?"

Odie smiled. "That might be fun. Let me see if Emerald is up for it." He put a hand on the dragon's nose and pictured the dragon flying to Tyran with the two of them on her back. She got down low, which Odie took to mean she was all right with it.

"Let's do it," Odie said. "Do you want to be in front or in the back?"

"Have you ever flown one?"

"No. Well, I thought I did once, but it was Garin and he went where he wanted to."

"Then I'll go to the front. I've flown an alicorn a few times and I know how to ride a horse." She climbed on Emerald's back and Odie climbed on behind.

Emerald stood and Odie focused on not squeezing Kaylee. He felt less stable than last time. Putting his arms around Kaylee didn't feel natural like it did with Claret.

"Wow, she's big," Kaylee muttered.

Emerald spread her long red wings and took off into the sky. Kaylee let out a small yelp and then laughed as they shot higher and higher. Odie thought it was fun but also worried about falling off. When they were high above Dragon's Cove, Emerald leveled off and Odie let out a sigh of relief.

"The breeze is so cold!" Kaylee yelled. "We should have waited until I dried off."

"Well, we are about to fly over the desert, so I bet you dry quickly."

"Oh no. We're going to get sunburned."

Odie hadn't thought of that. He had some of his sun balm in his bag, but he didn't want to let go to try to get it. As soon as the desert started, the pleasant breeze turned into a hot wind.

"Whoa, I can almost feel myself drying!" Kaylee said. "I wonder how big the desert is."

"Big enough. Dragons are fast, so I'm not too worried."

"I wonder how Mateo is doing. If he's not back when we return, we should go to Colter's Lake and try to find him."

23

— · —

CHAPTER 23

M ateo sat up and scowled. The goblins had moved them. Claret slept on the black floor, her long hair covering her face. The room didn't have any furnishings, and the walls and ceiling were as black as the floor. His tunic was next to him, so he pulled it over his head. It was dry but a little stiff. His arms had something sticky on them. They were definitely still in the goblin castle. A black door on one wall had a small window toward the top with bars. A window against the wall was the only thing giving any light.

Mateo stood on his shaky legs and looked out the small window on the door. All he could see was a dark hallway. The window showed him a view looking down the goblin mountain. He tried to do magic, but they must be blocked.

He thought about waking Claret but decided to let her sleep. Being awake here wasn't pleasant. Keys turned in the lock and he faced the door, ready for anything. Four goblins pushed a long table into the room. Mateo studied them. They weren't very big. He could probably take them. He jumped over the table and slammed the door.

"What is the purpose of this?" one of them said as they pushed the table into one corner. They didn't look concerned.

"Claret!" Mateo said loudly.

"I hope you don't think you can escape just because the door is unlocked," a goblin said. "There's an enchantment on the door."

He frowned and opened the door. He tried to stick his hand out, but it hit an invisible barrier.

"Why are we here?" Mateo asked. "Why aren't we in the dungeon?"

A goblin with spiky black hair turned and put his hands on his hips. "Because the dungeon is the first place your friends will look for you. Garin wanted you in a place no one would look. Now move away from the exit."

Mateo crossed his arms and leaned against the door. "I don't think I will. If King Ummi wants me to let you go, he's going to have to let us go."

The goblins all shared looks and shook their heads. "You do not seem to know how goblins work. The king has plenty of servants. If we stay in here, it will not inconvenience him."

"Do you want to stay in here? Let us out and you can go."

"We don't mind staying here," one goblin said. "It's probably better than working."

Mateo sighed and moved away from the door. The goblins all left, sending him nasty smiles.

Claret sat up when the door slammed. She looked around and pushed her hair into place. "They moved us?"

"Yes. It's not cold like the dungeon, but there aren't any beds or anything. The goblins just brought a table. I don't know what they expect us to do with that."

Claret stood and looked out the window. "We're up high. No one is going to find us up here."

"Probably not. When I was here with Odie, we walked around and there had to be hundreds of rooms. I doubt anyone would even think to look anywhere but the dungeon."

"It doesn't smell as bad as the dungeon, but I still would prefer it over this. It's going to be really uncomfortable."

"You can sleep on the table. It might be better than the floor but not much."

"They could at least give us a pillow to sit on."

"The goblins brought the table in before you woke up. Maybe they'll bring other things."

"Why a table? There isn't a lot of space."

"Who knows? Goblins are weird."

The lock sounded in the door again and a line of goblins came in with armloads of containers and bowls. They placed them on the table and left. Mateo went to the table and opened a canister.

"I think it's flour."

Claret opened another. "Baking ingredients? How odd."

"Dang. I bet they're going to make me mix up cookies all day. I guess that's better than doing nothing. If Vivi is the one baking them, they're still going to end up burned. Should I start now or wait until they command me?"

Claret shrugged. "Will you teach me?"

"Sure. It's pretty easy. Start opening things and see if you can find some butter."

Mateo opened a container full of eggs. "These are definitely cookie ingredients. That means the king still has some power. I don't know how much Garin is controlling him, but Garin wouldn't have me make cookies. Goblins think with their stomachs."

A tap at the door caused them to pause. It opened and Vivi came in with a jar of chocolate chunks. She handed it to Mateo. "I was sorry to hear you were both back."

"Can you help us?"

"I did. I talked the king into allowing you the ingredients. That's all the help I can give you. I didn't want you to go mad in here, so now you have a purpose."

Mateo sighed. "Great. My purpose is to bake cookies for goblins."

Vivi laughed. "And goblins eat a lot, so you can do it all day long if you want."

"Any chance of getting some pillows or cushions?"

"I'll try. King Ummi doesn't believe in having uncomfortable prisoners, but that man Garin is a different type. He ordered this. He's proud of himself now because almost as soon as you were moved, someone broke into the dungeon."

Claret frowned. "Who?"

"The man who was here once before. Back the first time the queen was here."

"Dovin."

"That's it."

"Was he captured?"

"No. He got in, knocked out the guards, ran to the dungeon, came back up, and disappeared before anyone knew what was happening."

Mateo grabbed a mixing bowl. "At least we know they're trying to save us."

Claret looked out the window again. "Perhaps if we watch, we might see them and we can call to them."

"I'm not sure that would help. We're pretty high up here, and they aren't going to walk up to the front door," Mateo said. "They're going to sneak."

Vivi nodded. "I'm afraid you're stuck. I'll be back in an hour to get the dough."

Claret measured the things Mateo told her to and put them in the mixing bowl. She'd never baked before, but it didn't seem too difficult. It reminded her of Odie's experiments. She wished Odie were the one she was stuck with. Not that she had anything against Mateo. If she was wishing, she might as well wish she weren't here.

She stuck a piece of the stuff Mateo called chocolate in her mouth as she stirred. It really was a lot better the way he'd made it. It was amazing the way something so bitter could become sweet if you added the right ingredients.

"When Vivi returns, we could run out," Claret suggested. "I don't think she would stop us."

Mateo shook his head. "There's something blocking us. Some type of magic at the door. The goblins can get through, but not us."

"I should have had a better plan when I came. Everything happened so fast. I knew they wouldn't let me go when I brought Jayah. I couldn't let them kill you, though."

Mateo pointed at a canister. "Put in two cups of flour. I appreciate it, but I doubt they would have killed me. I mean, maybe, but I don't think they would have yet."

"I feel bad about returning Jayah, but Isadora wasn't going to stop putting people in danger until she was returned. I wish we could storm Isadora's manor and free all the creatures in there, but that would make her mad. We need to stop her first so she doesn't retaliate."

"You made the right choice. Well, you probably should've had Jayah come up here without you."

Vivi came back as soon as the dough was mixed. She had two pillows and two small blankets. "Don't tell anyone I'm the one who brought these," she said. "I don't think anyone will notice, but you never know."

"Thanks, Vivi," Mateo said, taking them, and placed them in the corner. He handed her the mixing bowl. She took it and left.

"Vivi could help us if she really wanted to," Claret said. "She could slip something into everyone's food."

"But then they would know it was her."

"She could leave with us."

Mateo sighed and began putting lids on canisters. "Vivi likes me, but I don't know how she feels about the goblins.

She might like it here and be loyal to them. I'm afraid if we push her too far, she'll stop helping us at all."

Claret grabbed one pillow and put it against the wall and sat on it. She wasn't going to do well here. At least in the dungeon, she could pace and sit on a soft bed. This room was too small to do much of anything.

Mateo grinned. "Don't worry, I'll clean up."

Claret blushed and got back up. "Sorry. I'm not used to thinking about things like that."

"It's fine, really. I was just teasing you. It's not very messy and we don't have a rag to wipe it up or anything."

She twisted the lid back on a container. "You don't seem upset."

"About what?"

"Being locked in here."

"I'm not thrilled, but I know the others will get us out."

"The thought of being stuck in this room for days on end makes me want to scream. Why does everything have to be black? They could put a painting on the wall or something a little cheery. Or a rug. Don't goblins believe in rugs?"

Mateo raised his brow. "Why don't you go sit back down on the pillow? Maybe take a nap."

"I can't just nap away my worries."

"I doubt Vivi can sneak in a rug."

"What if we take down Garin? He's going to come in eventually, and he wouldn't expect you to punch him in the face. He's not a goblin, so if he comes in, the goblins would have to take down whatever it is they have blocking the door. If you knock him out, we could run and teleport."

Mateo frowned. "Hmm. Contrary to what some people might say, I haven't punched that many people in the face, and it didn't knock any of them out. It might just make him more angry and they might separate us."

Claret rubbed her eyes. She didn't want that. She sank back down on the pillow and rested her head on her knees. Her britches were already getting dirty, and she hadn't been here long.

Tomorrow, Garin would come to see what her decision was. She was ready to tell him she chose Odie. She didn't feel old enough to get married, but if she had to, she knew who she cared about. Garin had to know making her marry Odie wouldn't put him in charge in any way. If he thought they would step back and let him rule, he had another thing coming. He probably thought they were silly children who could be put in their place.

"You all right?" Mateo asked.

"Yes, just tired. Do you think they're going to feed us?"

As soon as she said it, Vivi came in carrying a dinner tray. She put it on the table and smiled. "Your cookies taste so much better than mine. I made sure I brought you a pile."

"Haven't you been practicing?" Mateo asked, teasing the goblin.

She laughed. "A few times, but they take too much time. I like things that don't take a lot of effort."

"Do you think the king will let you bring us some books?" Claret asked.

"I can try."

Mateo wasn't great at reading people, but he was afraid Claret was on the verge of a breakdown. Her eyes kept scanning the room, and she kept fidgeting. He hoped Vivi found some books because she needed to get her mind off their situation.

He didn't blame her. Mateo was upset about being here, but he was trying to play it off for Claret. He thought if he seemed casual about their situation, it might make her feel better. Still, she had more to worry about than he did. She might end up married at the end of this. There was no way that would help Garin. Mateo didn't understand the way that guy's mind worked. Making Claret and Odie get married might in some ways unite Riviand and the goblins, but that wouldn't give Garin any power.

He sat down next to Claret and tried to get comfortable. "Did you know I have five brothers?"

"I remember hearing something like that."

"We used to get into so much trouble together, and we were always good at getting out of it. Even if Dovin can't save us, we'll figure out a way, all right?"

She nodded. Mateo told her stories about his childhood and some of the things he and his brothers had done. It wasn't long before she was laughing and by the time they curled up on the floor to go to sleep, he felt like she was feeling better. He'd made himself feel better in the process. With luck, tomorrow would see them back at Claret's castle.

CHAPTER 24

E merald landed next to the castle, and Kaylee and Odie slid off her back. The guards near the doors all hesitantly came near. Most people in Riviand hadn't seen many dragons, especially dragons that were as big as Emerald.

Dovin came out the front doors and studied the dragon. "She's a real beauty," he said. "Do you think she'll stay around?"

"I'm not sure," Odie said. "She's curious. The dragons don't leave Dragon's Cove much."

Dovin turned to a guard. "Will you please go tell Durdessa to come out here?"

The guard bowed and ran into the castle.

"Is Mateo back?" Kaylee asked.

Dovin ran a hand over the dragon's back. "No."

"Shouldn't we be worried?"

Dovin sighed. "Isadora captured him and took him to King Ummi's castle."

"What?" Kaylee exclaimed. "Then why aren't you over there getting him out?"

"I already tried. He isn't in the dungeon. I don't know where they're keeping him."

"If Isadora took him, he might be at her house."

"No, we know he's there. Claret as well."

Odie frowned. "They captured her again?"

"She went willingly, to take Jayah."

Kaylee crossed her arms. "She took Jayah to Isadora?"

"Yes."

"Why would she do that?"

"Isadora said she would kill Mateo if she didn't. Jayah made the decision to return. We will work on rescuing her later. We can't keep putting everyone we know in hiding. This should stop the vorcraws as well."

"What now?" Odie asked. "The goblins aren't going to let me walk into the castle again. If I show up, they'll lock me up."

"I haven't decided," Dovin said. "Since we don't know where they're being kept, it makes things difficult."

"Claret has an army," Kaylee said. "Why aren't we using it? Claret said the goblins are no match for Riviand."

"That may be true, but what do you suppose would happen if the army attacked the goblins? They are going to use Mateo and Claret and threaten to hurt them. We need to think this through."

Kaylee frowned. "We don't have time to think. What about the invisibility potion Odie made?"

Odie ran a hand through his hair. "It's hard to make and I don't have a lot. Searching the castle could take days, and what if they aren't even there? They could have put them anywhere. They obviously knew we would try something. That's why they weren't in the dungeon."

Kaylee glared at him. "So you think we should leave them there?"

"No, I just don't think that would work."

"What would?"

"I wonder if I can get Gregor to fly into the castle and find them. Now that I can communicate with him, I might be able to pull it off."

"But what would he do if he found them?"

Odie shrugged. "The idea just came to me. I haven't had time to think it through. I would say we could tie a note onto his leg or something, but anyone might find that."

"Would he be able to tell you where they were if he found them?" Dovin asked.

"It's possible. I'm still getting the hang of talking to animals, but they can picture things and I can see them."

"Then let's go find Gregor and see what he can do," Kaylee said, grabbing Odie's arm and dragging him up the castle steps.

"Don't do anything rash," Dovin said, following behind them. "Garin isn't going to hurt them, not yet. He'll try to use them."

They found Gregor in Odie's room. The puffin was sitting on the window ledge, looking out the window. Odie sat by him and closed his eyes. Kaylee forced herself to stay quiet so he could concentrate, but it was difficult.

"Did you spot Garin at Dragon's Cove?" Dovin asked quietly.

Kaylee shook her head. "No. The dragons said he hasn't been around. We found some beetles that grow super big and then pop if you stab them. I probably still have beetle guts in my hair."

Dovin rubbed his chin. "I've heard of bugs like that before, but I can't remember where. I'll look it up when I get a minute."

"The bugs are eating the fairy city, but the dragons are vomiting on them. I guess that kills them."

"Interesting. I've had dragons that vomited on bugs before. Dragon vomit is almost impossible to clean."

"It's all over the fairy city. Most of the fairies are gone. We only saw one. She spoke like the beetles being there was someone's fault. She didn't say whose."

Odie turned to them. "I think Gregor understands. If we can teleport him to the castle, that would save time. I'm not sure he can fly that far."

"We can do that, of course," Dovin said. "I'm not sure how useful this will be, but I suppose it's worth a shot."

"What if the goblins see him and get suspicious?" Kaylee asked.

"They won't," Odie assured her. "They're all used to seeing him. He had free run of the castle. They won't even think twice."

Kaylee was tired, and she needed a real bath, but how could she rest when Mateo and Claret were lost? "I think we need to do more. Gregor might not be able to find them. It's not like he can open doors or windows."

"Right now, this is all we can do," Dovin said.

Kaylee bit back a retort. "Odie? Don't you think we should do something more?"

"I'm not sure what," he said. "There really are a lot of places they could be. I bet Garin is planning on contacting us with some type of demand."

Kaylee didn't know why Odie and Dovin didn't seem as concerned as she felt. Odie had more reason to worry than all of them.

"What if Garin forces Claret to marry him?"

"I doubt he will. Not yet."

"But what if he does?"

Odie rubbed his lips together and frowned.

Dovin tilted his head and studied Kaylee. "I understand that you are upset, but we have to deal with this carefully. I need you both here for the ball. Without Claret, it's going to be strange enough, but I think having Odie here might be to our advantage. After the ball, there will be a meeting with a person from each city or village."

Kaylee shook her head. "That can be put off."

"No. The sooner everything is organized, the better. Claret is a good queen, but Riviand is not organized. It will benefit her greatly when there are other leaders. I will teach the people who attend how to hold elections, and with luck, all the cities will have a governor within the next few months. It's a short amount of time to accomplish so much, but it will make a great impact."

"Why would my being there be an advantage?" Odie asked.

"When I tell them about the threat to Riviand and explain that you have left the goblins, it will comfort people. You know the goblins and their lands."

"I don't need to be there," Kaylee protested. "I could go try to find the others."

Dovin put his hand on her shoulder. "You are one of the heroes who saved Riviand from drowning. You wielded the Blade of the Phoenix. That will also give the people a boost of confidence."

"Fine," Kaylee said. "But if Claret and Mateo are getting tortured or something, it's all on you."

Dovin smiled. "That's fine. Goblins aren't much on torture. I'm not saying they are enjoying their stay, but I wouldn't worry too much."

"I swear I'm never making cookies again," Mateo said, glaring at the flour-covered table. "How many cookies can a bunch of goblins eat?"

"A lot, it seems," Claret said, sitting in one of the two chairs in the room. A couple goblins had brought the chairs in yesterday, probably at the urging of Vivi. All they had done for days was make cookie dough, and Mateo's arm was tired from stirring. Claret took turns, but her arms were less used to it than his were.

Claret took a cookie from a plate and took a bite. "I'm just glad Vivi is letting us have some of them, but I've probably overeaten. I'll likely spend all night with a stomachache."

Mateo nodded. He'd eaten his fair share, and he didn't want to make himself sick. A small group of goblins took them to the outhouse four times a day, but there was no way to go when it wasn't the scheduled time. The goblins had wiped something on their arms that stopped them from doing magic when they weren't in their cell. Mateo thought about using brute force on them, but their sharp weapons made him rethink it.

Keys turned in the lock, and Mateo got the mixing bowl ready to hand over to Vivi. She entered with Gregor hopping at her side. Claret stood, then dropped to her knees and held out her hand. Gregor walked over to her, and she softly stroked his head.

"The little bugger has been flying around the castle all day," Vivi said. "No sign of Odie, though."

Mateo handed the bowl to Vivi. If Gregor was here, there was a good chance Odie wasn't far. He wouldn't let Gregor get too far from him unless the bird was lost and came here because he knew this place.

Vivi looked at the dough. "Everyone in the castle is going to be sick. All the goblins are gluttoning themselves on these things until they can't move. I'm tired of baking them, but what can I do? When King Ummi gives a command, I obey."

Mateo grinned. "You don't take me as an obedient servant."

Vivi laughed. "I can be when I try, but you're right. I break the rules often enough. It might be boring, but I don't want you two left with nothing to do. I'm sure this helps pass the time."

"I guess," Mateo said. "It's so boring, though."

"I'm sure your friends will get you out soon," Vivi said. "They have busted people out two times already."

"Can't you help us?" Mateo asked.

She shook her head. "I can't change the charm they placed on the door. I don't know that type of magic. Even if I did, if I helped you, they would know it. Last time, they let it slide when the queen got away. I could have gotten into a lot of trouble, but they thought I'd been overpowered. If it happened again, they would be suspicious."

Gregor jumped up between the bars on the window and flew out.

"We should have tied a note on his leg or something." Mateo looked out the window and watched the puffin fly down the mountain.

Claret stood. "That might go poorly if the goblins found it."

"That Greg is a smart bird," Vivi said. "He's been all over the castle since he came back. I bet he was looking for you."

25

— · —

CHAPTER 25

The ball was well underway and Odie counted down the hours until it would end. He pulled on his white ruffled shirt and scowled. He felt ridiculous in this outfit. Who put ruffles on shirts? He couldn't remember a time he'd ever worn white, and he'd never worn ruffles. He wished Mateo were here so they could look absurd together.

Odie wasn't happy with his outfit, but if the look on Kaylee's face was any sign, she was even more upset than he was. Her long pink dress trailed after her and the sleeves puffed up just enough to make them not sit flat against her arms. The material glistened and drew some attention away from her glare.

The music bounced around his head and he moved around all the dancing couples. He'd managed to avoid dancing himself, but he wondered how long he could do it. If Dovin or Durdessa caught up to him, they would make sure he was paired with someone. There were more women than men, but he didn't want to make an idiot of himself in front of all these people. If Claret were here, he would make an exception.

There was a middle-aged woman with a bright yellow dress and brown ringlets that kept coming near him, but he moved whenever she got too close. He couldn't imagine why she would want to dance with him. It was possible she only wanted to talk.

"This is awful," Kaylee said, coming up beside him. "And we still have hours to go."

"You look nice."

She rolled her eyes. "Purple braids and a pink dress? It's like my five-year-old self picked the colors."

"Someone delivered my clothes this morning," Odie said, glaring at the lace around his sleeve. "I'm not even sure I'm wearing it correctly."

"You look the same as the rest of the men, so you probably don't need to worry."

"Goblins don't have balls. I've never dressed up before."

"I don't mind dressing up, but a different color would have been better."

The ringlet woman was staring at him and walking quickly in his direction. He frowned and turned to Kaylee. "Dance with me?"

She wrinkled her nose. "Dovin made me take lessons, but I'm not very good."

"I can't do it at all. I'll make you look skilled in comparison."

"All right," she said, putting one hand on his shoulder and taking his other in hers. Ringlets frowned and stopped. Odie put his hand at her waist and they moved across the dance floor. He wasn't sure it counted as dancing. He let Kaylee pull him around, and he tried to follow what she was doing.

"There's a woman who keeps trying to get near me," he said. "I'm not sure why."

"You could ask her. Maybe she knows you?"

"No. The only humans I know are the ones I met at the castle."

"Is she the woman in the yellow dress? She's watching us."

"Yes."

"Talk to her. What's it going to hurt?"

Odie sighed. "I don't know. I'm not used to talking to people. It's awkward."

"And it will keep being awkward until you practice. Is your dad here? I haven't seen him."

"He said he doesn't do balls or parties."

"It must be weird having a dad all of a sudden. I mean, one who isn't a goblin."

"Yeah, I don't know how to act around him. He hated me until he found out who I was."

"I think he hated everyone. He's been through a lot."

"I guess." Odie didn't want to make an effort with Arving. He wasn't anything like Odie had always hoped.

Odie caught sight of the woman in yellow. "There's something strange about that woman. When I was younger, I used to get glimpses of a woman. She would hide and watch me from the trees or behind a rock. Whenever I saw her, she ran off. She looked similar to that woman."

"Do you think it's her?"

"Perhaps. I've seen her a few times in the last year, but not as often as when I was younger. I used to get scared at night, wondering what she was doing."

Kaylee stopped dancing and dropped her hands. "Could she be your mother?"

Odie laughed. "My mother? Why would she watch me from the trees?"

"What if she lost you and then by the time she knew where you were, the goblins had you? Maybe she didn't know what to do?"

Odie's heart began pounding, and he looked around. The woman was still watching him, a slight frown on her face. What if it was true? It seemed far-fetched, but something inside Odie told him it was true. "Where's Dovin? He would know. So would Durdessa."

Kaylee looked around, then pointed. They were dancing across the room from them. He didn't want to bother them.

"Go talk to her," Kaylee urged. "What's it going to hurt?"

Odie swallowed and made his way through the crowd. The woman straightened and waited for him to approach. "Hello," he said.

She gave him a slight smile. "Hello."

"I'm Odie. I suppose you know that. Who are you? I've seen you before. You used to spy on me in the forest."

She looked down at the floor. "I promised I wouldn't tell."

Odie tried not to fidget. "You're my mother, aren't you?"

She looked up with wide eyes. "How did you know?"

"I guessed."

Tears spilled out of her eyes and Odie shifted from one foot to the other. She wrapped Odie in a hug and he patted her awkwardly on the back. She only came to his shoulder. He looked around for help, but Kaylee only smiled at him. The woman let him go and wiped her eyes.

"I'm sorry. King Ummi told me to stay away, and I've tried."

Odie frowned. "King Ummi knew?"

She nodded. "You and I fell through Mermaid's Demise. I woke up near the lake and I couldn't find you. I searched for days. There was no sign of you. I thought you were dead, so I started doing odd jobs for people to survive. One day, I overheard someone speak of a boy who lived with the goblins. They said he'd come from the upper continent."

"And you knew it was me?"

"I suspected. I went to the goblin king, and I saw you. It had been two years, but I recognized you. King Ummi told me they would care for you and they didn't want me interfering. You appeared happy, and I had no way to care for you. I stayed close and found you played in the forest quite often. That's why I watched you. I almost didn't recognize you today in your white shirt."

"Yeah, I didn't choose it."

"Rumors said that you were living here at the castle. When I heard about the ball, I used all my savings to get this dress so I could come see you."

"You never saw Durdessa?"

She frowned. "Durdessa is here? In Riviand?"

Odie nodded. "She's Queen Claret's advisor."

"How did she get here? When she was a mermaid?"

"Yes."

"Where is she?"

Odie looked around. "She's dancing somewhere with Dovin."

"Dovin is here as well?" She put a hand to her chest. "I can't believe they're here."

"Dovin only came a few months ago. He helped save Riviand when the goblins stole the Blade of the Phoenix."

Her brow furrowed. "I thought that was done by children."

"Dovin led them."

"And you know he is your uncle?"

"Yes."

"How?" She looked like she might pass out.

"Let's go into the hallway," he said, taking her arm and leading her from the ballroom. The air was less stuffy in the hall. "I didn't know Dovin and Durdessa were my aunt and uncle until just recently. It was my ring."

"They hadn't ever seen it before. We had only just gotten it for you a week before we ended up here."

Odie wasn't sure how much she could take. She was trembling and an occasional tear still fell. "They didn't recognize it. Someone else did."

"Who?"

Odie took her hand and led her down the hallway and up the large red-carpeted staircase. He went to Arving's door and knocked.

"What?" Arving growled from the other side.

She put her hands over her mouth. "It's impossible." She took a deep breath and began banging on the door. "Arving! Open the door!"

There was silence on the other side, and then the door opened a crack. Arving peeked out and his eyes went wide. "Neva?" He pushed open the door, and she fell into his arms. "How is this possible?" he asked, squeezing her tight. She cried and held on to him.

"I need to go back to the ball," Odie said, unsure how to excuse himself. They either didn't care or didn't hear. Odie hurried back to the dance and went and got a cup of water.

"Is she your mom?" Kaylee asked.

Odie nodded.

"Where is she?"

"I took her to my dad. I thought they could use some time."

"I can't believe you found both of your parents in such a short amount of time."

"Yeah, it's strange. I have a feeling I'm going to like my mom more than my dad."

"Give him a chance."

"I know."

She looked around the room. "Should you tell Dovin?"

"Not yet. He has a lot to do tonight, and I don't think he needs the distraction."

"You're probably right. I don't know what to do or how to act."

"Around your parents? Just act normal. I watched your mom while you were talking. She loves you."

Odie felt funny talking about things like this with Kaylee. It was nice to have a friend who cared. That was something he'd never had before. "She said King Ummi knew about her. Any loyalty I felt to him is gone now. He knew, and he didn't tell me. She's been working for anyone she can just to get by. He could have at least taken care of her."

Kaylee nodded. "I'm sorry. Do you want to leave? I doubt Dovin will notice."

"No, it's fine. I don't have anywhere to go, and I'm not sure I want to think about any of it right now."

Kaylee stifled a yawn from her chair in the ballroom. The room had been transformed fast after the dance. Now there were rows of padded chairs that all faced Dovin. He had been explaining to the room full of people all the problems that might come from Garin and the goblins.

She had to admit Dovin was good. He had already given everyone assignments and taught them how to run an election in their cities. She wouldn't be shocked if most of the people in the room ran and became governors. Dovin had picked them all because they were respected in their towns.

Odie leaned his elbow against the armrest and looked like he might fall asleep. It had been a big day. Even bigger for him. It sounded like things were wrapping up, and Kaylee longed for her bed.

Someone shaking her forced her to open her eyes. She must have fallen asleep. Everyone was gone, except Odie, Dovin, and Durdessa.

"Why don't you go to bed?" Dovin asked.

She yawned. "Did you tell them?" she asked Odie.

He shook his head.

"What is it?" Dovin asked.

"My mom was here," Odie said.

Durdessa frowned. "How can that be?"

Odie quickly filled them in on their reunion. "I took her to see my dad. I haven't seen them since. She was a little emotional."

Dovin pursed his lips. "Should we go talk to them or wait?"

Durdessa took a deep breath. "Arving and Neva were always on the emotional side. Let's give them space and let them come to us. Perhaps at breakfast."

"And now that the ball is over, we can figure out how to save Mateo and Claret," Kaylee said. "That's top priority."

"I need to go see if Gregor is ready to come back. He can't fly this far. I teleported him near the castle and told him to meet me again when he learned anything."

"So you can teleport?" Kaylee asked.

"Yes, it's easy. I'm not sure what Mateo's hang-up is."

Durdessa smiled and mussed Odie's hair. "You were always like that. You should appreciate it. Some people never
learn to control magic."

Odie's face turned pink, but he looked pleased. "I'll
go check and see if Gregor's there." He disappeared and
Kaylee went to bed. He would probably wake her if Gregor
found anything.

26

— · —

CHAPTER 26

Kaylee rushed down to breakfast the next day to find she'd slept in. Everyone was eating. Odie was sitting by his mom. She kept turning and patting his hand. He looked uncomfortable, like he didn't know how to react. Arving was smiling and telling stories about when Odie was little. Durdessa and Dovin were both listening attentively, even though they probably already knew the stories. Arving looked like an entirely different person.

Kaylee sat on the other side of Odie and took a bite of room-temperature eggs. Everyone seemed so happy and she understood why, but she felt like they were all forgetting Mateo and Claret. Odie actually looked more nervous than happy, but she could tell he was pleased to be by his mom.

He leaned toward her. "Gregor found them," he said quietly. "They're in a room in the castle. It has bars on the door and windows. They must have just installed them because I've never seen it. Gregor showed me his memories, but he was confused, so I can't tell exactly where it is. They were safe and didn't look any worse for wear."

Kaylee nodded with relief. "That's good to hear, so can we find them?"

"It still won't be easy, but now we know we can look for a door with bars."

"What are you talking about?" Arving asked. "I hope you aren't thinking of going to the goblin castle."

Odie shrugged. "We've got to save our friends."

"And we will," Dovin said. "Don't worry."

Kaylee narrowed her eyes. "I worry."

"You don't have your ring anymore," Neva said, looking at Odie's hand. "You always wore it when you were in the woods."

Odie took a sip of water. "Oh. Right. Queen Claret has it."

Neva frowned and fiddled with her braid. "The queen has it? Why? Did she force you to give it to her? I've heard she's a kind ruler."

Odie's face turned red, and Kaylee took a drink to hide her smile.

"I... uh, I let her take it."

Arving frowned. "I wondered about that. She had it on a chain around her neck. What did she want it for?"

Neva looked thoughtful. "Maybe she wanted to study it. There aren't a lot of things that can block magic."

Odie looked like he would be happy to have the floor open up and pull him under.

Dovin chuckled. "I think Odie chose to give the ring to Claret. She didn't ask for it."

"But why?" Neva asked, not getting the hints.

Durdessa put her fork on her plate. "Odie and Claret... are good friends."

If Odie's face was red before, it was nothing compared to now.

Kaylee snorted and covered her mouth, trying to hold in a laugh. Everyone turned to look at her, and that made her giggle. "I'm sorry," she said. "I think you're going to have to be a little less vague."

"I think Kaylee and I should go to the goblins' castle with the invisibility potion and try to find the others," Odie said, trying to change the subject.

Kaylee dropped her fork. "Really?" She could tell from the look on his face that he hadn't meant it. He just wanted the topic to move off him and Claret.

"Wait..." Arving said. "Are you and the queen involved? Is that what you were all trying to say?"

Dovin laughed. "I knew Arving would catch up eventually."

"Really?" Neva said, beaming at Odie. "You and the queen? Tell us everything."

"There's nothing to tell," Odie muttered.

Kaylee smiled. Or nothing he wanted to tell.

"So when do we leave?" she asked.

"I don't think it's a good idea," Dovin said.

Kaylee frowned. "Do you have a better one?"

"Not yet, but I should be the one to go."

Odie scratched his head. "We can't stay invisible for long. It might be better if I go alone so we don't waste as much of the potion. I'm the best one to go because I know my way around."

"All right," Kaylee said. She didn't like it, but he was right. "But if you aren't back in a day, I'm going to come looking for you."

"This sounds dangerous," Neva said. "I don't want to lose you right when I finally get to be with you."

"I'll be fine. I have a few tricks up my sleeves." He patted his arm and Kaylee heard glass softly hit together. She shook her head. It literally was up his sleeves.

Odie drank the invisibility solution, then ran up the steps of the goblin castle. He didn't know how long he would be invisible and he didn't want to take any chances. He walked past the guards and opened the door, slipping in. The guards pushed the door shut behind him. They must have thought a breeze blew it open.

It would make the most sense to put prisoners up high, and from the images Gregor had shown him, he knew they were in a room looking out over the goblin village. He ran to the staircase, doing his best to make as little noise as possible. He rarely went to the top floor of the castle because there was nothing but a bunch of dirty rooms and there were a lot of stairs. By the time he was at the top floor, his legs were tingling.

He looked down one hall and then another. Rooms lined both sides of the halls, but none of them had bars. He went down a floor and rushed past all the black doors. He skidded to a stop when a door with bars at the top came into view. This had to be it, and it hadn't taken him long at all to find it.

He looked in the window and saw Claret and Mateo putting things in a bowl.

"Hey!" he yelled in a whisper.

They both jerked up and looked at the door.

"It's Odie," he said. "I'm going to get you out. Do you know what they're using to keep you in?"

Claret and Mateo came to the door and tried to see him through the window.

"I'm invisible."

Mateo nodded. "There's something going across the door. We can't leave even if the door's open."

"Hmm." Odie touched the door. There wasn't anything he could feel. "Any chance you know where the keys are?"

"Nope. Vivi probably has some. She comes the most."

Claret squinted at him. "I can see your outline."

Odie's mouth turned down. "That's not good. It lasted a lot longer last time. I'm going to run to the kitchen and get the keys, and with luck, I'll be back before I'm visible." He turned and ran, not waiting for an answer. He ran past several goblins, but none of them noticed him. Goblins weren't the most observant creatures.

Once he was in the kitchen, he hurried to the place Vivi kept her keys. The keyring was going to make a lot of noise if he wasn't careful. He tucked it into his pocket and began the long trek back up the stairs.

"I'm back," he said. He tried one key after another. "Why does Vivi need this many keys?"

"Maybe there are a lot of prisoners she takes food to," Claret said.

"I doubt it. As far as I know, you're the only ones." The next key went in but wouldn't turn.

"I can make you out now," Claret said, "but you are see-through."

"And I would love to know how you do that," Garin said from behind. Odie spun around and Garin punched him in the face. He fell into the door and Claret screamed. Odie narrowed his eyes and jumped up, punching as hard as he could. Garin caught his first and pushed him back, a small smile at the edges of his mouth.

"Let them go," Odie said with as much authority as he could muster.

"No, it's not the time. Would you like to join them or have a room for yourself?"

Odie dove at him and fell to the floor when Garin stepped to the side. Odie glared up and kicked him in the knee, then jumped to his feet. Garin hadn't been expecting that, and he'd fallen against the wall. He frowned and waved his hand in the air. The door unlocked and opened, then he pointed his arms at Odie and moved them quickly. Odie flew across the hall, into the room, and smashed against the far wall. He crumpled to the floor and ground his teeth to keep from screaming. The door slammed shut behind him.

Claret ran to his side and kneeled by him. His head throbbed and his right shoulder didn't feel normal.

"Are you alright?" Claret asked, gently touching his cheek.

"I'll be fine," he lied. "I can't believe I failed that badly."

"Kaylee isn't here, is she?" Mateo asked, helping him sit up.

"No. She wanted to come, but I didn't let her. She'll probably show up, though. It's been driving her crazy that Dovin hasn't had the guards storm the castle."

"That wouldn't be good," Claret said.

"I didn't think so, but I'm changing my mind. The goblins aren't guarding like they should be. I got in here without a problem."

Mateo raised his eyebrow. "Oh, yeah?"

Odie sighed. "I got in, just not out."

"We need to make some sort of pact," Mateo said. "If anyone can get out, they get out. The fewer of us here, the better, and I'm not sure how easy it will be for us all to escape at once. If you get a chance, take it."

Claret agreed to Mateo's pact, but she doubted she would be the one able to escape. She hoped Odie's head was all right. He'd hit the wall hard and she could tell he was in pain and trying to hold it in. She wasn't happy Odie had been captured, but she was glad to see him. He scooted himself back against a wall and closed his eyes.

She glanced at Mateo, but he didn't seem concerned. He stuck an entire cookie in his mouth and chewed. Claret sat next to Odie and touched his arm. He opened his eyes and gave her a half smile, but she knew he was forcing it.

"Are you all right?"

"I'll be fine. I'm a little dizzy, but it'll pass."

"Did you go to the ball?"

"Yes."

"How was it?"

"Long. But I met someone."

Claret sat up tall and prepared herself to get her heart broken. "Oh?"

"My mom was there. She's still alive."

Claret's eyes opened wide. "Whoa. That's huge. What's she like?"

"She seems nice. She's been living in the forest and doing odd jobs all these years. You should see Arving. He's like a different person. I think they're going to be happy now that they're back together."

She smiled. "That's good."

"Did you dance with anyone?" Mateo asked. "I can't picture you dancing."

He laughed softly. "You should have seen me. I was wearing the most horrid white lacey shirt. It even had ruffles."

Mateo grinned. "I wish I'd seen it."

"I wish you had been there so you would have had to wear one as well."

Claret tilted her head. "What's wrong with a white shirt with lace?"

"It's not my style, I guess."

Mateo grinned. "You didn't answer my question. Did you dance?"

"Only once."

"With who?"

Claret wanted to tell Mateo to be quiet. She didn't want to hear about Odie dancing with anyone else.

"Kaylee. Don't punch me."

Mateo grinned. "I won't. I'm maturing."

Claret leaned her head against Odie's shoulder. "Did Dovin talk to the people he wanted to? Are the elections all set?"

"Yes. I think they will be. Dovin wants to train all the people who get elected."

"I hope that means he's going to stay in Riviand for a long time. I'm going to be lost when he leaves, and even more when Durdessa goes. She's gotten me through a lot and she makes sure I don't make poor decisions."

"You'll be fine without her. I believe in you."

Claret smiled and kissed Odie's cheek. "Thank you."

Mateo groaned. "I hope you guys aren't going to spend all your time kissing and stuff while we're here. I'm not sure I can take that."

Claret smiled and snuggled in closer to Odie, and he put his arm over her shoulders. She wouldn't think of kissing him in front of Mateo, but it lifted her heart to know he was here.

"What's going on with you and Kaylee?" Odie teased. "I feel like something has changed between the two of you, and she was ready to come and take on all the goblins by herself to get you out. The only reason she hasn't is because she can't get anyone to teleport her here."

Mateo's eyes widened, then narrowed all in a moment. "Kaylee has certain plans about what she wants from life, and I don't think I fit into them."

"So nothing happened between you?" Odie asked. Claret kept her mouth shut. She wouldn't tell anything Kaylee had confided.

"Well, there's always the lip balm," he said with a grin. He pulled it from his pocket and turned it in his hand.

"I thought you didn't use stuff like that," Odie said.

"Not usually, but Kaylee insisted."

Claret smiled since she knew the story.

"She smeared it all over my lips... with hers. Best moment of my entire life."

Odie laughed, then cringed and touched his head. "I guess that's something. It seems out of character for Kaylee."

Mateo nodded, still fiddling with the lip balm. "I think she likes me but doesn't want to. Hopefully, something will happen, but who knows? I can't ask her to choose me over her life plans, can I?"

Claret's mouth turned down. "Would you choose her over your life plans?"

Mateo sat on the chair backward. "What do you mean?"

"Your plans are in this world. Hers are on Earth. That is the biggest thing that might keep you apart. Would you be willing to live on Earth for her?"

Mateo leaned forward on the chair and frowned. "I don't like living on Earth."

"If you both feel so strongly about where you have to live, then you might as well give up now. I would give up my throne and everything I had if it was the only way I could be with... the person I love."

She felt her cheeks turn pink. She didn't want to say outright that she would do it for Odie, but she would. He wouldn't ask her to, but she knew her life would be better if she followed her heart.

Mateo looked like he wanted to argue but thought better of it. He rested his chin on the top of the chair and sighed.

27

— · —

CHAPTER 27

Kaylee didn't like to lie, and she really didn't want to lie to Dovin, but she couldn't think of any other way to get where she wanted. She wasn't telling a complete lie. She was just leaving things out. It was still a deception, but she needed to do this. They stood inside the cave on the goblin mountain and she held on to him as he teleported them to Basura. He took them to the front of Graham's business.

"I don't see why you have to talk to Graham right now," Dovin said.

Kaylee shrugged and knocked on the door. Her friends weren't going to be saved if she waited for it to happen. The door opened and a pretty woman with long red hair opened the door. Kaylee was pretty sure she was the same girl Graham had brought to her house years ago.

She looked from Kaylee to Dovin and smiled. "Hi, Professor Dovin. And you must be Kaylee," she said. "It's been a while."

Kaylee nodded.

"Come in. Graham isn't here, but he should be back soon." They followed her into a room that was full of shelves covered in different vials. There was an empty desk, and in one corner, a large cushion, almost like an oversized bean bag.

Dovin looked thoughtful. "I have a few things I want to check while I'm here. I'll meet you in an hour. All right?"

"Okay," Kaylee said. Dovin went back out and shut the door. Kaylee looked at the beautiful girl and tilted her head. "Are you one of the people Graham brought to my house a few years ago?"

She nodded. "I'm Wren."

"Are you Graham's girlfriend?"

She smiled and nodded.

"Do you know how to teleport? I need to go see Sen."

Wren's smile faded. "Right now?"

"Yes."

"Why didn't you have Professor Dovin take you?"

Kaylee ducked her head slightly. "Because if he knows why I want to see him, he won't take me."

Wren studied her carefully. "Why do you want to see him? I'm sorry to pry, but if you want my help, I need to know."

"His brother's in trouble. No one will do anything, but I bet Sen will."

Wren nodded. "Probably. Why won't Dovin help?"

"He thinks we should wait, but the longer we wait, the more likely he'll get hurt."

Wren nodded. "I'll take you to the castle, but you need to hurry. Dovin said he'll be back in an hour and I don't want him to get mad at me."

"I'll hurry."

"Have Sen bring you back here."

Kaylee frowned. "Wait, did you say castle? Why is Mateo's brother at a castle?"

Wren smiled. "Mateo didn't tell you? Sen is married to the Queen of the Northern Kingdom."

Kaylee blinked twice. "That seems like something that would come up in conversation."

She smiled. "I don't know Mateo well, but Sen doesn't talk a lot. If Mateo is like Sen, I'm not surprised he didn't mention it."

"No, Mateo talks a lot."

"Well, we don't have a lot of time. I'll take you now." She held out her hand and Kaylee took it. Before she could say anything, they were inside a large throne room. The golden throne was empty, and a guard stood by the door. He looked surprised but not worried when he saw Wren.

"Can you tell Sen that there's someone here to see him?" Wren asked.

The guard nodded and stuck his head out the door and said something to a guard on the outside.

"I'll come back in a half-hour if Sen doesn't bring you back." Wren smiled at her and disappeared.

Kaylee waited for what seemed like an hour, but it was probably only ten minutes. The door opened and a man in a fancy blue tunic came into the room. He looked a lot like Mateo, just a little older.

"Are you looking for me?" he asked.

Kaylee nodded. "I'm Kaylee. I'm from Earth." She didn't know why she added the last part. "I've been in Riviand the last few months with Mateo."

He raised his brow. "My parents told me Mateo was down there. It's hard to believe it actually exists."

She nodded again. "I came here to get help. Mateo was captured by goblins, and I don't know what to do. I thought you might help me."

Sen frowned. "Captured by goblins? My mom said Dovin was with him."

"Yes, but Dovin's moving too slow. He keeps telling me to wait, but I think we need to save him now."

"Is he the only one?"

"No. They also have the Queen of Riviand and another friend."

"Does Dovin know you're here?"

"He knows I'm in Basura but not that I'm talking to you. He thinks I'm with Wren, but she brought me here. I'm not magic. Graham's my cousin." She didn't know why she was spitting out useless facts.

He rubbed his chin. "I need to talk to my wife first."

Kaylee nodded. "Thank you. I'm sorry to barge in like this. I've just been nervous about the goblins and there's this guy, Garin. He's trying to control the goblins."

Sen's eyes narrowed. "Garin? Blond man with strange orangish eyes?"

Kaylee nodded.

"I knew he wasn't dead," Sen muttered under his breath. "I saw him jump into the ocean and swim toward

Mermaid's Demise. Let me tell my wife and then I'll be back." He turned and jogged from the room.

Kaylee felt relieved. Sen looked and sounded like someone who was going to get things done. She waited for a few minutes, and he returned with a sword at his waist and a small brown pack.

"Can you take us to Graham's place?"

He nodded and grabbed her hand. When they arrived, Wren was sitting at the desk, writing something.

She looked up and smiled. "Oh good. You beat Professor Dovin. I didn't want to face him without you. Hey, Sen."

He nodded.

The door opened, and Dovin came in carrying a basket of rolls. He looked at Sen and frowned.

"Sen's coming to help us," Kaylee said.

Dovin shook his head. "I should have known you were up to something."

Sen frowned. "You should have come for me when Mateo was taken."

"We're working on it."

"I'm coming."

"Fine," Dovin said. "I've learned not to argue with certain people."

Sen smiled.

"Do you want the rest of us to come?" Wren asked. "Graham should be here any minute, and I could get Tal and Ming Li."

Dovin shook his head. "First, I think we should try something more subtle. If we end up needing help, I'll come for you."

"All right. Good luck."

"Claret should try to get out of here," Mateo said. "She has more chance than we do."

Claret stared at the wall as she listened to Mateo and Odie talk. She had just woken up and was trying to go back to sleep until she started listening to them.

"More chance, how?" Odie asked.

"Claret is a queen. The goblins probably don't expect her to try anything without us. If she can get the goblins to take her outside, she could probably outrun them."

"She's not terribly fast," Odie protested. "I mean, most goblins aren't either, but they have magic."

Claret frowned. She was the obvious choice to escape because she was weaker than the other two. That's what they were saying. No one expected her to have a spine.

"I still think it would be possible. They won't guard her the same as they do when they take us all out."

She rolled over and frowned at them. Odie was on a chair and Mateo was looking out the window. "I'm not as useless as you think."

Mateo rolled his eyes. "That's not what I'm saying. You've got more to you than people might expect. You could surprise them because they don't know what you can do."

"That's right," Odie said. "You took out that vorcraw at Dragon's Cove. That has to be harder than outwitting a goblin."

She sat up and looked thoughtful. "I could try, but how would it help? You two would still be here."

"Yes, but the goblins wouldn't have the leverage of having the queen," Mateo explained.

"Fine. What should I do?"

"You need to get them to take you out without us. Then I think you have to improvise."

She looked at her arms. "I can't do magic with this stuff on me."

"No, but you might have a chance to slip away or grab something and knock them out."

Odie frowned. "It might be too dangerous."

"I can do it. Should I yell for someone?"

Mateo nodded. "Tell them you need the outhouse and it's an emergency."

Claret nodded and felt her face get warm. She was raised to not talk about things like the outhouse.

She looked out the small window on the door and yelled. "Hey! Hello? Is anyone there?" No one came. She spent the next ten minutes trying to get someone's attention. When she was about to give up, Vivi came into view, carrying the breakfast tray. She entered and set it on the table.

She turned to Claret. "What's with all the yelling? The guard down the hall said you're screaming and bothering him."

Claret crossed her arms. "I knew someone could hear me. I need to use the outhouse. It's an emergency."

"I'll let someone know." Vivi shuffled off, and Claret sighed.

"If I get out, I'm coming back with guards and getting you out."

"Just be careful," Odie said. Claret threw her arms around him and hugged him tight. She ignored Mateo's snort. She didn't know how long it would be before she saw them again.

The door opened, and a goblin ran a finger in an odd pattern over the doorframe. They did this almost every time they took the prisoners out. It must have something to do with the spell that kept them in.

"The queen can come," he said.

She stepped out of the room and glanced back at Odie. He gave her a small smile. Mateo put both of his thumbs in the air. She wasn't sure why. It must be some type of upper world thing.

There was another goblin in the hall. She followed one, and the other walked behind her. Her legs should be getting stronger from going up and down all the stairs several times a day, but it still felt difficult.

They walked through the black halls and out into the sun. Several outhouses stood in a line behind the castle. An enormous pile of boulders stood behind them, but if she hid, that would be the obvious place. Trees grew on the mountain but not in abundance. She couldn't count on them for cover. She'd already tried to rub off whatever was on her arms so she could do magic, but that hadn't come to anything. With no branches lying around, there wasn't anything to use as a weapon. If Kaylee were here, she would think of something.

Claret went into one of the small, smelly outhouses and tried to think. She wrinkled her nose and frowned. There was nothing to use in here. Flies buzzed her, and she swatted them away from her head. The wood planks that made up the outhouse were weak and rotted in some places. They could easily be broken and used as a weapon, but the goblins would hear if she kicked it. She didn't really want to touch it, anyway. She doubted anyone ever cleaned in here.

The longer she stood in the smelly structure, the more unsure she became. The two goblins began talking about whether they should make her come out. She opened the door a crack and saw them in a heated discussion. She pushed the door open just enough and slipped out and around to the back of the outhouse.

"Hey, you gonna live in there?" one goblin yelled.

"Sorry," Claret called. "I think I'm ill. I'm going to vomit!"

"Two more minutes!" one said. They began arguing again, and Claret took the opportunity to run behind the boulders. She sat on the ground and breathed deeply. Her heart was pounding so loud she could feel it in her head. She looked farther up the mountain. It was steep. She needed to go down, but that wasn't an option. She would be seen for sure and that was where they would search for her.

The goblins would be checking the outhouse at any moment, so she turned and ran up the mountain as fast as she could. Her feet kept slipping on the loose dirt, but she didn't let that stop her. If the goblins came around the outhouse, they would see her. She prayed they would keep arguing and that they would be too nervous to actually open the outhouse door.

She changed her course slightly when she spotted a clump of trees. She ran into their cover and kept going. Her heart was pounding, and she was sweating. She grabbed the only tree branch she could see to use as a weapon. It wasn't as thick as she would like, but it was better than nothing. Even if she wasn't found, she didn't know what she would do. Being up high on the mountain was hardly liberating and she would eventually have to make her way down. It might be better to go around the back side where the goblins didn't live and climb down there.

She must be missed by now. Even tolerant goblins wouldn't leave her in the outhouse for this long. There was a cave up ahead, so she made that her goal. Its dark entrance seemed to be the most welcoming thing she could see at the moment. A cave would be an obvious place to look, but with luck, they would assume she snuck past them and went down the mountain.

She glanced over her shoulder and saw no sign of the goblins. She got to the cave and went inside and scanned it for a place to hide. It was small and didn't have any crevices she would fit in. She hoped with everything in her that the goblins would go down.

The cave felt dark and closed in and made her nervous. She tried to quiet her breathing, but running up here had been exhausting. She kept her hold on her branch. It was only a little better than having nothing. It had leaves all over it and several smaller branches protruding from it.

"I'll check the cave!" a voice yelled.

Claret's heart stopped, and she leaned against the side of the cave and held her branch up, ready to swing.

The goblin stepped into the cave and Claret swung with everything in her, connecting with the goblin. He stumbled back and fell to the ground. She smacked him over and over while he tried to cover his face. He rolled backward and stood on his feet.

"That was foolish," he said, wiping blood from the corner of his mouth. "All you have done is ensure you are more carefully guarded." He wiped more blood from his lip and Claret ran at him and tried to swing her branch again. He held up his hand, and the branch was yanked from her hand and hovered in the air. She ignored the pulsing pain in her hand. It was probably bleeding from how hard the branch had been ripped away from her, but she didn't have time for that.

Claret kicked the goblin, and he fell back. She leaped forward before he could react and sat on him before he could do any more magic. She heard the branch fall behind her, and she grabbed the goblin's hands and held them down. Goblins were small but supposedly fierce, so she wasn't giving him a chance to act.

A small popping sound behind her made her turn her head. Dovin, Kaylee, and a man she didn't know stood there, staring at her with their eyes bulging.

Dovin let out a small laugh and waved his arms. The goblin went stiff beneath her. She got up to her feet and took a shaky breath. The goblin looked frozen. Only his eyes were moving. Kaylee stepped forward and wrapped her in a hug.

"There's still another one out there," Claret said. "I'm sure he'll be in here any minute."

Dovin stuck his head out of the cave. "There he is." He waved his arms again. "He's taken care of."

Kaylee shook her head. "If you can do things like that, you should be able to save everyone faster."

Dovin tilted his head. "Goblins are obnoxious, but not much of a threat in small numbers. Witches and sorcerers, on the other hand, are not to be taken lightly."

Kaylee looked around the cave. "Where are Mateo and Odie?"

"Still locked in the castle. They told me to escape."

"It's fortunate we came at just this time," Dovin said. "Let's go back to your castle."

Claret nodded and grabbed Dovin's cape. The others did the same. She hoped Garin wouldn't punish the others for her escape.

28

CHAPTER 28

Odie sat at the table, his leg jiggling up and down. "Do you think she got away?"

Mateo had been watching out the window for the last hour. "I don't know. If she did, she didn't come down this way. She must have gone around the other side of the mountain or gone up."

"What if they caught her?"

Mateo shrugged. "Something must have happened. She's been gone too long, so either she succeeded or they caught her and put her somewhere else."

"This was stupid. We shouldn't have had her do it."

"But what if she escaped?"

Footsteps coming down the hall quieted them. The door opened, and Garin and Isadora entered. Garin looked serious, and Isadora was smiling.

"We've come to get..." Garin trailed off and looked around the room. "Where's the queen?"

Odie shrugged. "She wasn't feeling well, so some of the goblins took her out back."

Garin nodded. "We'll wait for her to return."

Isadora stood next to Mateo and looked out the window. "It's quite the view, isn't it?"

Mateo glared at her. She smiled and brushed her hand over her bright green dress.

Odie's mind was racing. Magic couldn't be performed inside the room. That must also apply to Garin and Isadora. He studied them both and wondered if he and Mateo could take them in a fistfight. He was sure Isadora would fight dirty, but she looked like she spent more time on her perfect hair than building muscles. If it all came down to it, he could probably take her. Garin looked strong, and he had a sword. If there was a fight, Garin and Mateo were probably evenly matched, except for the sword.

Garin's cool smile landed on Odie. "I can tell what you are thinking, and you wouldn't win."

Odie glared at him and frowned.

Isadora leaned against the wall and sighed. "How long do we wait? There are so many things I would rather be doing."

Garin crossed his arms. "I've given the queen longer than I should have to make a decision. It's time she agreed to something so we can get things in motion."

Isadora walked up to Garin and cupped his cheek in her hand. "I don't see how you could even consider marrying that girl. It's one wasted step in our plan to rule."

Garin took a step away from her. "The people love Claret. It will be harder to have their loyalty if we get rid of her."

"She chooses Odie anyway," Mateo said. "She already told me."

Odie frowned and scratched his head. "Chooses me for what?"

"To marry."

Odie's eyes went wide, and Isadora laughed.

"I'm confused," Odie admitted.

Garin looked amused. "I assumed she would, and that works just fine with my plans. Claret and Odious will marry. It will signal an alliance between the goblins and the people of Riviand. To keep peace, I will be their advisor. If they don't like that, they can be kept out of the way with only a few public appearances to keep the people happy. I prefer working in the shadows to being in the public eye, so this is perfect."

Odie shook his head. He couldn't understand Garin's game.

"You don't want to be king?" Isadora asked Garin.

"I want money and power but not the tedious parts of running a kingdom. I don't need the title of king to get what I want."

"Claret will not be your puppet," Odie said.

Garin's orange eyes sparkled. "She will if I keep the rest of her friends locked up. If we have to kill one off to let her know we are serious, so be it."

Isadora looked irritated. She didn't like Garin's plan. "I thought the two of us would eventually marry and rule Riviand."

Garin ignored her. "Something is wrong. The queen should be back." He turned and left the room with a swish of his cape. Isadora glared at them and followed. The door slammed behind them.

"I thought you were going to attack Isadora," Mateo said. "You looked ready to pounce."

Odie shrugged. "I thought about it, but I wasn't sure you could take Garin."

Mateo frowned. "I think I could, but not if he had time to draw his sword." He glanced out the window. "When they first put me in here, there were goblins patrolling the ground every fifteen minutes. Now it's about every five. I'm surprised there aren't guards standing all around the castle."

"Most people don't bother goblins, so they aren't as careful as they should be. I think someone's coming," Odie said. Someone fiddled with the keys and then opened the door. Isadora entered and shut the door behind her.

"It seems your little queen has escaped and left the two of you to rot."

Odie released a sigh of relief.

"Now let's talk about the way things are actually going to go," she said. "Garin is delusional if he thinks I'll be happy as a person who works behind the scenes. I will be Queen of Riviand, and Garin will be king, whether he wants to be or not. All you get to choose is whether or not I kill you before it happens."

"I'd prefer not," Mateo said.

"Then you will be obedient and cooperate. I might allow Garin to force the queen to marry Odious, but they will rule the goblins and not Riviand. Garin can manipulate how he sees fit, but Riviand will not be influenced by you."

"You seem to forget that Riviand isn't going down without a fight," Mateo said. "And they are better prepared for war than you."

"Claret won't allow her people to go to war if she can help it."

Odie stood, and before he could talk himself out of it, he grabbed his wooden chair and swung it at Isadora. It hit her on the shoulder and knocked her to the ground.

She looked up and laughed. "What do you want to accomplish here? You think you can defeat me?"

"You are such a stereotypical villain," Mateo said, pulling her to her feet. "It's almost sad. I can predict the next stupid sentence you are going to say. Odie, rip pieces from the bottom of her dress so we can tie her up."

Odie raised his brows. How was he supposed to do that with no knife? He didn't have anything useful since the goblins had taken everything from his pockets soon after he arrived.

Mateo put his arms around Isadora so she couldn't move her arms. She threw her head back, hitting his nose. He released her and stumbled back. Odie charged her, pushing her back into the wall with his shoulder. She tried to bite him but missed.

"You two are idiots," she said through clenched teeth. "Even if you tie me up, what then?"

Odie held her arms down and stayed away from her head.

"Then Garin lets us go so we don't hurt you."

She laughed. "If you know typical villains, as you say, then you better think this through. Garin will not give up what he wants to save me. That isn't how people like us work. In his mind, everyone is dispensable."

"And you like hanging around people like that?" Mateo asked. "People who are only loyal if it suits their purposes?"

"It's the only way to get ahead."

Mateo ripped a long strip from the bottom of his own tunic, and Odie held her hands behind her while Mateo tied them.

"I'm only allowing you to do this so you can see how pointless it is," she said.

Mateo ripped off another piece and tied it around her ankles.

"Sit," Mateo said.

Isadora tossed her brown hair over her shoulder and sat carefully against the wall, glaring at both of them.

"You can't rely on magic in here," Odie said.

Mateo grinned. "Yeah, it's too bad that it's your only talent."

Garin's face appeared in the door window. His eyes narrowed. "Isadora, what are you doing?"

"Baking cake," she said sarcastically. "What do you think? Get me out of here."

Garin frowned and then smiled. "I have more important matters to attend to. The queen can't be far. I'll be back for you later. Enjoy the company." His footsteps retreated, and Isadora's face turned the color of a tomato.

"Don't leave me here!" she yelled. "Garin! Get back here!"

Odie grinned. "And you want to marry him?"

She scowled.

Mateo smirked. "Don't worry. We'll keep you company. Hey, Odie, you want me to teach you a really annoying song?"

Odie smiled. "Sure."

Kaylee wanted to scream. She thought once Sen came, they would storm the goblin castle and save the others. It turned out Sen was a careful thinker, and he wanted them to have a plan before they acted. Claret had taken a bath and was resting. Her hands had been bloody and raw from having a tree branch ripped from them.

Kaylee sat outside on the castle steps, thinking about how unfair it all was. She pulled her cloak tighter. The seasons were changing, and it was getting cold. Claret told them they hadn't been hurt or mistreated aside from being locked up, but Kaylee still wanted to run over and fight off all the goblins. Sitting here wasn't helping anything. She walked down the city street past all the small shops. She took a key from her pocket and unlocked the bakery she had planned to start with Mateo.

Everything was dusty. They'd cleaned it once but then neglected it. They didn't have time for hobbies. She looked at the sign they made. *Kaylee's Snakes and Bakes*. She touched the letters that were carved into the wood. Mateo was right. Having a business with animals and food wasn't a good idea. She'd loved the idea of it, so she hadn't taken time to give it enough thought.

Movement from the corner of her eye made her turn to face the window. Someone had been looking in, but they ran when she spotted them. Frowning, she rushed out the door just as someone disappeared around the corner. She raced after them, her cloak flapping behind her. She turned the corner and came face-to-face with Chad.

Kaylee skidded to a stop. "Chad? How did you get down here?"

He shrugged. "I don't know. I woke up, and I was here."

He wore jeans and a blue T-shirt. He was going to stand out here.

Kaylee narrowed her eyes. "That's hard to believe. Even if that happened, why spy on me through the window? Why run?"

His jaw moved from side to side. "I wasn't sure it was you."

"How did you find this place?" she asked, pointing at the bakery.

"I saw you walking from the castle."

She took a step forward and poked him in the chest with her pointer finger. "If you followed me, then you knew it was me. Why are you lying?"

He threw his hands up in surrender. "Hey, I was far away. I saw you walking, and I thought it was you, but it was a guess."

Kaylee couldn't figure Chad out, and she didn't want to, but something was up. "You're supposed to be hiding in Basura."

"Do you know how boring that is? I was there with all these people with nothing to do. I mean, if they had TV or video games, it would be one thing, but they don't. Time was hardly moving. I tried playing some weird sport with Mateo's little brothers, but those boys are brutal. I left, then ended up here."

"You can't just end up here. It doesn't work like that. People have been trying to find this place for thousands of years. You don't just wake up one day and you're here."

He walked out from behind the house and looked both ways down the street. "Then how do you explain it? I'm here, so what happened?"

"I don't know. Why don't you tell me?"

Chad opened his mouth, then closed it and a determined glint sparkled in his eyes. He turned and darted off down the street.

"No, you don't," Kaylee muttered, running after him. He was surprisingly fast and Kaylee quickly began falling behind. She touched the Blade of the Phoenix with one hand and frowned. She couldn't zap Chad with it, no matter how much she wanted to. If she wasn't lugging around the sword, she might catch him, but she couldn't leave it behind.

She pulled out the sword and swung it forward, but angled it slightly to the side and past Chad. Blue light flashed from the sword and lightning struck a few feet in front of him. He yelled out in surprise and changed direction. She kept the sword in her hand as she ran. She didn't want to hurt him, so she didn't use the sword again.

He ran past all the shops and into an alleyway. It was a dead end. She walked toward him, frowning.

Chad breathed loudly and bent over to catch his breath. "What are you going to do? Stab me?"

"Not unless I have to. Go back to the castle. I'll follow you."

He looked around for an escape.

"If you weren't up to something, you wouldn't be running."

"Who made you the police?"

Her eyes narrowed.

A bright silver portal opened behind Chad and he jumped through. Kaylee frowned. Chad couldn't do magic. She jumped after him, and when she landed, she was standing in front of Isadora's home.

He looked at her and grinned. "She said you would follow me, but I didn't believe her."

"You're working with Isadora?" Kaylee spat. "Even you should have higher standards."

"I have high standards. That's why I chose you."

Kaylee wanted to make fake barfing sounds, but that would be immature. "Well, I don't choose you."

"You don't have a choice. Isadora is powerful, and she's going to help me."

"I have a choice. Do you really want to be with someone who doesn't like you? It's pathetic."

He grinned. "Isadora has a love potion. She's going to give it to me now that I brought you to her."

Kaylee tilted her head. "Think this through, Chad. You're a smart guy. What was wrong with everything you just said?"

Chad just squinted at her.

"Isadora wants me. You brought me to her. She gives me a love potion and then what? Then she has me, not you. She's going to lock me up, and if you're lucky, use you as her little messenger boy."

"No. She wants you out of the way, but she doesn't care if you're hurt or not. We'll stay together in her basement. You won't even want to leave because you'll be so in love with me."

"A spell isn't real. I won't really love you. Isn't that hollow? And why do you want to be with me, anyway? We've never gotten along."

"I've been in love with you since seventh grade. Doesn't that mean anything to you?"

Kaylee sighed. "Chad, it's never going to happen. I don't get why you want it to. You drive me crazy, and not in a good way."

"Well, it's going to change. Once you drink the potion, you'll be mine."

Kaylee arched a brow. "Well?"

"Well, what?"

"I was waiting for maniacal laughter."

He scowled.

"What makes you think I'm going to follow you into Isadora's house? I'm not. I'm the one with the sword here."

"Sorry about this," said a voice from behind. Kaylee turned to see Korum. "I can't fail Isadora again. She won't be forgiving." He raised his arms, and Kaylee sheathed her sword against her will. How had he done that?

"Korum? I thought you were a good guy," Kaylee said as her legs began walking to Isadora's house like they had a mind of their own.

"I want to be, but Isadora is terrible to those who betray her."

"So you choose to be a coward?"

He rubbed his head and frowned. "I am."

Chad smiled as he walked next to her.

"I didn't know magic could control people," Kaylee said as she tried to force her legs to obey her.

"I'm half leprechaun," he said. "My magic is more potent than any you have known."

"Then why can't you defy Isadora?"

"She's a witch, she's evil, and she has no morals. I can't fight against that."

"You still get to choose. You are choosing to be a coward and if you obey her, that makes you as bad as she is."

He looked ashamed, but Kaylee's feet kept walking. He led her into the house, this time through the front door. Isadora's house was fancy, with crystal chandeliers and fluffy red carpets. Vases and art filled the hallway. Kaylee would bet it was all stolen.

"This is your last chance, Korum. Make the right choice."

He shook his head sadly. "I have no choice."

29

CHAPTER 29

"Ninety-seven, ninety-eight, ninety-nine, one hundred." Mateo stopped his push-ups and got to his feet. He stretched his arms and then went back down for sit-ups.

"I'm going to kill Garin when I get out of here," Isadora muttered. "It's bad enough being stuck in here without the smell of sweat."

Mateo smirked. "You don't get to be in awesome shape by not sweating."

"I've never seen anyone do these exercises before," Odie said. "I wonder if I should try."

Mateo nodded. "Might as well. We aren't going anywhere. Start small. Just a few a day and work up to it."

"Please don't," Isadora protested. "One smelly little boy is enough."

"Little?" Mateo asked. "I could bench-press you."

She looked confused.

"I think you and Garin need to work on your relationship," Mateo said. "He's left you here for an entire day."

"He's made his last mistake," she said. "He doesn't know my power. Release my hands and feet, and I will end him the next time he enters."

Mateo raised his brow. "Do we look stupid?"

"You really do."

"Ouch."

"I think we'll leave you where you are," Odie said.

"I will need to use the outhouse soon," she said.

The door opened, and Garin entered. "I'll have someone bring a bedpan. We can't have anyone else going out and escaping."

Mateo wrinkled his nose. "A bedpan better not be what I think it is."

"If you don't let me free, I swear I will turn you into a rat and I will feed you to my dragon," Isadora threatened.

Garin grinned. "That might be threatening if you were ever going to get out. I've been thinking about it and I think you are a liability. It's time to sever our alliance, don't you agree?"

Isadora growled. "You need me."

"Why? What have you contributed?"

"More than you'll ever know."

Garin looked at Odie. "I want you to make a sleeping potion. Don't tell me it will take time. I know you stalled last time. I want it tonight."

Odie held up his empty hands. "And how do you want me to do that?"

"Write the ingredients and I'll get them."

"Isn't it great?" Chad asked when they got to the cell they would be staying in. It was the first one after the stairs where the monkeys used to be. It looked completely different. The cell was decorated in pastel colors. It all looked like the set from a TV show with three decorated walls and then an open one. Except this one had bars. There was a kitchen area and a space with a sofa and a chair.

"What's wrong with you?" Kaylee asked. "You want to spend your life as a zoo exhibit? You know people will come in and out and stare at you? Isadora will probably put a plaque out that has your name and says you are a person from an alien planet or something."

Chad crossed his arms. "But I'll be with you."

"So? Don't you want a life?"

"We won't be here forever. Isadora said she'll send us back to Earth after she takes over here."

Kaylee turned to Korum. "Did you give him something? Chad's always been... unique, but this is over the top."

Korum shrugged. "Only something to exaggerate his emotions."

She sighed. "Chad, did you hear that? These aren't your actual feelings."

"They are," Korum said, "just amplified."

"I don't care," Chad said. "Once you take the potion, we're going to be happy."

Korum opened the cell and shooed them in. He took a small tube of red liquid and handed it to Kaylee. "You can take it of your own accord, or I can force you. Believe me when I tell you that won't be pleasant."

Kaylee threw it at the floor. She cringed at the sound of shattering glass. Red liquid ran across the wooden floor.

Korum snapped his fingers. The mess disappeared, and the tube was back in his hand. He handed it to her. "We can do this all day. It's only going to get more frustrating."

Kaylee looked at the red liquid. She was stuck.

"Last chance to do it on your own," Korum said.

Kaylee frowned and thought of throwing it again. She lifted it and opened it. She frowned. Korum was controlling her again. She lifted the tube to her mouth and drank it. The taste of strawberry hit her tongue, and she swallowed. She felt a little dizzy. Korum grabbed her hand and led her to the sofa. She sat down and covered her face with her hands.

"How long does it take to work?" Chad asked.

"It's immediate, but it makes the person a little woozy," Korum said.

Kaylee's heart began pounding. She looked up at Chad. How had she failed to notice how attractive he was before? She frowned. That was the potion talking, not her true feelings. Her eyes narrowed as she fought the urge to throw herself into his arms and kiss him. This was taking away her will, and she hated when people did that.

She stood and slowly walked to Chad.

He smiled at her. "So how do you feel?"

How did she feel? If she wasn't careful, she was going to promise Chad to love him and follow him until she died. How could Korum do this to her? When she was in front of Chad, he leaned in toward her. Her lips wanted to pucker, but she bit the inside of her cheek instead. She pulled her arm back and punched Chad in the face.

Chad stumbled back and put a hand to his eye. "It didn't work!" he exclaimed, glancing over at Korum.

Korum smiled. "Oh, it worked. It's a love potion. It makes the person fall in love with you, but it doesn't change their free will."

"You're lucky I didn't use my sword. It's horrible to do this to someone," Kaylee said, wanting to punch him again or maybe kiss him. It was hard to know for sure. "And just because I feel this way doesn't mean it changes anything between us."

"It will change," Chad said. "Isadora promised."

"And the promise of a witch is something to trust?" She looked at Korum. "Does it last forever?"

"It lasts until you kiss someone you love. Someone who you haven't been manipulated to love."

Chad grinned. "And I know you lied to me when you said you and Mateo were a thing. He was way too pleased when you smeared that lip gloss on him. You'd never done it before, I could tell. So who do you love?"

Kaylee made a fist and took a step toward him.

Korum left the cell and locked it. "Try not to make him bleed. Blood is hard to clean." He went up the stairs. Kaylee stared after him. She unfisted her hand and wiped the sweat from her palm on her pants.

She sat back on the sofa and messaged her forehead. Who did she love? Mateo had filled her mind lately, but did she love him? Right now, all she could picture was Chad. She'd been trying to snuff out any feeling she had for

Mateo, but there was definitely something there. As much as she tried to ignore it, she found herself thinking about him more and more, and now that he was locked up, it was driving her mad. But it didn't seem as urgent anymore.

She frowned. It was still urgent. She was drugged. Her mind wouldn't be right until she kissed someone she loved, and if she wasn't in love with Mateo, she wasn't in love with anyone.

Chad sat on the sofa and put a hand on her shoulder. She looked up at him. He was going to have a black eye. She touched it softly and frowned. "I don't believe in solving problems by hitting people, but I'm kind of glad Mateo punched you. You've passed the line of just being a bully."

"But you love me, right?"

Her eyes narrowed. "Whatever I just drank tells me I do, but it's not real."

Chad sighed. "You are so stubborn."

She grinned. "I really am."

"What can I do to prove we belong together?"

"Help me get out of here. I don't want to be an exhibit. Help me save my friends from the goblins."

"But I want us to be together."

"It would be better if we were together somewhere else."

Chad sighed. "If that's what it takes, then I'll do it." He pulled a key from his pocket and unlocked the cell.

"They gave you a key?"

"No, I stole it."

Kaylee just shook her head. "Let me check something," she said. She ran down the long hallway of cells. They were full again. Isadora had even gotten a new dragon. She avoided eye contact with the mermaids. A white alicorn in one cell caught her eye. "Can you free her?"

Chad nodded and unlocked the cell. Kaylee led the alicorn from her prison.

They left the cell and climbed the steps. She hoped Korum wasn't waiting for them when they got to the top. She opened the door and peeked out. No one was there, so she led the alicorn out and through the house. Isadora wasn't the best at keeping prisoners secure.

She climbed onto the alicorn and took Chad's hand and helped him up. Part of her wanted to leave him, and the other part wanted to cuddle the entire flight. She shook her head and signaled the alicorn. The majestic beast ran and took off into the sky. Kaylee had experienced a lot of strange days since she'd been in Riviand, but this one definitely was the weirdest.

Mateo watched Odie measure ingredients. "What's going to stop it from making us fall asleep? I remember what happened to Claret last time you did this."

Odie shook his head. "I've done a lot of stupid things when I'm experimenting. I have an idea, though. I've thought of it before but never tried it. It's a sleeping potion that has to get ingested."

"I doubt that's what Garin wants. That's harder if you want the entire room to fall asleep."

"I think it will work both ways. By setting it on fire or ingesting it. I can't figure out a way to do it without fire that doesn't put the other person to sleep."

"I hope you aren't going to make me drink it," Mateo said.

"Nope, I have another idea," he said, looking at Isadora.

She glared at them. "I'm not drinking anything you give me."

Odie poured some into a cup and handed it to Mateo. "She only has to drink a little. Think you can get her to drink it?"

Mateo shrugged. "I can try."

"Stop!" Isadora said. "I'll tell you something if you don't make me do it. The spell on the door. It has to be activated every time someone leaves. It's only been activated a few times. Most of the goblins forget when they leave, and Garin doesn't take the time to do something like that. If you can open the door, you can leave."

Mateo looked at Odie. "Do you think she's telling the truth?"

Odie shrugged. "If so, we're stupid. We've been sitting in here when we could have left."

Mateo took the cup over to Isadora. "Open up."

"But we had a deal."

"No. We never agreed. Open up. It won't hurt you. It will only put you to sleep."

She grinned. "You know I'm more dangerous when I'm asleep?"

"Fine, take it."

She scowled. When she opened her mouth to protest, Mateo tossed the contents of the cup into her open mouth. Some went in and some hit her face and ran down her chin. She spat and glared at him. "How dare you?" Her eyes rolled up in her head and she tipped over.

"Success," Odie said.

"That took forever for you to mix. I didn't think you would be finished in time."

Odie smiled. "That's because I was making two things." He grabbed a gray bowl and held it out. "I made some glue once that was almost impossible to get off, so I created this stuff to get it off. I bet we can use it to wash the stuff from our arms and then we can do magic once we get out of the room. You remember the glue. We used it on the Blade of the Phoenix."

"Right," Mateo said, taking some of the mixture and rubbing it on his arms. "How do we wipe it off?"

"I don't know."

Mateo kneeled down and wiped it on Isadora's dress.

"That seems a little low," Odie said.

"Low? She keeps people locked in her basement."

Odie put some of the mixture on his arms and wiped it on his own pants.

"The next goblin who comes in, we charge past them. All right?"

Odie nodded. "What about Isadora?"

Mateo weighed their options for a moment. "When a goblin comes in, I'll grab Isadora, we run out, and you teleport us."

Odie nodded. "It sounds complicated, but it's probably best to take her."

Keys in the lock quieted them. They shared a look, and Mateo picked Isadora up. Vivi walked in and tilted her head when she saw them.

"Sorry, Vivi," Mateo said. "We have to go."

She sighed. "I can't be found locked in your room again. It won't go well for me. Take me with you."

Odie held out his hand, and she grasped it. They stepped out of the room and Odie put his hand on Mateo's arm and took them all to Claret's castle. They were in Odie's room. Mateo dumped Isadora on the bed, then ran into the hallway.

"Guards!" Mateo yelled. Four guards came running from around the corner. Claret's guards had a much better response than the goblins'. "The witch is in here."

They all paused and looked at one another.

"She's asleep from a potion. She won't wake up for a while."

They ran in and one of them picked her up and they took her away. "Make sure you do something to block her magic!" he called.

Dovin and Sen came walking around the corner and stopped.

Sen grinned. "Mateo!"

Mateo ran to his brother and threw his arms around him. "What are you doing here?"

"Kaylee went and got him," Dovin said. "She wanted someone who would barge into the goblins' castle and save you."

He smiled. "That would be Sen."

Sen nodded. "I was about to come, but then Kaylee disappeared."

Odie joined them in the hallway. "You don't suppose she went to the goblins, do you?"

Dovin rubbed his temples. "I wouldn't be shocked. She doesn't enjoy waiting for well thought out plans."

"Did Claret make it back?"

"Yes. We ran into her on the goblin mountain."

"Where is she?"

Dovin shrugged. "Probably sleeping. She had a headache earlier."

"Have you looked for Kaylee?" Mateo asked.

"We just started. She's not in the castle."

Kaylee and Chad watched the alicorn fly away.

"We should have kept it," Chad said.

Kaylee clung to Chad's arm. She tried to force herself to let go, but it was all she could do to force herself not to kiss him. She settled for pinching his arm.

"Ouch! What was that for?"

She glared at him. "I'm going to hurt you every minute until this spell is broken. Now let's go into the castle and make a plan to save my friends."

They walked up to the steps, and the front doors opened. Dovin, Mateo, and Sen came out. They all stopped when they saw Kaylee and Chad.

"Mateo!" Kaylee said. "We were just about to go save you!"

Dovin frowned. "Where did Chad come from? Please tell me you didn't figure out a way to teleport, and why in the world would you choose Chad, of all people, to bring back?"

"And why are you... hugging his arm?" Mateo asked.

Kaylee punched Chad in the arm, then kissed his cheek. Mateo, Sen, and Dovin all stood staring in disbelief.

Kaylee glared at Chad and his attractive lips. "Ugh! I hate you!"

Chad grinned. "But you love me."

She narrowed her eyes. Her feelings were such a mess right now she didn't know how to respond.

Mateo rushed down the stairs and crossed his arms. "What's going on? Why does Chad have a black eye?"

"Because I punched him in the face. You would have been proud." Kaylee told herself to let go of Chad, but she snuggled her head into him instead. He smirked at Mateo and put his arm around her shoulders. Mateo looked ready to hit someone.

She looked up at Mateo, and her mouth turned down. Whatever she was feeling for Chad was fake, she could tell, but it was strong. She could feel her feelings for Mateo bubbling up in her, but they didn't replace what she was feeling for Chad.

"Please get me away from him!" she begged.

Mateo scratched his head and frowned. "Why don't you let go of him?"

Kaylee rolled her eyes. "Isn't it obvious? I can't! If you don't get me away right this second, there's going to be some seriously embarrassing PDA going on."

Mateo's eyes narrowed. "What's PDA?"

"Public display of affection," Dovin said.

"How do you even know that?"

Dovin rolled his eyes. "I was around a lot of teenagers while on Earth. Chad, did you give Kaylee a love potion?"

Chad sighed. "I didn't give it to her per se…"

Kaylee looked up at Chad and wondered why she was fighting it. Chad really was cute. Did it really matter that he had a horrible personality? Mateo yanked her away from Chad. She wondered if she should fight Mateo or kick Chad. She needed to do something, but she was at a loss.

"How do we break it?" Mateo asked.

"Don't let them take you from me!" Chad said. "You know you want to be with me."

Kaylee took a deep breath. Was he right? He took a step closer and Kaylee slapped him. "How dare you do this to me!" As soon as she did it, she regretted it. She tried to move away from Mateo and go to Chad, but Mateo held her back.

"Most love spells can only be broken by the person who casts it, or by kissing the person you truly love," Dovin said. "Who cast it?"

"Isadora or possibly Korum," Kaylee said. "But who knows where she is?"

"She's in the dungeon," Dovin said, "but she's in a deep sleep."

Kaylee covered her face with both hands. She wanted to kill Chad and kiss him. It was the worst feeling she'd ever had. She might puke. She'd battled her feelings for Mateo and she didn't know exactly how she felt about him. If she kissed him and she didn't love him, it wouldn't work, but if she kissed him and it did, she would know for sure, and she wouldn't be able to tell herself any differently.

Chad sighed and rubbed his face. "I don't even want her like this. Sorry, Kaylee. I shouldn't have done it."

Kaylee looked over her hands and glared. She tried to break away from Mateo, but he wasn't letting go. She would probably thank him later. This was going to be embarrassing and weird, but could it really get worse? She turned around in his arms and threw her arms around his neck and kissed him.

All the confusion and frustration immediately faded from her mind and she was filled with a feeling of peace. Mateo put his arms around her and kissed her back. She loved Mateo, and not because of a spell. She would worry about what that meant later.

She broke the kiss and pushed her face into his shoulder. She didn't want to see the looks on any of their faces.

"Kaylee?" Mateo said softly. She looked up into his brown eyes. "Are you all right?"

She nodded.

He gave her a half smile. "You don't want to kiss Chad anymore?"

"No, but I still want to hurt him." She looked around. Everyone else was gone.

"You didn't actually kiss him, did you? Before you got here?"

She shook her head. "Every time I wanted to, I hit him instead. Not my best moments."

"You can't blame yourself for a spell. Most people can't resist love spells. You're strong."

She smiled. "And you didn't punch Chad."

He grinned. "You did that for me."

"I'm such a hypocrite."

His smile faded. "The spell was broken when you kissed me."

She looked down at the ground as millions of thoughts raced through her head. All the arguments from before filled her head. They were from different worlds, for goodness' sake. But did it matter? Maybe she didn't have to figure it all out at once.

"I can almost see you talking yourself out of it," he whispered.

She looked up and swallowed a lump in her throat. "I love you."

He smiled. "I love you too."

He leaned forward, and she put a finger to his lips. "I can't promise I'll stay in this world forever, and I know you aren't happy on Earth."

"I can compromise, and we don't have to plan our entire lives right now, all right?"

She nodded. "I can't believe I kissed you in front of Dovin and your brother."

Mateo chuckled. "No one's here now."

Kaylee tried not to smile when Mateo kissed her. It was a perfect ending to an otherwise terrible day.

30

CHAPTER 30

Claret sat at the dining room table with Mateo, Odie, and Kaylee. It wasn't dinnertime, but most of them had missed the meal and they were eating sandwiches. It was nice to have all of them together again.

"Does anyone feel like we get captured way too much?" Mateo asked. "How many times have we all been in the dungeon since Kaylee and I came to Riviand? I say we make it our goal to stop doing that."

"I can agree to that," Odie said.

Claret put her sandwich on her plate. "Isn't it odd that we think of Isadora and Garin as being our powerful enemies, but they can't seem to hold us long? Perhaps we are giving them more credit than we should."

Odie nodded. "The goblins aren't very organized. Garin didn't choose well when he went with the goblins. They're already questioning their loyalty. I don't think he's going to motivate them to war like he thinks he will."

"When they first captured Dovin, he said he had to try really hard to get the goblins to even notice him. They don't patrol as well as they should."

"They were getting better," Mateo said. "They have more guards circling around than they did."

Kaylee leaned forward. "I think it's time to free everyone who has been captured by Isadora. If she's in the dungeon, she has no more hold on them."

Claret nodded. "That should be a priority. We have so many things that should be priorities. I worry about missing something. Captain Nerman has doubled the guard. Once all the cities have governors, we are going to need to get organized and work together. Also, Odie needs to spend more time getting to know his parents."

Odie raised his eyebrows. "That's a priority?"

"I think it should be. Things have been so chaotic you haven't had time. Your mother has had a hard life since she came here and your father... well, you need to give him a second chance."

Odie didn't look thrilled but nodded.

"You probably shouldn't flinch every time they call you Pax."

"It's just so strange, trying to answer to a name you don't know. I've spent all my life hating my name, but I don't know that I like Pax either."

"I've gotten used to Odie," Kaylee said with a smile. "When I first met you, I thought of a yellow cartoon dog every time someone said your name, but I don't anymore."

Mateo grinned. "Me too."

Claret didn't know what they were talking about, so she moved on. "We should also have a meeting with the giants and trolls to see where they stand on everything. They could prove to be formidable allies if we end up fighting the goblins. I feel like they will take our side, but it's hard to know for sure. We need to stop doing things like going to Dragon's Cove and hoping something important happens. We need to do things that move our cause along,"

Odie smiled. "Listen to you sounding all queen-like. I haven't heard you sound like this in a long time."

Claret tried not to smile. She hadn't felt like this in a while. Now that they were all safe and united, she felt motivated in ways she hadn't.

"I'm going to ask Williams if he will teach us again. When I was escaping the goblins, I couldn't help but think how much easier it would be if I could run longer and faster. So many things can get in the way of magic and I want to feel more prepared."

"What are we going to do about Isadora?" Kaylee asked.

Mateo grinned. "Leave her to rot in the dungeon. What else?"

"She scares me more than Garin. I don't think Garin knows what he wants. He's changed his mind multiple times."

Claret shuddered. "I don't know why so many of his plans involve me getting married."

Odie threw a piece of fish to Gregor. "He wants control. If he can control who you marry, that can be big."

"Yes, but one of his options was for me to marry you. I don't see how that would help his cause."

"It would show a partnership between Riviand and the goblins," Odie explained. "The people would trust the goblins more because they trust you as their queen."

"And Garin thinks we would sit back and let him make the decisions? He should know we aren't that passive."

"He's hopeful."

Kaylee tapped her fingers on the table. "The people in Riviand know we're having problems with the goblins. Wouldn't they know something was up?"

Mateo rested his folded arms on the table. "Not necessarily. It's no secret that Odie and Claret have become... friends."

The door opened, and Sen entered. "Hey, Mateo. Dovin's going to take Chad back to Basura. I'm going with them unless you still need me."

"Someone better watch Chad," Kaylee muttered.

"Dovin's going to put my dad in charge of him," Sen said. "My dad knows how to keep people in line. I don't think Chad will cause any more problems. I didn't even get to use any of my skills this trip."

"What skills?" Odie asked.

Before Claret could blink, Sen was holding a knife in his hand.

"That was fast," Odie said, impressed. Sen walked over and handed Odie the knife. "You can never have too many knives. He pulled out another just as fast as the first time.

"Where was it?" Claret asked. "In your sleeve?"

"No. This is the one that was in my sleeve." Another knife appeared in his other hand.

"Are you sure you can't stay and teach that to us?" Odie asked.

"I might come back sometime. I don't trust Garin. We have a history and it's not good. Stay away from him if you can."

"Thank you for coming," Claret said. "It's good to know there are people we can call on if we have to."

Sen nodded. "Call on me anytime. Well, preferably not for the next two months, unless it's an emergency."

"Why two months?" Mateo asked.

Sen grinned. "I forget you haven't been around. You're going to be an uncle."

Mateo grinned. "Really? I'm already planning to be the favorite."

Mateo followed Sen from the dining room. He wished he could stay.

"You're different here," Sen said. "I think Riviand agrees with you."

"It does, but not any more than Basura. I'm going to stay once this is all over. Not here, but up above."

"You're growing up, saving the world, and kissing girls. It's so weird."

Mateo grinned sheepishly. "You did all those things."

"Yep. My jaw almost hit the floor when Kaylee kissed you. I knew she wanted to save you, but I didn't know you had that type of relationship."

"We don't or didn't. I don't know where we're headed. I hope things work out, but I think she's still unsure about me."

Sen winked. "We all are."

"Thanks a lot."

Sen patted him on the back. "I'll see you soon, all right?"

Mateo nodded. It was always hard to say goodbye to his brother. They had always been the closest growing up. He went back to the dining room and sat down. He wasn't sure what everyone was talking about, so he spaced out and thought back to the first time he saw Kaylee. She'd been sitting in Dovin's classroom taking notes. There had been something even then that drew him to her.

"Mateo?" Kaylee said, getting his attention. "What do you think?"

"Oh... uh... yeah."

"You weren't listening, were you?"

"Sorry. What were you saying?"

"We were talking about the big beetles on Dragon's Cove. Do you think they might be a bigger threat than we think? The dragons don't like them."

"You might just be prejudiced because you got beetle juice in your hair," Mateo teased.

Kaylee shivered. "That was so gross."

"I could talk to Emerald about them," Odie said.

Mateo frowned. "But that would mean going back to Dragon's Cove."

"No, Emerald stayed here. Haven't you noticed her? She's been behind the castle. She sticks mostly to the gardens. I think she likes Dovin, and he's been training her a little."

Gregor bit Mateo's pant leg, so he tossed him a piece of sandwich. "Having dragons on our side could be a good thing. I keep expecting Garin to turn into a dragon every time I see him."

"I bet he's keeping it a secret, the whole dragon thing," Kaylee said. "He probably thinks it will be to his advantage."

"Is it getting dark in here?" Mateo asked, walking to the window. He frowned. "Hey, Kaylee, come look out here." The green and purplish clouds sent a feeling of panic through his stomach. "The clouds remind me of that time at school when the goblins came, and we thought there was a tornado."

Kaylee looked out. "I think you're right. And the wind is picking up."

Odie came and stood by them. "The goblins do that when they want to distract people from something. We should ignore the weather and make sure we don't miss anything."

Claret rubbed the goose bumps on her arms. "I thought we were going to have a few days of peace. Can the goblins cause a tornado?"

"I'm not sure," Odie admitted. "I've never seen it."

Claret frowned when she looked outside. "I've never seen anything like that. This wind is going to destroy things. I should send the guard out to see if anyone needs help tying things down."

A blinding flash of lightning caused them all to close their eyes. It was followed by the loudest boom Mateo had ever heard, and the castle shook.

"That must have hit something nearby," Odie said. "Stay away from the windows." Rain pelted the windows and soon became hail. "This isn't good."

Yelling in the hall caught all of their attention. They rushed out to see guards running in different directions.

"What's going on?" Claret demanded.

"There was an explosion," a guard said.

"From the lightning?"

"Perhaps. There's an enormous hole in the backside of the castle." He hurried away.

Claret stood tall, but Mateo could see the stress in her eyes. She shook her head, then ran down the hallway. Odie and Kaylee followed, so Mateo did as well. They turned a corner and almost ran into Captain Nerman.

"They blew the back of the castle off," he said to Claret. "It went down deep enough to open up some of the dungeon. Three prisoners escaped. We caught one. My men are on it."

"Please tell me one wasn't Isadora."

Mateo could tell from the captain's face that it was.

Kaylee turned to Captain Nerman. "What did you mean when you said, 'they blew the back off.' Wasn't it the lightning?"

"I didn't see it clearly, but I believe the lightning was caused by fairies. They were all over the castle grounds, dancing around in the rain and laughing."

"Be careful," Claret told him. "Odie thinks the weather is caused by the goblins. If the goblins and the fairies are working together, we might be in for a tough fight."

Captain Nerman nodded and left.

"I thought goblins and fairies didn't get along," Claret said.

Odie frowned. "They don't."

Odie walked around and looked at the damage the next day. The wind had ruined several roofs and fences, but most things looked like they could be easily fixed. He jumped over tree branches and moved some of the bigger ones off the road.

He had slept poorly the night before, wondering what the goblins and fairies could be doing together. They knew the fairies were at least informing Isadora of things, but if they were working with the goblins, that changed every-thing. If there was a war, Riviand would have no trouble beating the goblins. The fairies were a different story.

He'd asked Vivi what she knew, but the goblins didn't confide in the castle staff.

Since fairies kept to themselves, there was no way to know how many of them there were, and everyone knew fairy magic was strong. They wouldn't fight with their fists or weapons like the goblins would. They would do everything with magic and probably from out of sight.

Shopkeepers were out now, sweeping the branches away from the front of their stores. Some were on the roofs, hammering down patches or securing loose pieces. A lot of them turned and gave Odie curious looks when he passed. He was used to being stared at and found it more tolerable here than in the goblin villages. Here they only looked curious, not angry.

Circling around the main area of the city took about an hour, then he returned to the castle. His mother was waiting for him in front of his bedroom door. Her face lit up when she saw him.

"Pax!" she said, opening her arms. He hugged her and tried not to feel awkward. Having a mother who loved him was great, but since he hadn't had a lot of affection in his life, he didn't know how to take it. "Can we talk for a minute?"

"Sure," he said, opening the door to his room. She linked her arm with his and they went in and sat on the bed.

She turned to him and frowned. "I hate Riviand. I've wished to go back to Basura every day since we ended up here."

He nodded. "So you're going back?"

"Yes. After all these years, I can finally go home and relax and not worry about when my next meal will come. I've missed Arving."

Odie put his arm over her shoulder. He couldn't imagine the things she'd been through. "Now that I can teleport, I can visit," he said.

"I had hoped you would want to join us," she said. "If you feel you belong here, we understand."

Odie frowned. "I can't leave Claret, especially when so many things could go bad really fast."

"Will you be upset if we leave?"

"No. It's probably safer up there."

She nodded. "You will come often?"

"If I can. Once the problems here are over, it will be easier."

"Teleporting only takes a minute. I hope you'll check in at least weekly."

"I'll try."

"Dovin can take you the first time so you can find us."

"I saw Arving's house once."

She rolled her eyes. "Yes, he said he's been living in a little dumpy house because he didn't want to stay in our house with the memories. We have a nice house in Akkron. I think you'll like it. Your friends are welcome anytime as well."

There was a knock on the door and Claret's voice came through. "Odie? Are you back?"

He walked to the door and opened it. Claret was wearing a bright blue dress. Her blond hair fell in soft curls over her shoulders. He smiled down at her.

"I want to go back to Dragon's Cove," she said. "The cave and the beetles have been on my mind. I want to see if I can see one for myself. Will you come with me?"

"Yes. When?"

"Twenty minutes?"

"I'll be ready."

She smiled and went on her toes and kissed the tip of his nose. "Thank you."

Odie watched her rush off down the hallway. He turned and shut the door. He was sure he had a goofy smile on his face. He was still amazed to know Claret liked him. His mother sat, smiling from his bed. He'd forgotten she was there.

"I see why you would want to stay. She seems like a nice girl." She laughed. "That seems like a weird way to describe a queen."

"Claret is one of the best things that's ever happened to me," he said, sitting on the edge of his table. "She has every reason to hate me, but she's forgiving and sweet."

"Well, I wish you all the best. We would stay to help, but Arving and I aren't the best in these situations. Dovin and Durdessa will guide you. I doubt anyone can ever get the best of those two."

Odie nodded. "They've been helpful."

She stood and gave him one more hug. "Remember, you can come to me anytime. All right?"

CHAPTER 31

Claret ignored the spray from the waterfall as she went around it and into the cave. Odie followed behind her, his sword drawn. Claret's sword was at her side. She'd chosen to wear a tunic, just in case there was any running.

When she stepped inside, her eyes went wide. "Oh, my." The fairy city was no longer covered in broken houses and dragon vomit. Everything was clean, and the houses had all been fixed. "How did they clean this up so quickly?"

Odie's eyes scanned the city. "I don't know. Magic, I'm sure."

"There aren't any dragons in here that I can see."

"Perhaps they were able to get rid of all the beetles, and now the fairies don't need the dragons' help."

A fairy with long white hair flew past them. As she did, she quietly whispered in Claret's ear, "Follow."

Claret and Odie went back out from behind the waterfall and ran after the fairy. She wasn't going to slow down for them. She flew part of the way around the lake before stopping and growing to human height.

"My name is Rilla. We cannot have humans going into our underground cities. I am only taking the time to warn you kindly because you are the Queen of Riviand. You were fortunate I saw you before any of the others. Their welcome would not be as pleasant."

Claret nodded. "We came to see what was happening with the beetles and the dragons."

Rilla sighed. "I hope you have ways of getting rid of the beetles. The dragons kept them from completely overtaking us. The witch is keeping them from us now, but you will not be as fortunate."

"We haven't seen any."

"Not yet, but the witch will see that you do. We hate being indebted to the witch, but she is the only one who can keep them away. They hatch underground and once they reach the outside, they grow at an alarming rate."

"Did the fairies help the witch escape?" she asked.

Rilla nodded. "The goblins and the fairies."

"If the fairies align themselves with the goblins and Isadora, Riviand will fall."

Rilla's head hung down. "We do the best we can. The witch has the power to destroy us, so we will do what we must."

Odie's eyes narrowed. "I don't believe the fairies can't defeat Isadora. Fairy magic is more powerful than one witch."

"Yes, but she is holding off the beetles. If she were to die, they would come at an alarming rate."

"But we could work together to defeat them. She might only be telling you that to keep you on her side."

"We can't risk them destroying our homes again."

"If you give in to her, she will never let you be free. She will always have something to hold over you."

"We know this, but she has also promised us many things if we help her. I need to go now before I am missed. Don't enter our world again." She shrank and flew away.

Claret kicked at the dirt. "This is so frustrating! We can't beat the fairies."

Odie took her hand. "We can. I can probably find something that will kill the beetles."

She shivered. "I'm sure you can. I get all itchy every time I remember the time the bugs were raining from the dungeon."

Odie grinned. "It solved the problem, though. The goblin castle is bug-free."

"That was one of the most terrifying experiences of my life."

He grinned. "Mine too."

"Really? I didn't think the bugs bothered you."

"They didn't. It was the terrified queen clinging to me that really scared me."

She laughed. "I was terrified." She looked into the sky and saw dragons flying overhead. Her smile faded when she saw a blue one. The only blue dragon she had ever seen had turned out to be Garin.

"What's wrong?" he asked.

"Is that Garin?" she asked, pointing.

Odie frowned. "I think it might be. I hope he isn't trying to get the dragons to follow him. Hang on." He jogged over to the side of the lake where a silver dragon was drinking. He held out his hand and slowly rubbed it over the dragon's head. From this distance, Claret couldn't hear whatever it was he was muttering.

She watched the flying dragons while she waited. None of the dragons seemed to stay close to the blue dragon. When he flew near, they went the other way. She hoped that was a sign that the dragons still didn't like him.

Odie came over. "It is Garin. The dragons are flying around so they don't have to interact with him. That dragon only landed because he was thirsty."

"Should we leave?"

"I'm not sure. I don't want to leave the dragons with Garin. Who knows what he might do?"

"I don't think there's much we can do to stop him."

Odie nodded. "I suppose you're right." Odie took her hand and teleported them to the castle. It was suppertime, so they went to the dining room. They were the last to arrive.

"The fairies are obeying Isadora," Odie said. "One of them told us."

Dovin put his fork on the table. "It's good to have confirmation. Now we know what we are up against."

Claret sat at the head of the table. "She must have control over the beetles. The fairy seemed to think Isadora is going to unleash them on us."

Kaylee wrinkled her nose. "Those beetles are gross. I can't imagine dealing with more than one at a time."

"I took Arving and Neva home," Dovin said. "We can put all our focus on Isadora."

"What about Garin?" Claret asked. "He was at Drag-on's Cove flying around."

"Garin is planning, and he might be a little more patient than Isadora. She's probably going to come at us first."

"But aren't they working together?" Kaylee asked.

"They were, but I doubt they are anymore," Mateo said. "Garin left her tied up with us. She won't forgive that."

Dovin nodded. "But the fairies and the goblins were behind the bad weather and breaking Isadora from prison. It's possible she has forgiven Garin if he helped save her."

"What now?" Kaylee asked. "I hate waiting to see what's going to happen."

Dovin rubbed his chin. "Durdessa and I are going to talk to all the new governors to train them. We'll gather groups of them so they are easier to manage."

Mateo leaned forward. "They were already elected?"

"Yes."

"That was fast."

"We don't have time to be slow. We also don't have time for them to be governing on their own with no direction. I think it's important to make sure we are all in this togeth-er."

"What do we do while you're gone?" Claret asked.

Dovin grinned. "Stay out of trouble and don't get thrown in the dungeon."

Kaylee stood with Claret, Odie, and Mateo on Claret's large semicircle balcony. They all rested their elbows on the three-foot wall and stared up at the ominous sky. Green and gray clouds once again swirled around each other, putting Kaylee in mind of a tornado. It was the middle of the day, but you would never know it.

"What do you suppose the goblins are trying to distract us from?" Claret asked.

Odie reached over and squeezed her hand. "It could be anything. They might be trying to scare us."

Kaylee flinched as a bright bolt of lightning flashed through the sky. "It's working." A raindrop hit her face and ran down her cheek. She looked over the city. The empty streets made her feel sick to her stomach. Tyran was usually busy at this time of day. The only people she could see were the guards surrounding the castle.

"I bet they want to draw us out," Mateo said. "Have us come looking for them."

"Do we?"

"No. Let's wait and see what they do."

"I bet they won't do anything. Not yet," Odie said. "They just want to keep us nervous. I remember King Ummi telling me once that it was a great strategy. Make your enemies scared and unable to sleep, and they make mistakes. We can't let them."

"I agree," Claret said. "We go about as usual. We can't guess what they might do, so there's no reason to try. Once they act, we will decide what to do."

Kaylee wasn't sure she agreed with that tactic, but she didn't have any better ideas. The rain was coming down harder. She closed her eyes and raised her face to the rain. She would see the rain as renewing and not something to fear. Thunder rattled the city. Kaylee kept her eyes closed. They were going to save Riviand again. She didn't know how, but they would save it as many times as it was needed.

—·—

ALSO BY KRISTY DIXON

<u>Cozy Mystery</u>
Murder With a Side of Bacon
Murder With a Hint of Cinnamon
Murder With a Fudge Brownie to Go

<u>Young Adult</u>
Akkron (The Silver Eclipse Book 1)
Boztoll (The Silver Eclipse Book 2)
The Other Continent (The Silver Eclipse Book 3)
The Amethyst Crown
More Than Once Upon a Time
Trapped In Once Upon a Timen
The Beginning of Once Upon a Time
Blade of the Phoenix (Riviand Lost Book 1)
Mermaid's Demise (Riviand Lost Book 2)

<u>Coming Soon!</u>
Fairy Lies (Riviand Lost Book 4)
Murder With a Splash of Vanilla
Murder With a Drizzle of Syrup

— • —

ABOUT THE AUTHOR

Kristy Dixon received a degree in English from the University of Utah. She started writing stories when she was seven and never stopped. She enjoys writing fantasy books for middle grade and teens and cozy mysteries. At home, she spends her time playing board games with her husband and kids and writing. Occasionally she takes part in a Super Mario marathon. She has six chickens and a cat that help keep life amusing. If she isn't playing with her kids or writing, she is usually eating cookies, or wishing she was eating cookies.